Those Who Can, Date

Barbara Meyers

THOSE WHO CAN, DATE

This edition published by Barbara Meyers, LLC

First pass edits by Noah Chinn

Cover by Steven Novak, Novak Illustration

Print ISBN: 978-1-951286-19-4

Digital ISBN: ISBN: 978-1-951286-18-7

1. Contemporary Romance – Fiction. 2. Hollywood (U.S.) – Fiction.

3. Family Relationships – Fiction.

4. Gambling – Fiction. I. Title.

Contents

For Adrienne and Kellar

Chapter One

♥

Day rounded the corner toward the elevators, just as a man old enough to be his father barreled into him.

Somehow, Day managed to keep his balance and grasped the other man's arm to stop his forward momentum. "Whoa, there, buddy, slow down."

The man gave a terrified glance over his shoulder. "Shit! Here he comes. If he's got a gun, we're in trouble." He tugged on Day's sleeve. "Come on. Hurry!"

"Hey, wait. What?" Day reluctantly let himself be led, glancing back, but he had no idea who the man was referring to. This was Vegas. Someone carrying a gun in a hotel wouldn't be all that uncommon but using one here, where the main concourse buzzed with activity, people, and security cameras seemed highly unlikely.

They dodged through the sea of people who were streaming out after the end of a show and crossed the expanse of the lobby. Day allowed himself to be tugged into the nearest lounge. The man's hold loosened, and he took a seat at the far end of the nearly deserted bar. Day's lips twitched, but he was intrigued now, even though the last thing he needed or wanted was a cocktail. He'd ducked out of the launch party of yet another high-end brand of vodka, this one partnered with late night talk show host, Jamie Falcon.

All Day wanted was the king-sized bed in his suite and a decent night's sleep before he headed back to LA tomorrow. He'd get there, too, just as soon as he could extricate himself from his new acquaintance. If nothing else, he might get a good story out of it. One he could use the next time he guested on Jamie's show.

"We're safe here," the other man said.

"*We*?" Day looked around. Only a few of the small tables were occupied and there was a cluster of twenty-something guys good-naturedly ribbing each other at the opposite end of the bar. Pop music from two decades ago played in the background. It didn't escape Day's notice that his seat was between his companion and the entrance. "What am I? Your human shield?"

"Nah." The guy glanced at the corridor. "He won't try anything until he can get me outside... or more likely, the parking garage."

"Is that so?"

The bartender appeared in front of them. Day decided he might need something after all. Plus, his new buddy shouldn't be drinking alone. He decided not to mix things up and stuck with top shelf vodka and cranberry juice in a tall glass. "And for my friend?"

Day noticed the guy perked up when he heard what

brand of vodka Day had ordered. He asked for an equally high-end Scotch on the rocks.

When the bartender stepped away, a lightbulb came on over Day's head. "Wait a minute. Did Ryan put you up to this?"

The man frowned. "Ryan?"

"Ryan Grayling. This is one of his pranks, right?" Day waggled his fingers in an encouraging gesture. "Come on. What's the rest of it? I get jumped as soon as I leave the bar? Hog-tied and left in a laundry cart?"

The guy shook his head, his expression glum. "This ain't no joke, buddy. This is my life."

The drinks arrived in record time. Day signed for them with his room number. He leaned back against the stool's padding and swiveled to face the man, who stared into his drink. If this wasn't one of Ryan's elaborate practical jokes, he wanted to know what was going on even more. "I'm Dayman, by the way." He offered his hand.

The man barely gave him a glance but shook the hand Day offered. "Rory."

Day knew his longer than usual hairstyle, along with the beard he'd grown for his latest role, kept the average American from recognizing him in public which pleased him. When he'd left the launch party, he'd donned a pair of round tortoiseshell glasses to further insure his anonymity. He said, "I guess you don't want the police involved, otherwise you would have called them. What's this guy going to do when he gets you outside? Shoot you?"

Rory gave a bitter laugh. "Pistol whip me, more like. Break a kneecap or two. Dead guys can't pay up."

Just as Day suspected. "Loan shark."

"Muscle for him, yeah." Rory continued to contemplate his glass, though he'd yet to take a sip.

Day glanced into the corridor where a guy leaned against the wall across from the lounge entrance, studying his cell phone. Or pretending to. His gaze flickered up and caught Day's for a fraction of a second before passing on to Rory. Seeming satisfied his quarry was in plain sight, he returned his attention to his phone.

There was something feral about the man, but Day couldn't decide if that was due to the tailored leather jacket, the snakeskin cowboy boots, or the attitude emanating from him that spoke of violence beneath an ironclad control mechanism.

"That him?"

Rory straightened and looked past Day. "Yep." Defeated resignation swamped his features.

"How much?"

"Pal, you don't even want to know."

"Try me."

"A hundred Gs," Rory admitted.

Day emitted a low whistle. "How?" he asked.

Rory began to explain, but Day stopped him. "Do you mind if I record this?"

"What for?" Rory asked, looking around as if he might spot hidden cameras.

"I'm in the movie business," Day explained. "I'm always looking for stories. Yours sounds like an interesting one."

"You'd pay me?"

"Maybe."

"How much?"

"I can't say. Could be enough to save your kneecaps. This time anyway."

Rory dropped his head.

"I don't want to talk here," Day said. "Let's go up to my suite."

Rory eyed the muscle, who behaved as if he had all the time in the world to wait. "He won't let us get by. Me anyway."

"Sure, he will." Day signaled the bartender. After a brief conversation with him out of Rory's earshot, Day used his phone to send a text message.

Minutes later, two of the hotel's security guards arrived. Day used his chin to indicate the guy who'd already pocketed his phone, straightened away from the wall, and took off. "You requested an escort to your suite, Mr. MacDay?" the older of the two said.

"Yes, thanks. Along with my companion here." He signaled to Rory, who looked at the three of them and checked the corridor, before he downed the rest of his drink.

Rory stood, adjusted the belt at his waist, and smoothed down his shirt. "Let's do this."

For the next four hours, Rory talked while Day and his assistant, Chazz, listened. Day only interrupted when he had a question or needed clarification. Day's text to Chazz earlier was to make sure a video recorder was available. He wanted to be able to reference everything Rory said, including his agreement to sell his life's story. He also wanted quality reference material for when he played the character, capturing his various nuances and mannerisms. Day introduced Chazz to Rory as his creative director, which wasn't far from the truth.

Day began to see what Rory described—the family he left behind to follow the siren's call of Vegas, the new family he'd begun, only to have it disintegrate before his eyes, ups and downs from glory to despair, the trail of destruction left in his wake. Day could see how Rory's story would unfold on screen. This was exactly the kind of vehicle he needed to launch his production company. All he needed was the right to tell it.

Day and Chazz stood. "We're going to step into the other room," Day said, "and when we come out, we'll have a decision."

A bleary-eyed Rory waved them off. "Go ahead. I've got nowhere to be."

Chazz followed Day to the far side of the bedroom and into the luxuriously appointed bathroom. Day closed the door. "What do you think?"

"It's got possibilities."

Day loved how low-key Chazz could be. He probably had a better poker face than Rory. Even after the years Chazz had spent as Day's assistant and closest friend, Day sometimes still found him hard to read.

"My gut says go for it," Day told him. "While he talked, I kept visualizing scenes. I've already got most of it shot in my head."

Chazz offered one of his rare smiles. "I figured. It's a decent story, and he's an interesting character."

"Destructive."

"Destructive and clueless about how destructive he is."

"A lot of facets there."

"Exactly."

Back in the living room, he pitched the idea to Rory. "We make contact with your loan shark," Day said. "Tell him to back off until tomorrow. I call my legal team. They get a contract to us. You sign it. We go to the bank, get the money. Pay off your debt. And you'll have some left over."

"You really want to make a movie about me?"

"Not about you, per se," Day corrected. "A guy like you. Who's lived a life similar to yours. Who's ended up where you are right now."

Rory lifted an eyebrow. "Two hundred thousand, you said?"

"That's what I said."

"How about you up the ante to two-fifty?"

"Nope. This is a one-time offer. No negotiation. Take it or leave it. You're welcome to walk out of here and take your chances with the muscle downstairs."

Rory slid a glance to the door before he offered Day his hand. "You've got yourself a deal."

Chapter Two

♥

O*ne Year Later*

Kellar Kennedy fought the urge to lick her lips, a habit she'd been trying to break for years. It wasn't her fault that God had gifted her with the driest lips in the world. She'd tried balms, moisturizing lip gloss, every treatment under the sun, but nothing seemed to work as well as good old petroleum jelly. She kept tubes of it in every purse and piece of carry-on luggage she owned and jars of the stuff in both bathrooms in her townhouse.

But after the hair stylist and makeup artist spent over an hour making her look presentable enough to be a guest on Jamie Falcon's late night talk show, time had taken its toll. She refused to be seen in anything less than pristine condition, so the urge to chew off the lip color that had been so carefully applied five minutes ago would have to wait. Even if it drove her crazy.

"Here's the green room," the production assistant said. She opened a door. "We'll call you in about thirty minutes to get you mic'd up before your segment, okay?"

Kellar nodded. The assistant took off and all Kellar could think was *thirty minutes*? Already she wanted to take a damp paper towel and wipe off the lip stain the makeup girl had so painstakingly applied.

But Kellar was in the big leagues now, so she'd have to suck it up and act like she belonged there.

Stepping into the green room was like walking into a bachelor pad circa 1995. A black leather sofa and two matching chairs faced a large wall-mounted flat-screen TV. A wet bar, complete with an ice maker, small fridge, cabinets, and drawers occupied one wall. The adjacent countertop was set up as a buffet and held a variety of pre-packaged snacks: crackers, chips, pretzels and peanuts; as well as a tray each of sliced fruit (strawberries, pineapple and kiwi) and one of vegetables (carrots, celery sticks, broccoli florets and grape tomatoes). A bowl of gummy white dip sat in the middle of the tray.

Kellar had no intention of eating. Anything could happen if she did. Seeds in her teeth. A dribble down her carefully selected navy blue knit dress. Plus, it would put her lips at risk of losing their carefully applied color. She had so much makeup on, she felt as though she was wearing a mask, but she had to trust the people running the show. The last thing she wanted to do was make a fool of herself in front of a national audience. This was her make-or-break golden moment of opportunity.

A bottle of water would be harmless enough, however, especially if she could find a straw. Otherwise, she'd have to wait until after the show. Her mouth became as dry as her lips just thinking about it.

She approached the wet bar and opened the refrigerator. Sure enough, an entire shelf of bottled water greeted her. She took one and set it on the counter. Straws...now where would they be? She opened the overhead cabinets and saw an array of glasses in one and an assortment of drink mixers in another. Jars of olives and cocktail onions, small bottles of tonic and soda water. Another cabinet held the makings for coffee and tea.

She tried the drawers and found utensils. Strainers, corkscrews, bottle openers.

In another drawer she found a supply of cocktail napkins with the Jamie Falcon Show's logo on them.

"There must be straws here somewhere," she said when she located swizzle sticks in a smaller drawer. Finally, in what was probably the last unopened drawer in the room, she found what she was looking for.

"Ah hah!" She opened the water, stuck the straw in and sipped carefully with pursed lips before she caught sight of herself in the wide, full-length mirror.

She took another sip, puckering her lips as she sauntered toward her reflection exaggerating her imitation of a model on a catwalk. She studied herself critically.

"Ooh, baby, you look fantastic," she purred. Her hair was her natural mahogany, enhanced with a few honey-colored highlights. It fell in thick layered waves to her shoulders. She considered her hair one of her best features. She rearranged the ends, but otherwise it looked perfect.

She checked the flawless makeup, the liner, shadow, and mascara showcasing her hazel eyes. The foundation covered every freckle or tiny blemish she might have. The coating of blusher enhanced her cheekbones.

A silver necklace, which she'd carefully chosen, complemented the neckline of the dress which plunged into a vee that showed enough cleavage to be alluring but still leave plenty to the imagination.

She was never going to be runway model thin, nor would her proportions qualify her for a plus-size gig, either.

She was what she looked like. A well-fed girl from Indiana who'd grown up on meat and potatoes. She had the sturdy frame and the curves to prove it.

Daily she said a prayer of thanks to Kim Kardashian and Nicki Manaj for making curves cool. Kellar had firmed up every one of hers with regular workouts in the gym, hiking in the summer and skiing weekends each winter. There were no jiggly parts except where they were supposed to be. Her breasts were a hundred percent natural, and she'd been told they were awesome by male admirers.

All in all, she was pleased with her appearance. She set the water aside and smoothed her hands along her thighs. She bent and lifted the hem of the dress. Even though it fit perfectly, and she had no body image issues, she adjusted the edges of the body-shaping undergarment.

A voice behind her said, "Why do women wear those?"

She whirled, allowing the dress to fall back into place,

to discover a man stretched out full-length on one of the sofas. He was dressed in black. Perhaps that's how she'd missed him before. He had his arms crossed under his head and a lazy, but amused smile on his lips. And she knew that face.

"From what I can see, you really don't need anything at all under that dress. Explain it to me."

Kellar was rarely at a loss for words, but none came immediately to mind. Instead, her brain flooded with a memory dating back to her senior year of college when she'd first met this man.

Her small college town had been the setting for his second movie, and she'd been given the honor of interviewing him for the school newspaper. They'd clicked, or so she thought when he made a date to meet her at a local pub. Then, as now, she'd dressed carefully. She'd wanted to look her best. Make herself memorable. To impress him.

Only he hadn't shown. She'd waited an hour, thinking she knew how unpredictable the movie business could be. He could have got held up for one reason or another. She fended off the unwanted attention of the bartender who'd hit on her previously before she'd walked back to her dorm alone. But along the way, she'd passed the best restaurant in town. Laughter and light spilled from inside. She saw her date at a table, surrounded by movie people, his gorgeous blonde co-star, Willow Thorne, whispering in his ear. Kellar stalked back to her dorm, the lines of her next blog writing themselves in her head.

Certain he had no memory of their previous meeting, she watched him unfold himself from the couch and come toward her. "Sorry if I startled you."

It wasn't something she normally did upon introduction to a man, but she backed up a step. She bumped the edge of the countertop behind her, where she'd set her bottle of water.

He extended a hand in her direction. "I'm—"

Her eyes went wide with alarm when cold liquid splashed against her back, propelling her straight into his chest, a move for which he was not prepared. To maintain his balance, he grasped her upper arms as he staggered back and fell onto a glass and chrome coffee table. The glass shattered under their combined weight and the frame collapsed around them.

Kellar found herself neatly wedged on top of the man, her breasts smashed against his chest. Her thighs pressed snugly atop his, the entire length of his body secured against hers. His eyes were closed.

Her first thought was she'd killed Dayman MacDay.

Day-Day. Big Mac. DMD. The entertainment press had a hundred nicknames for him, and they were always coming up with new ones. Especially couples' names when he was entangled in one of his famous romantic relationships. DayLee when he'd been with super model Lee Masters for a few months. DayLo during his brief engagement to rock star Lorrie Foster. DayLight because of his on-again off-again relationship with actress Julie

Lightner.

If she'd killed him, her name would be linked to his for-ever. DayKell. Knowing the press, they'd probably add their own twist and make it Day*Kill.* Forever after she'd be known as the Day Killer.

Oh God oh God oh God. "Please don't be dead," she whispered. She couldn't tell if his heart was still beating beneath hers. He lay so still. Was he breathing? She managed to disentangle one of her hands from the wreckage of the coffee table. Luckily, neither she nor Day appeared to be bleeding. She pressed her fingers to his lips. He didn't so much as twitch. If he was breathing, surely, she'd feel his exhaling breath on her fingers. Wouldn't she?

She desperately tried to remember how to give mouth-to-mouth resuscitation. No wait. That was for drowning victims, wasn't it? Or was it for anyone who'd stopped breathing? *Had* he stopped breathing? She couldn't tell.

She pressed her ear to his lips and nose. She detected something. A swirl of air against her lobe. No wait. That wasn't air. It felt more like... the tip of a tongue. And now she felt his goddamn teeth. He nipped playfully at her earlobe. She pulled back, bracing herself on his shoulders, too stunned for a moment, too *relieved* if she was honest, that he was alive. That she wouldn't be known as *DayKill* for the rest of her life.

His eyes were now open. Those silvery gray-blue eyes that had seduced millions of women on screen and probably hundreds off screen. She wanted to smack that lazy grin off his face. "I thought you were dead."

"If I was, you'd be the most popular woman in the world."

"You mean notorious. Tarred and feathered and run out of town. I'd never be forgiven for killing every woman's dream man."

He snorted. "Hardly. Do you have any idea how many women never want to lay eyes on me again? How many have told me to drop dead?"

"Probably just those whose hearts you broke. That still leaves a lot of women in the world who think you're the cat's pajamas."

He laughed. His glee seemed genuine. She felt his chest rumble beneath hers as if he couldn't control himself. "The—the—cat's—pa—pa—" He couldn't get the words out, he was laughing so hard. Kellar narrowed her eyes. She did her best to edit herself, to keep the old-fashioned Midwest euphemisms she'd picked up during her formative years out of her everyday speech. But sometimes they still slipped out, often when she was stressed or when she needed one to avoid using profanity.

Most of the time, the reaction was a lot like this. Laughter. Asking for an explanation of the obscure term. Depending on the age of her audience, what she said could be so completely over their heads there was no point in trying to explain.

Kellar, like most people, did not like to be laughed at. Especially not by this guy. A mega movie star. A notorious heartbreaker. The guy every woman in America dreamed of having as her very own.

She became aware of the water that had soaked the back of her dress, trickling between her legs and landing on the inside front of her dress. If it soaked through... between her legs... before the show...

Oh God oh God oh God. Please no. She'd prepared so meticulously for her appearance. She'd been so careful. And now, because of him, she was ruined.

She pushed herself up, using his shoulders, all too aware of her position and his proximity to the vee of her dress. His laughter dissipated and his eyes went where any red-blooded, heterosexual male's would go. Right to her cleavage.

She crawled backwards down the length of his body, not caring how much weight she put on his chest, his rock-hard abs, his thighs and shins. He moaned while she did so and said, "Hey, watch it there!" when her fingers came perilously close to his crotch. Then she was back on her feet.

He was surrounded by crushed glass and bent metal, his body surrounded by the skeleton of the broken table. He held his arms up. She didn't want to touch him again and did her level best to deny the impact of what being on top of him had felt like. He'd upset the equilibrium and self-control she tried so hard to maintain.

But she couldn't ignore the fact that he might be injured and that she'd been the indirect cause of their accident. She stared into his eyes and thought she saw the challenge in his. Reluctantly, she bent down so he could grip her hands and leaned back to counter his weight.

She was a substantial woman, but she was wearing not very substantial Louboutins. And he was a very solid hunk of man wedged between four metal poles. She grunted with the effort of helping him extricate himself from the mess they'd made. His fingers gripped her so hard she thought for a moment he might pull her back down. But then he was free of the wreckage, on his feet, and the momentum propelled him right into her.

She fell back under his weight once more, straight into the pool of water that was now dripping from the counter onto the carpet.

She tried unsuccessfully to avoid getting any wetter than she already was, but the high heel of her shoe caught in the wet pile of the carpet. She went one way, and her heel went the other. But this time, Dayman caught her and kept them both from crashing into any other pieces of furniture or the floor.

His fingers still gripped hers and he'd pulled her hard against him when she thought she might fall and take him with her once more. She looked up at him, into his eyes, and became breathless. Maybe he'd have to give *her* mouth to mouth. She contemplated his lips and realized she wouldn't mind that at all.

She was acutely aware of her chest pressed to his, of her nipples tightening in awareness, of heat pooling in her lower body. Of a throat clearing.

It hadn't come from him, that attention-getting,

"Ahem." At the same time, they turned their attention to the open door.

The production assistant signaled to her. "We're ready for you, Miss Kennedy."

"All right. Just a minute." Nervously, she licked her lips as she glanced at Dayman. She could see that smile of his play around his mouth. Under other circumstances, she would have found what just happened hilarious. It *was* hilarious. But that it had happened to her at such a critical moment made it considerably less funny. This could ruin her.

She stepped away from the water unevenly, because of her missing four-inch heel. She grabbed some paper towels from the holder next to the sink and began to dab at the spots of water on the front of her dress.

Dayman moved past her. She couldn't focus on him right now. She had about two minutes to repair the damage to her appearance. She straightened suddenly when she felt pressure on her backside. She tried to turn to look behind her, but he had a firm grip on the hem of her dress. "What do you think you're doing?" she hissed.

He glanced up. "Helping?" He pressed a wad of paper towels to her bottom, and that pressure affected every nerve ending she had.

"Stop it. You've done enough." She licked her lips again and looked beseechingly at the assistant who was lounging against the doorjamb, taking everything in. *Oh, God. I'm ruined.*

She batted at Dayman's hands and stumbled away. She

knew what she had to do.

"Nice meeting you," he called.

She shot daggers at him with her eyes, wanting nothing more than to wipe that amused grin off his face once and for all.

Chapter Three

❤

Day watched the woman limp lopsidedly toward the door. He noted the sway of her hips, the ramrod straightness of her back, every ounce of her oozing determination.

What a woman. He'd been thinking that from the moment he opened his eyes and saw her primping in the mirror. She was the stuff his teenage wet dreams were made of.

He hadn't met or even seen a woman like her in a long time. Not here in La-La Land, where women were Botoxed up one side and down the other. Where their boobs were too big for their thin frames and were hard as rocks. Where noses and chins and foreheads and God knew what else had fallen prey to the surgeons' knives. Where nothing and no one was real.

Day was so sick of it sometimes he wanted to puke. Which is why he'd put his escape plan into motion years ago. He got smart with his money and invested in land. Wyoming. Colorado. Utah. New Mexico. He now owned hundreds of acres in those states. He planned to move to one of those properties. Raise horses or cattle or grow Christmas trees or avocadoes or something. That part was a little blurry. But he was going to escape LA soon, and if he was very lucky, he was going to find a woman who wanted to go with him.

He held his shirt away from his back and shook the bits of glass still clinging to it out onto the floor. Fortunately, the table had been made of tempered glass. Carefully, he brushed his backside, dislodging more of the crushed bits. His gaze caught on the broken heel from the woman's shoe. He picked it up. It was delicate, silvery, glossy, about four inches long with the signature red strip inside. He dropped it into his shirt pocket.

Ignoring the broken glass, he plucked up the TV remote from the rubble of the coffee table and turned on the sixty-inch flat screen television. It was the only thing that had been updated in the green room in years.

Of course, it automatically tuned to the feed from The Jamie Falcon Show. A commercial for the latest pharmaceutical miracle played, but Day had done the show enough times to know Jamie would be pretending to fight his way through the curtains in about two minutes.

He always opened his show that way, pretending to be a cat caught in a wet-paper bag. His shenanigans got a big laugh from the audience, and he maintained his popularity with a winning brand of self-deprecating humor.

Day had known Jamie since he'd been a regular doing standup at clubs on the West Coast. They were friends of a sort. Jamie was one of the few real deal guys Day had met since he'd started in the movie business. Although Jamie always went for a laugh during an interview, and sometimes his jabs and questions hit a little too close to home, he never set out to intentionally humiliate a guest.

Day sat through Jamie's appearance and his opening monologue. He promised his audience that right after the upcoming commercial they'd meet his first guest, dating coach, Kellar Kennedy.

Day narrowed his eyes as something pinged far back in his brain. He'd never met Kellar Kennedy before. Why then, did her name—and now he realized the woman herself—seem so oddly, hauntingly familiar?

Kellar stood nervously, waiting in the wings. She was mic'd and ready to go as soon as Jamie introduced her. The production assistant hovered next to her. Kellar had worn exactly the wrong thing because with a dress like hers there was nowhere to clip the sound box at her waist. They'd had to improvise with some heavy-duty tape. Kellar hoped her dress would still be wearable after the show given how much she'd paid for it.

The assistant had offered to locate another pair of shoes for her as well as a blow dryer, but Keller had declined. She knew exactly how she could play the results of the mishap in the green room to her advantage, and that's exactly what she planned to do.

She'd probably chewed off the carefully applied lip color by now, but she didn't care. She'd had to improvise so often in her life, she'd become an expert.

"And now, for our first guest," Jamie Falcon was saying. "She's a well-known dating expert, podcaster, and blogger. Her monthly column is featured in *Out and About* magazine and she's just written her first book entitled, *Those Who Can, Date*. Please welcome, Kellar Kennedy!"

Jamie stood and took a few steps away from his desk.

"Go!" the assistant hissed.

Kellar did her walk/limp/wobble across the stage where Jamie greeted her with a close handshake, a press of his cheek to hers and a look of concern on his face when he stepped back. He swept an arm toward the guest chair next to his desk and kept one hand on her elbow until she made it there.

He slid back into his seat and said, "Kellar, there's so much I want to ask you, but first I just gotta know, what the hell happened to you?"

The audience roared. Kellar grinned. This was so much better than how she thought the interview would go.

"I—uh—well..." She pretended to stumble over her words. "I had a little mishap in your green room."

Jamie's eyebrows rose as high as they would go. "A mishap? Were you running for your life from resurrected dinosaurs?"

More laughter from the audience while Kellar kept her smile in place to let them know she was in on the jokes about her appearance.

"Art?" Jamie looked across at his long-time producer. "Send a security team to the green room, stat. They'll need the big tranquilizer guns."

The audience tittered.

"Seriously, though. How did this happen?" Jamie asked.

"I was trying not to mess up my lipstick," Kellar began.

"Wait. You're telling me this." He waved a hand from her head to her feet. "Is the fault of a lipstick? Art," he deadpanned, "Tell them to be on the lookout for Revlon Number 226. Accidental Red." The audience chuckled. Jamie turned back to her. "Go on."

"Do I have any lipstick on my teeth?" She bared her teeth and leaned toward Jamie.

He inspected her teeth. "Maybe a little." He swiped at her front teeth with his forefinger for a second, then pretended to inspect them again. "Got it."

"Now, what if I showed up for a date like this? Would you still go out with me?"

"Unh. I would, but my wife made me stop dating shortly after we got married."

Kellar chuckled along with the audience. "Seriously, though. Pretend you're still single. I've agreed to meet you at a restaurant for dinner. And I show up looking like this. What would you do?"

"Wow. That's a great question. But this is my show and you're supposed to be responding to my questions. So why don't you tell us since you're the dating expert.

What's the average guy going to do?"

Kellar looked Jamie in the eye, knowing the camera was on her. "Bail." She said it emphatically. The audience applauded.

"Bail? But he's already there. He invited you to dinner."

"Of course, he did. But now I'm not what he expected. He's probably embarrassed to be seen with me. Look at me." She spread her hands wide and lifted her foot to display her shoe with the broken heel. "I look like something the cat dragged in."

"Actually, you look like something the cat dragged in, played with for a while, drooled on, and then lost interest in."

"Exactly!" Kellar agreed. "I'm not saying the guy wouldn't ask what happened or if I'm alright. But he also might be thinking I'm a trainwreck or a drama queen, so chances are he'll play it safe and hit the escape button. I predict the guy who asked me out is going to toss me aside the moment I don't live up to his expectations. Or the second I don't look exactly the way he wants. Or, God forbid, if I do something to embarrass him."

"You're saying men are shallow."

"I'm not, but how about if we ask your audience how they'd react?"

"Sure. Okay, men, you expected to have dinner with the lovely and talented Kellar, and she arrives looking a bit disastrous. Who's going to stick around, pick up the tab and ask her out on a second date?"

He waited for the smattering of applause to peter out. "And who's planning to bail first chance they get?"

The applause this time was much more uproarious and enthusiastic and took longer to die down.

"I guess we just proved your expertise in the world of dating," Jamie conceded.

Kellar didn't hide her pleasure at how helpful the men in the audience were in making her point.

"Women often have a hard time being themselves around men they're interested in. Sometimes they're so desperate to hang on to a guy they don't show their true selves because they're afraid if they do, he'll walk away."

"Interesting. And your book is about...?

"Changing the way women view men and dating."

"I'm curious about the opposite side of the equation. If those who can, date, what about those who *can't*? Those who can't...teach? Are destined to live with a houseful of cats and die alone?"

The audience chuckled politely.

Jamie continued to riff on possible answers to his question. "Those who can't, swipe left? Compensate in some other way? Get mom to fix them up with the neighbor's child? Eat lots of ice cream?"

"Those are all possibilities, certainly, but I think for all of us out there in the dating world the answer is never give up hope of finding that special someone. Even when it feels like all you're meeting are a lot of not-right-for-me people, first."

"Well, we've got to go to a commercial break, but I

want to hear more about this when we come back. Don't go away."

"You're doing great," Jamie said to her in a low tone, the moment they stopped recording.

Kellar allowed herself to breathe. "Thanks. You're making it very easy for me."

"That's my job. But I've got to know what happened in the green room. Do I have a lawsuit on my hands?"

Laughter bubbled out of Kellar. "Not from me." She held up her foot. "Although I wouldn't mind if you felt bad enough about my accident to replace my Louboutins.

"Oh, God, Louboutins. I know what those cost. Do you have any idea the budget we've got to put on this show? We're operating on a shoestring here. But I'll see what I can do."

"A shoestring, huh? The top-rated late night talk show? If you say so. I hope you can find room in the budget to replace the coffee table in your green room."

"Wait, *what*?" Jamie was equal parts intrigued and horrified.

"Back in five, four, three, two, one," a production assistant counted down.

Like flipping a switch, Jamie returned to his on-screen persona. "We're back with dating expert Kellar Kennedy. Kellar, you have a chapter in your book about dating talking points. Tell us about that."

"Sure. As I said earlier, it can be hard to be yourself on a first date for whatever reason. You're nervous or feeling anxious. Maybe you've set high expectations in the past and been disappointed. Instead of fumbling around for something to talk about, I think it's a good idea before a date, to have a mental list of subjects which can keep a conversation going. This is especially crucial on a first date."

"Why's that?"

"Because the truth is, most men aren't great conversationalists. Their verbal skills lag far behind that of women's."

Jamie's mouth dropped open in shock, which got the desired reaction from his audience. "I beg to differ but go on."

"This isn't my opinion. There's scientific evidence to back this up. I encourage women to have a mental list of things to talk about just in case the conversation lags. For example, an incident that happened that day at work or a problem with their car. A pet, a family member, a quirky neighbor."

"You advise women to talk about themselves on a date. Just in case they aren't already inclined to do that." He winked at the audience, which got more laughs.

Kellar chuckled right along. "Well, Jamie, it's a good way to find out if the guy's ever going to listen to anything you say. If he does, encourage him to share the same sort of information with you. If he doesn't—"

"Don't tell me, let me guess. Bail?"

Kellar smiled until her cheeks objected. "You got it. And frankly, this is a good tip for men as well, especially if they're conversationally challenged. I'm not saying anyone needs to delve into their family drama or a play-by-play of their dog's digestive issues. Keep it light. If you've got a good sense of humor, let it shine. Remember, you're looking for a way to connect while also gauging the other person's level of interest."

"Great advice," Jamie told her. He held up her book for the camera. "The book is Those Who Can comma Date. Dating expert Kellar Kennedy, everyone." Applause began as the band started up to play them into the break. "We'll be right back to talk with Dayman MacDay about his latest sure-to-be-blockbuster film."

Day applauded with everyone else from behind the curtain, after watching Kellar's performance on the monitor. He all but ignored the assistant who attached the mic box to his belt and the microphone to his collar, craning his head to see over hers.

Kellar Kennedy was dynamite. The real deal. He tried to imagine which other women of his acquaintance would have dared appear on national television in such a state. She hadn't whined. Hadn't thrown a fit. Hadn't burst into tears over her ruined shoe or her less-than-perfect makeup. She'd leaned into it, turned it to her advantage, and the audience loved her for it. He bet her book would be on every bestseller list by this time next week.

During the break, she relocated to the armless sofa next to the guest chair. She licked her lips and crossed her legs to hide her broken shoe from view. The makeup team rushed in to dab Jamie's nose with powder, then did the same to Kellar. Day thought he heard her say, "What's the point?" but he couldn't be sure.

Soon, everyone scurried back to their places and settled. The countdown came and Jamie was back. "My next guest you know as the Oscar-nominated megastar of the big screen. His new movie is *Break of Dawn*. Please welcome back, Dayman MacDay."

Applause thundered as Day stepped out of the curtains. He waved to the crowd, stopped mid-stage, pressed his hands together and bowed, then moved in to greet Jamie. They did their signature close-in hand grasp and whispered a few words to each other. Jamie slapped him on the back and Day took the chair as the applause died down.

"How have you been?" Jamie asked. He stared down at his finger, then bent to look closer at it. He picked a tiny shard of glass out of it. "I'm bleeding. Good God, man, what did you do to me?" Jamie held up his hand and motioned for the camera to get a closeup. Which it did. There was a mild gasp from the audience, and chuckles as most assumed this was all part of a bit.

Day shifted so he could pull out a clean white handkerchief from his pocket and hand it to Jamie.

Jamie pressed the cloth to his wound. "Seriously? You carry around white linen handkerchiefs? I did not know this about you."

"It's one of my many, deep dark secrets," Day said with a smile.

"Are they monogrammed?"

"I save those for ladies in distress."

The audience laughed.

"So, any idea how I got glass in my hand when I slapped you on the back?" Jamie pulled the handkerchief away from his finger. The tiny bit of bleeding had stopped.

"Well, there was an...incident...in your green room." Day glanced at Kellar when he said this. He swung his gaze back to the host. "You're going to need a new coffee table." The audience tittered.

"I take it you two have met?" Jamie said.

"Not exactly," Day said, looking once again at Kellar.

"Just briefly," Kellar said at the same time. "We didn't have a chance for introductions."

"Oh, allow me," Jamie said in a gallant tone worthy of British royalty. Kellar Kennedy meet actor Dayman MacDay. Dayman, this is dating expert, Kellar Kennedy."

Dayman turned fully so he could face her. He extended his hand leaving her no choice but to take it or appear rude. She slid her fingers against his. It was only a fraction of a second, but it seemed much longer that they looked at each other. The moment went on until he lifted her hand to his lips and kissed it. Cheers and whistles erupted from the audience. He grinned and let go, turning back to Jamie.

"Art, make a note," Jamie said to his producer. "Install

security cameras in the green room."

The audience approved.

"Okay, time to fess up. Tell us what happened."

"First of all, she arrived looking one hundred percent stunning from head to toe." Day looked first at Kellar, then the audience, then at Jamie. Kellar rolled her eyes, but smiled when she did. "And I accidentally ruined her. I'm responsible for this." He indicated her. "And for that." He pointed at Jamie's finger.

"Art, get the insurance company on the phone. We know who broke the table and her shoe, and why my finger is injured. Tell them Dayman MacDay's responsible for the damage. You're insured, aren't you, Day?"

Everyone laughed.

"This is your new thing?" Jamie asked Day. "Breaking tables and shoes instead of hearts?"

"Apparently. Oh, wait!" He withdrew the heel of Kellar's shoe from his shirt pocket and held it up for a moment before he got down on one knee next to her. He tapped her ankle until she uncrossed her legs. He picked up her foot and did his best to reattach the heel to her shoe.

More hoots and hollers, whistles, and shouts of encouragement erupted from the audience.

The camera shot back to Jamie, who rolled his eyes. "He's a movie star, a heartbreaker, and now I think he's auditioning for the role of Geppetto. We'll be right back and talk more about Day's new movie *Break of Dawn.* Don't go away."

During the break, Day said to her, "I'll buy you a new pair of shoes."

Kellar shook her head. "That's not necessary."

"Of course, it is." He eyed her critically. "What about the dress? Donna Karan?"

"MaxMara."

"What size?"

"You don't have to replace the dress. Or the shoes. Let's just forget this whole incident, shall we?"

"No chance in hell," he said before he leaned forward and whispered something to Jamie.

Kellar allowed her nose to be powdered *again*. She wished desperately for a tube of petroleum jelly. Or some moisturizing lip gloss. Her lips were beyond dry. She licked them again. It didn't help because her mouth was dry too. She had no idea why she kept doing it. Instinct, she supposed. Nervous habit. She'd started off strong, lemonading the hell out of the lemons life had thrown at her, but now she just wanted the show to be over. The makeup artist pointed to a mug on the low table in front of the sofa. "There's water there for you. I've given up on the lip stain."

Afraid of what might happen if she so much as looked at the water, Kellar gave her a weak smile. "Thanks." She couldn't wait to get back home. Get out of this dress and her heels—er, heel—and take a nice long bath.

She envisioned it now. Candles. A glass of white wine. A magazine or two. Her favorite scented bath oil. Her face and lips free of makeup and lavishly moisturized. Teeth brushed. Body lotion smoothed over her arms and legs and then bed. Soft sheets. Down pillow. Sleep.

She almost missed the countdown before the cameras were back on. She sat still, hands in her lap, and listened politely to Day's patter about his new movie. A clip was shown.

Day was known for doing truly fine plot-driven action/adventure films. But he'd also done a few dramatic roles and several romantic comedies. Those were Kellar's favorites. She was a sucker for romance, even though there'd been precious little of it directed her way.

"I'd love to take you to dinner. What do you say?"

Kellar realized she'd completely spaced out when Dayman MacDay addressed her. Jamie Falcon looked at her expectantly.

"Excuse me?" The audience laughed at her obvious confusion.

"Jamie's offered to buy us dinner at Shariffe after the show. How about it?"

"Oh, no. That's very nice, but I can't."

"Can't?" Day fixed her with a look. "Or don't want to?"

Kellar read the challenge in his eyes.

"Those who can, date, right?" Day said. "I guess that means those who can't, eat alone and write advice columns."

She looked at Jamie hoping he'd help her out. "The serial dater and the dating expert. It's a match made in heaven, right folks?"

The well-trained audience whooped and cheered.

Day leaned over and whispered in her ear. "You're not afraid I'll bail on you halfway through, are you?"

"I'm not afraid of anything." She hoped he didn't catch the slight quaver in her voice. He'd bailed on her once before, so she wouldn't be at all surprised if he did it again. She almost hoped he would. Then she'd really have something to write about. "I'd *love* to." She smiled and bobbed her head, hoping that would stop the obnoxious though enthusiastic cheers which threatened to give her a headache.

"She said yes!" Day hollered. Applause surged again. Jamie did his sign-off, announcing tomorrow's guests, and the taping was over.

A dinner date with Dayman MacDay was the kind of publicity money couldn't buy and Kellar knew it. She just hoped she was strong enough to survive it.

Chapter Four

♥

Day had his phone out and began furiously texting the moment the cameras were off. Then he pocketed the phone and helped Kellar up. Of course, the broken heel did not stay up with her. "Maybe you should just take those shoes off," Day said.

She slipped out of them, and he picked them up, tucking the broken heel inside its shoe. They said their goodbyes to Jamie, who seemed pleased with their performances. He kept repeating "great show" as if those were the only two words he knew.

Kellar sighed with relief as they made their way down the corridor. She retrieved her purse from security and Day escorted her to the exit and into a waiting limo. She slid over to make room for him. She opened her purse and pulled out a tube, squeezed some of the soothing jelly onto her ring finger, and smoothed it over her lips. Instant relief. She capped the tube and dropped it back into her purse.

She caught Day staring. "What?"

"Did you...? What did you just do?"

"My lips are dry. *Were* dry. It's the only thing that helps."

"It makes them look kissable."

She fixed him with a look. "Is that so?"

A wiser man would have shut up. "More kissable. Not that your lips didn't look kissable before. But now you look like you're waiting for a kiss."

"Do I?"

"Oh, yeah."

"And I suppose you're just the man to do it?"

He pretended to think about that. His eyes twinkled. "I might be. But not on the first date." She couldn't tell if he was teasing her or dead serious. *That's what you get when you're with an actor.*

Unlike Day, Kellar knew when to shut up. She didn't bother pointing out that this wasn't a date and regarded him as if she had no opinion on the subject one way or the other.

"I guess you get kissed pretty regularly, huh?" he said.

"I don't see how that's relevant. Nor is it any of your business."

"You're a dating expert, aren't you?"

Again, she didn't respond.

"You only get to be an expert on something after lots of practice."

"That is not true. Besides, I never claimed to be a kissing expert."

"Name something you can be an expert at without actual practice."

"English literature, for one. I could read it. Study it. Memorize it. Get a degree in it. A PhD, even. I'd be an expert on it without ever having written a single novel."

"Touché."

"Or men, for that matter. I learn all about men by studying their behavior, their biology, researching their psychology. I could be an expert on men without, thank God, being one."

"I thank God for that, too." When he smiled, Kellar warned herself not to be taken in by his charm. Maybe he wouldn't bail on her tonight. Not now that the press was involved. He'd bask in the publicity he'd get from a well-publicized "date" with her for his new movie, just as she would for her book. Jamie Falcon had done them both a favor and he certainly knew it.

But she was under no delusion, if they were to really *date,* Dayman MacDay would bail on her if something or *someone* better came along. That's what he did. She was an expert on Dayman MacDay. He just didn't know it.

"Excuse me," he said. He withdrew his phone from his pocket again. "I need to take care of a few things."

"By all means." She had a phone, too. She also had a bunch of text messages. She scanned through them. Her assistant, her editor, her agent, her sister, and her mother.

Kellar started with the one from Adrienne, her sister, updating her on Adrienne's six-year-old daughter, Gracie, who was undergoing treatment for a rare form of leukemia. She was doing great and might be able to leave the hospital sometime next week. Kellar breathed a sigh of relief.

The news from Kellar's mother, however, was not as good. Kellar's grandmother had been moved to a hospice facility. It was only a matter of time.

Kellar was not unprepared for this. Her grandmother, Pearl, whom everyone called Poppy, had been sick for a long time. Kellar would miss her as would the whole family. Poppy had always been there for everyone. She had a giving soul and a way of making whoever she was with feel like they were the most important person in her life. She listened. She loved. She taught.

Many of the things Kellar had learned in life she'd learned from Poppy. How to make brownies. How to sew and knit and quilt. How to butcher a chicken and make a flaky piecrust.

Kellar looked out the limo's tinted window, thinking of all the times she and Adrienne had spent at her grandmother's house. How she'd let them stay up late and watch scary movies against her mother's explicit orders. How they all swore each other to secrecy every time they broke one of Mom's rules.

Poppy had been woven into the fabric of their lives. No one else would fill that space.

Kellar blinked away the tears, the phone forgotten in her lap.

"Everything okay?"

Lost in her reminiscences, Kellar had almost forgotten Dayman was there. She sniffed, hoping he didn't notice the telltale moisture at the edges of her eyelids. "Fine.

Why?"

"Something made you sad." He indicated her phone. "Just then."

Poppy would have loved meeting Day. She adored his movies. Kellar could almost feel Poppy's bony elbow nudging her during one and whispering, "He's hot."

Keller would egg her on with a reply like, "Meh. If you're into that type."

Poppy would pretend outrage. "Every red-blooded woman in the country is into abs you could cut a diamond on and eyes that would melt chocolate."

"If you say so." And here, Kellar would have to grin.

Then Poppy would get sentimental. "He reminds me of your grandpa."

"In what way?" Kellar knew for a fact there were zero physical similarities between the two men.

"In the way that I'd like to wake up and find him in bed with me."

Then they would giggle at their silliness.

If Poppy knew that her granddaughter was, at this very moment, in a limo on her way to dinner with him, she'd declare herself ready to die and go to heaven... right after she grilled Kellar for every dreamy detail.

"You can tell me, you know. I may be a man, but I'm not *completely* insensitive."

"I never said men were."

He didn't look like he believed her.

"It's my grandmother if you must know. She's—she's—" if she said the words, they'd be true. Kellar didn't want them to be true. "Dying."

"I'm sorry to hear that." He paused a beat. "Is there anything I can do?"

"What could you possibly do?" Her tone had been sharper than she intended.

Not knowing how to answer her question, he looked out the window.

"Sorry. I didn't mean to sound snarky. But unless you've got a cure for old age and congestive heart failure, there's nothing anyone can do."

"Good thing this isn't a real date," he said. "Because you're not taking your own advice. Where's your list of light-hearted topics to kick things off?"

For some reason she'd have to examine later, that startled a laugh out of her. "You're right. I should have one prepared for these unscheduled outings."

He grinned. The car slid to a stop. Kellar looked out the window. "Where are we, anyway? I thought we were going to Shariffe." She hadn't paid the least bit of attention to the direction they'd been traveling. It appeared they were in one of the exclusive shopping areas of Beverly Hills.

"We are. I'll be right back." The door sprung open, and Day exited. He stepped into a boutique and a young woman handed him a shopping bag with a smile and wave. Day slid back into his seat and the limo pulled out into traffic. The whole event took less than a minute.

He leaned over and set the shopping bag in Kellar's lap.

She frowned as she slid the shoebox out of the bag and

chanced another look his way. He looked pleased with himself. She picked up the box to discover that, according to the label, it held a pair of shoes exactly like her ruined ones.

She lifted the lid. "How did you know my size?"

"I checked when I carried your shoes out of the studio."

"That's what the urgent texting was about?"

"Most of it."

She'd thought he was ignoring her. That he had more important things to do than have a conversation or entertain her on the way to the restaurant. She wondered now how long he'd been watching her while she read her own texts, while she was lost in her memories of her grandmother. Was Day more observant than and, dare she think it, *sensitive* than the average man? Could he possibly be even more thoughtful?

Don't be ridiculous, she warned herself. She could hardly walk into one of LA's hottest new restaurants barefoot or wearing one good shoe and one with a broken heel. *Movie Star* Dayman MacDay had an image and a reputation to uphold. Bad enough he was showing up with a relative nobody like her.

She crossed one leg then the other to slip the shoes on, aware of Day watching her every movement. She put her old shoes into the box and set them aside. "Thank you. Now at least I won't embarrass you."

"I thought you'd be more comfortable—wait, is *that* why you think I got the shoes? To protect my image or something?"

"Isn't it?"

He sat back as if she'd shot him. His jaw set and he looked out the window, his fingers tapping on the leather seat.

Kellar had not only managed to piss him off, she'd also hurt his feelings. Maybe she wasn't as much of an expert on Dayman MacDay as she'd thought.

"I'm sorry. I'm so bad at this. I say all the wrong things. I do all the wrong things. I haven't been on a date in about two years. Not that this is really a date. For a dating expert, I really, truly suck at it."

Her speech appeased him. "Stick with me then, kid. I'm the crown prince of the dating world, or so the press would have everyone believe."

Kellar scrambled for something else to say, to make some effort at small talk and came up blank. Day didn't seem to mind her silence, and she began to relax. *This isn't a date.* Reminding herself of that helped immensely. One dinner. One evening which her companion would barely remember by next month. Any publicity this non-date generated for her book could only help sales. She hadn't been able to make much of an impression on Dayman MacDay ten years ago nor would she now. She gazed out the window at the passing LA landscape, a part of her wishing that wasn't the case.

After a few more minutes he glanced out the window again, then back at her. "We're here. Any last-minute adjustments you need to make? Need to touch up your lips?"

She almost laughed. "Sorry to say it, but this is as good as I'm going to get."

"You look pretty damn good to me. I thought we'd catch a break since it's so early, but it looks like the paps are already out in full force. Just stick close. You don't have to say anything if you don't want to, but it's a good idea if you smile."

"To make them believe I'm enjoying myself?"

"It just looks better when the pictures show up in the gossip columns and entertainment mags."

He pulled out a tube of lip balm and ran it across his lips. It didn't make them shiny or anything. If she hadn't seen him do it, she wouldn't have been able to tell.

"What's that?" she asked before he put the tube back in his pocket.

He held it out to her. "It's made from bee pollen or beeswax or something like that." She picked up the tube and examined it before handing it back to him. He said, "You're not the only one with dry lips, you know."

Her eyes met his. "I guess not."

"Ready?"

"Ready."

He rapped on the window and the driver opened the door. Day stepped out and offered her his hand. She slid across the seat and stood next to him.

What felt like a million flashbulbs went off. Reporters yelled questions, which Day ignored. She remembered to smile. Day released her hand and kept his on the small of her back while he slow-walked her to the restaurant entrance. She was vaguely aware of him acknowledging the crowd gathered on either side of the roped-off walkway.

Then they were inside. The door whooshed closed behind them. As if a director had suddenly yelled, "Cut!" Day dropped his arm and greeted the hostess.

Chapter Five

♥

They were swept past a few other patrons waiting for tables and through the sparsely occupied dining area. Day paused to briefly greet a couple of people. The director of his last movie, if Kellar wasn't mistaken, and a well-known screenwriter. Both times he said, "Meet Kellar Kennedy," in an off-hand way, but didn't bother to introduce the men to her. They nodded politely to her before she and Day moved on to where the hostess waited at a corner table for two.

Day pulled out Kellar's chair. He took the one that kept his back to the room.

"Shouldn't this be the other way around? Don't you want to see and be seen?"

"I've been seen enough. It's your turn. What would you like to drink?" he asked as the server appeared.

Her dress was almost dry and probably unaffected by the green room mishap. She'd like to keep it that way. "White wine. Preferably pinot grigio."

The server wrinkled his nose. "We also have a lovely Riesling madam might enjoy."

Kellar wrinkled her nose back at him. "Pinot. Grigio. Thank you."

She caught Day trying not to smile. He ordered a brand of beer she'd never heard of before. Not that she was an expert on beer brands.

"How are you doing?" he asked, placing his crossed arms on the table, and leaning forward.

"Other than the apparently glaring faux pas of ordering something as mundane as pinot grigio in a place like this, you mean?"

"That and being seen in public with the likes of me."

"It's not exactly a hardship. I expect it will do wonders for my book sales."

"Will the increase in revenue make up for me messing up your look?"

"You're kidding, right? Thanks to you, I'll get more publicity out of tonight than any marketing campaign my publisher could have come up with."

Their drinks arrived. Day waved the server off when he tried to offer them menus.

He picked up his glass. "Let's have a toast."

"To what?"

"To the runaway success of the dating expert."

"And to the continued success of the serial dater. May he find what he's looking for."

They clinked glasses and sipped, but she noticed Dayman's demeanor subtly changed after her words.

Kellar said, "You know, I use my experiences and observations in my blog and on my podcast. I *will* be mentioning what happened tonight."

"Honey, there's nothing you could write or say about me that hasn't been written or said before. Whether it's true or not."

Kellar bristled. "I don't make things up and I don't embellish."

"That makes you different from about ninety-seven percent of the journalists I've encountered in my career."

"You seem a little bitter."

Day sat back. Kellar got the impression that he was forcing himself to appear relaxed. "Nah. I'm used to it. I don't expect the truth from anyone anymore."

"That's kind of sad."

He sipped his beer. "That's Hollywood."

"Not that it's much of a reassurance, but you can always count on me to tell the truth."

"Always?"

"*Always.*"

"That might explain why you're... less than successful at dating."

"True. Most men don't want to hear the truth."

"Most people, I should think."

"But if there's no honesty, then everything's an illusion. Nothing's real."

"That's what makes this town so great." He smiled when he said it, but the smile didn't quite reach his eyes.

Kellar cast about for a change of subject. "I'm going to need to eat something soon. If I don't—" She gestured at her half glass of wine. "And I keep drinking, I'll not only be honest, but I'll turn snarky. Trust me, it won't be pretty."

This time his smile appeared genuine, but he was a gifted actor, so how could she be sure? "A lightweight, huh?" He signaled the waiter.

"Let's just say I'd prefer to get through the evening without any further incidents."

When an appetizer of grilled calamari and baby scallops appeared a short time later, Kellar agreed to a refill of her wineglass.

They'd made small talk waiting for the food. Kellar'd had the opportunity to check out her surroundings. She wasn't exactly surprised to find a few curious glances directed her way. The dining room was set up to appear formal, yet intimate. Tables of twos and fours were arranged to take advantage of the space. Their corner table was the most isolated since it sat along a wall and was half hidden by the hallway to the restrooms. She supposed in most restaurants it wouldn't be considered a prime location, but if a diner wanted privacy, it was ideal.

"How'd you become a dating expert, anyway?" Day asked.

Should she tell the great Dayman MacDay that *he* was responsible for the start of her dating blog? She'd been half-heartedly blogging about all her college experiences, including dating, before he'd stood her up all those years ago. She hadn't used his name when she arrived back at the dorm that night and poured her heart out on her computer screen. She'd titled it, "The Guy I Really

Liked."

The response had been surprising. She'd struck a chord, tapping into her feelings about something many young women could relate to. So, she expanded on dating in future blogs. Using her friends' experiences, interviewing students on campus for their reactions and feelings, and her own observances.

She'd stuck with it after graduation, parlaying the blog's success into a career writing for dating web sites and women's magazines. She'd started offering advice to her peers when asked. Meanwhile, she pursued her master's in psychology. Credentials were important for credibility. Even though much of what she wrote was theoretical, her ideas worked for many of her followers. More recently she'd begun her weekly podcast. Her popularity grew and the book deal materialized.

Which had led to her coming full circle somehow, sitting across from Dayman MacDay who seemed intent on being the one conducting the interview this time.

She condensed her answer as much as possible. "I got either stood up or dumped one too many times. I decided to figure out what I was doing wrong. And the rest, as they say, is history." She helped herself to a scallop. Spice and citrus cut through the buttery richness, the flavors bursting on her tongue.

"You got stood up? The guy must have been an idiot."

"That's certainly what I thought at the time, although I also thought I had evidence to the contrary."

"What kind of evidence?"

"I'd spent some time talking to him. He seemed sincere. And not an idiot."

"Then why assume *you* did anything wrong?"

Kellar polished off the scallop. Explaining how Dayman's behavior had affected her without him knowing was kind of fun. "Like I said, it wasn't the first time a guy I liked didn't... perform as expected." She eyed the calamari and the accompanying dipping sauce. "There was a pattern. I decided I needed to take a hard look at the common denominator."

They reached for the same piece of calamari at the same time. Dayman withdrew his hand. "Please."

Kellar smiled. She hadn't been out with a gentleman in a while. She dipped the calamari and leaned forward. She closed her eyes, chewed and swallowed. When she opened them, she found Day staring at her. "Mmm. That was good." She licked her lips.

"You've got a..." He leaned forward and brushed his thumb along the corner of her mouth. She felt his touch all the way to her toes. She straightened and dabbed her lips with her napkin.

Nervously, she slid her tongue across her lips.

"Are your lips dry again?"

"A little."

He withdrew his lip balm from his pocket and offered it to her. "Here. Try this." He uncapped it and handed it to her.

She took it. Dayman MacDay sharing his lip balm came as a surprise. She glanced around the dining room. Most of the other diners seemed to be going about the business of eating or talking amongst themselves. No one stared. Yet the moment still seemed surreal.

"I'm clean, if that's what you're worried about," Day said.

"What?"

"I'm careful. You won't catch anything from me."

"You mean like...?"

"I've got the last set of test results at my house. Nothing to worry about."

"Do you normally feel compelled to reassure your dates in this regard?"

"Depends on where I think the date might end up. I will tell you one thing, though. I've never shared my lip balm with a woman before."

"I'm your first?"

"You're my first."

"I'm honored."

She rolled the balm up and applied it to her bottom lip, then pressed her lips together before she handed it back to him. He recapped it and replaced it in his pocket. "It's soothing. I sense a hint of mint."

"It doesn't make your lips shiny. Although I think I like the wet look on you."

Keep doing what you're doing then.

The waiter approached with menus. "How do you think our not-a-date is going?" Day asked. "Should we order dinner?"

"By all means. In fact, since you've been here before,

why don't you order for me? I'd like to go to the ladies' room."

"What do you like?"

You. "I'm not picky. Stay away from organ meats and tofu, though."

"Noted."

He stood and helped her with her chair. She didn't feel quite steady on her feet, but she made her way to the restroom okay. Her head spun because she couldn't process everything that had happened in just a few short hours, and she couldn't sort out how she felt about any of it. Or perhaps she'd sipped too much wine on an empty stomach.

No. It wasn't the wine. It was Dayman MacDay. She'd been zapped back in time to ten years ago. This is *exactly* how she'd felt during that interview. Wildly attracted, her nerves thrumming with excitement. She'd loved talking to him and she'd resented it when the publicity coordinator signaled their time was up.

Following right behind those memories was the one of him standing her up. The crushing weight of his rejection followed her around for months.

She stared at herself in the mirror while she washed her hands. "Do *Not*. Set Yourself Up. *Again*."

She dabbed on a bit of petroleum jelly for more of a wet look, even though her lips weren't the least bit dry.

Chapter Six

♥

When she returned to the table, Day appeared to be deep in thought. His glass of beer was still half-full. He didn't have his cellphone out, but he was a million miles away mentally and her reappearance startled him.

"Penny for your thoughts," she said.

"I doubt they're worth that much."

"Oh, I don't know. I'm sure there are any number of people who would pay big bucks to find out what goes on in the mind of *People Magazine*'s Sexiest Man Alive."

Day winced. "That was two years ago."

"True." She gave him a once-over. "But it doesn't appear that anything's changed."

He laughed. "Is that your subtle way of telling me you think I'm sexy?"

"Why? Is your ego not happy unless *every single woman* of your acquaintance says so?"

"Is that the snark making an appearance? I like it. Have some more wine."

Kellar dutifully sipped. Damn. She *liked* him. She enjoyed their conversation. He made her enjoy herself. She liked it when he laughed at something she said. This was bad. Very bad. She should get up and walk out. Save herself before it was too late.

No. She wasn't a starry-eyed college student anymore. She wasn't going to cry into her pillow because her crush stood her up for some leggy blonde. She was a dating expert. She could handle the likes of Dayman MacDay. Handle him like he'd never been handled before.

That silent unintended inuendo lingered and brought a flush to her cheeks. She sipped some more wine. Was it hot in here?

"You do know that's all publicity."

"What?"

"Sexiest Man Alive. Hottest Actor. Best Abs. Forbes Highest Paid Celebrities. Whatever some magazine's got going that month. It doesn't mean anything."

"Surely Forbes does their research."

"Sure. But the rest? It's what studio or record label or modeling agency pulls in the most favors or generates the most advertising dollars for the rag. Or which publicity department is the media darling of the moment. Those lists draw in readers, but it helps us, too."

"So... you don't think you're sexy?"

"You're asking if I believe the hype printed about me?"

"That's not what I asked. Do you think you're sexy?"

"I have my moments." He gave her a look that made her think he knew exactly how it affected her. "Which makes me exactly like every other guy."

"You are *not* like every other guy." For some reason she felt compelled to assure him of this. She drank some more wine. Where the heck was dinner?

"Don't you think almost every guy is considered sexy by someone? His wife or his girlfriend—"

"Or boyfriend."

"Exactly. Sexy is in the eyes of the beholder."

"You don't think we can manufacture sexy for ourselves?"

"To a certain extent. Play up your assets, downplay your flaws. Try to look your best. Be genuine. Be confident. The sexy will follow."

"Is that what you've done?"

"I suppose."

"Then you *do* think you're sexy. I win." She lifted her wineglass. There wasn't much left, so she drank the rest.

He said, "I can't decide if talking to you is stimulating or merely exhausting."

She licked her lips. *Stop that!* "Do I get a vote?"

"By all means."

"I vote for stimulating."

He lifted his beer glass. "It's certainly been interesting." He took a drink.

"Uh oh. That's like telling your buddy the girl you want to fix him up with has a great personality. She's... *interesting.*"

The waiter appeared. Finally. He refilled Kellar's wineglass. "Your salads will be out momentarily."

"You know, if you'd rather not do this, it's okay. We can

go," Kellar told him. "We had drinks and an appetizer. That ought to be enough to satisfy the paparazzi, right?"

"Is that what you want?"

"No. I just meant you got rooked into taking me to dinner on national television. And I sense you're too much of a gentleman to make up some excuse to—"

"Bail?"

"Yes."

He leaned forward. "Let me explain something to you, although as a dating expert you should already know this, about guys in general and me in particular. We don't do anything we don't want to do. If I didn't want to have dinner with you, we would not be here. I've become an expert at extricating myself from situations I don't want to be in. At the moment, I have no desire to be anywhere else. Or with anyone else."

She felt a glimmer of a smile hovering around her lips. She couldn't contain it.

Their salads arrived. She sipped some more wine.

Day poked at his salad, but most of his focus remained on Kellar. Not that she seemed to be aware of it. She'd given him an out! He could imagine how she would have portrayed *that* in her blog tomorrow. He could write the headline himself: "Dayman MacDay Bailed On Me."

However, negative publicity was not the reason why

he stayed. Meeting Kellar Kennedy had brought home to him once again how tired he was of the life to which he'd once aspired. A life he'd worked hard to obtain. Sure, he was a well-respected actor. His movies were consistently successful. He'd made *a ton* of money in the past ten years. Professionally, he had no complaints. His personal life, however, was a disaster.

His last two relationships had been more publicity stunts than anything. Probably the ones before that were as well, but he'd been too naïve to realize it at the time. He'd stopped expecting to find anything real in the world of fakery in which he lived.

Which was why he was ready to bail on Hollywood. He'd done what he'd set out to do here; now he could do what he wanted. Start his own production company. Produce. Direct. Write. He could still take acting roles, but he could afford to be choosy. And he planned to be *extremely* choosy about his next relationship. It would have to be with someone who wouldn't use him. Preferably someone who didn't even know who he was. Although that could be difficult unless he expanded his search way outside the U.S. Even then, it could be tough.

The important thing was that it was with someone real who wouldn't use him as a steppingstone in her own career, someone he could have a conversation with that wasn't about "the industry," someone who challenged him, someone he was attracted to—

"This is delicious. Is that goat cheese, do you know?"

Someone with a healthy appetite who wasn't afraid to

eat the cheese in her salad or anything else on her plate. Someone who didn't feel compelled to wear makeup to bed and who could leave the house without an hour-long consultation with a stylist.

Someone like Kellar Kennedy, as a matter of fact.

"No clue. My palate's not very refined."

"With all the great restaurants you frequent?"

"I grew up eating at truck stops. Scallops and goat cheese weren't usually on the menu."

Kellar knew that about him, of course. It was one of the first things she'd asked him about in that long-ago interview. Several years after their marriage, his parents were told they couldn't have children and decided to partner with each other as long-haul truck drivers. As their only child, he'd come as a surprise to them, born in Manchester, New Hampshire, but, according to their calculations, likely conceived in Dayton, Ohio—thus, the unusual spelling of his first name.

Home-schooled until he started middle school, he traveled with his parents and watched a lot of movies to waylay boredom when he wasn't studying. He'd moved to LA for college and did some modeling to support himself before he broke into acting.

Kellar smiled. "I love truck stops. We took a road trip to visit cousins in Nebraska when I was a kid. I'd never been out of Indiana. We'd stop to eat, and I loved everything about those places. The semis. The gift shops. The drivers who all seemed to know each other. Oh, and the food! Cheeseburgers and fries, but the real thing, you know? Nothing like fast food. Hashbrowns and runny egg yolks for breakfast. And pie! Those wedges of pie in those round display cases. With dishes of pudding and slices of cake."

Kellar sat back and closed her eyes for a moment, the goat cheese in her salad forgotten. She opened her eyes. "I haven't thought of that trip in a long time. It's one of the best memories from my childhood."

"Why's that?"

Her face clouded, making Dayman sorry he'd asked. "We didn't go on many trips. We didn't have a lot of money and my parents... didn't always get along. They split up when I was fifteen, as a matter of fact, and I didn't see my dad very often. Sorry, I'm rambling. This isn't good date talk. I think I've had a little too much wine.

"It's just that when we were on that trip, it was the first time my eyes were opened to new places and people who weren't all the same as where we lived. There was a whole world out there I knew nothing about, one I wanted to explore. I found it all fascinating."

She leaned forward. "Sometimes, oh, maybe a couple of times a year, I'll take a weekend and just drive. No destination in mind. I drive and stop and explore and do whatever I want. I eat cheeseburgers and pie and runny eggs with hashbrowns at truck stops. That's my idea of fun. Probably sounds stupid to you. I should stop talking now.

"This is why I don't drink very much. I get very chatty. I ramble on about whatever pops into my head. Guys hate it. I can just hear them telling their buddies. 'All she did is talk about herself.'

"This is why I'm bad at dating. Well, another reason, anyway. Word vomit. That's from *Mean Girls*. Do you know Tina Fey? She's had quite a career, hasn't she?"

Day said nothing as the server returned. "Finished with your salad?"

Kellar licked her lips and looked at her plate before answering. "I guess so. No wait, can you leave it? Is this goat cheese?"

"Yes ma'am. And yes, it is goat cheese. Your entrees will be out shortly." He picked up Day's plate and left.

"Don't let me drink any more wine." She said after taking another bite of salad. She pushed her glass a few inches away. "Otherwise, I won't stop talking.

"I do know Tina Fey, by the way. We were presenters at the Oscars last year."

"Is the Oscars fun? It seems like it could be. Except you have to be so careful about how you look, or you end up getting trashed online. That's the part I like. Seeing the dresses and the jewelry and the hair. The awards? I mean, I couldn't care less. But the *clothes*. I'd love to have designers sending me dresses hoping I'll wear them so when a reporter asks, who I'm wearing I can say, Carolina Herrara or Givenchy or Prada." Kellar giggled. "Like that's ever going to happen."

"It might."

"How?"

"They could make a movie out of your book."

"And call it what? *Dating Hell*?"

"Or you could go as someone's date."

"Ugh. Except, as you've discovered, I'm horrible at dating." She lowered her voice. "You won't tell anyone, will you? It can be our little secret."

"Is it a secret? The guys you've dated must be aware."

"There haven't been that many. And they probably don't remember me anyway."

"I find that hard to believe."

"What? That there haven't been that many? Or that they wouldn't remember me?"

"Both. My impression is you'd be hard to forget."

Kellar pushed her salad away and reached for her wineglass. "You might remember me for a while. Because of the way we met. But ten years from now? A month from now? You'll have forgotten everything."

"Somehow I don't think so."

In answer, she took a healthy swig of her wine.

Her salad plate disappeared to be replaced by her entrée. She stared at the steak and frites and her mouth watered. She glanced at Dayman to see an exact duplicate sitting in front of him. Their water glasses were refilled by an attentive busboy. A fresh glass of wine appeared next to her plate. Dayman declined the offer of another beer, and they were alone again.

"I can't believe you ordered steak."

"You're not a vegetarian, are you?"

"God no." She narrowed her eyes. "But I think you knew that."

He cut into his steak. "You look like you're in pretty good shape. You need protein to maintain a body like yours."

She picked up her knife and stole a potato from her plate. "Oh. My. God. This is beyond a French fry. This is... heaven." She cut into her steak and took a bite. After her third bite, she said, "Wait. What do you mean, 'a body like mine'?"

"Just what I said. You landed on top of me, remember? I'm something of an expert on the female form. You obviously work out. And you've got curves everywhere you're supposed to have them."

"You can take the farm girl out of Indiana, but..." She ate another potato. Then another. Sipped some more wine. "Another faux pas. White wine with red meat. How shall I ever redeem myself?"

"Are you enjoying yourself?"

"Yes."

He liked her prompt answer. "Then no redemption necessary. You're perfect just the way you are."

"Who said that? Wait, I know." She snapped her fingers. "Colin Whatshisname. Firth. *Bridget Jones's Diary*. Except I think his line was, 'I like you just the way you are.' Right?"

Day wondered when the last time was he'd smiled this much. Enjoyed a 'bad' date this much. "Fine. Have it your way. I like you just the way you are."

Kellar giggled, picked up her wineglass and drank some more.

Chapter Seven

♥

"Have you seen this?" Day's assistant Chazz was perched on a barstool at the center island. Day hadn't rolled out of bed until 7:30. He'd done a half hour of meditation before his trainer arrived. Now he wanted caffeine and food.

Chazz got up to prepare Day's breakfast.

Day helped himself to coffee and took Chazz's seat. Chazz had Kellar's *Those Who Can, Date* website up on his laptop. She'd posted an article a half hour ago. The title was, "I'm Horrible At Dating."

While Chazz prepared an omelet Day sipped his coffee and started to read.

I'm Horrible at Dating

♥

I'm horrible at dating. I'm a dating expert who's bad at dating. There. I've said it. Now you all know my dirty little secret.

Worse? I put America's Sexiest Man Alive (from two years ago, but it still counts) through one of the worst evenings of his life.

If you tuned into the Jamie Falcon Show last night, you saw my disastrous appearance and heard Jamie goad poor Dayman MacDay into having dinner with me at Hollywood's hot new restaurant, Shariffe (more about that later).

I then proceeded to:

a) drink too much wine

b) lick my lips far too often (I do this when I'm nervous or when my lips feel dry—which is all the time)

c) talk way too much (mostly about myself)

To be fair, I offered to let Mr. MacDay off the hook

after the appetizers arrived. Gentlemen that he is, he refused to leave, although now I'm sure he wishes he had. He might have been afraid that my blog today would be about how he'd bailed on me. Not that, realistically, a star of his stature has anything to fear from little ole me. But I digress.

I ate an entire steak and the fried potatoes that came with it. Without regret. Even this morning, I'm feeling quite satisfied with myself and my tummy is very happy. (Though I will be hitting the gym later, make no mistake.)

Unlike me, Dayman MacDay was a dream date. The perfect date. Granted, he's had considerable practice in that area, and he might be more of a dating expert than I am. I'd say he should be writing this column, but where would that leave me? I'm not much of an actress.

Mr. MacDay insisted on walking me to the door and no he did NOT kiss me goodnight—I'm sure I'd remember if he had.

All in all, considering how my evening began (more about THAT later) I had a lovely time.

Which means there's hope for all of us, right? Don't give up, because the lesson here, my chickies, is that you can have a pleasant date even if you're not particularly good at dating.

Day rubbed his hands together and placed his fingers on the keyboard. He thought for a minute before he hit the "Leave a comment" button and started to type.

Chazz glanced over his shoulder and raised an eyebrow. Day read back over what he'd written before he posted the comment. Then he exited the site and opened his email program.

A few minutes later, Chazz set a plate next to him. Two slices of toasted organic bread bracketed a perfect omelet filled with veggies, cheese, and chunks of chicken sausage. Day pushed the laptop across the counter to Chazz and shot instructions to him regarding replies.

Chazz had been a find. Day didn't know what he'd do without him. His title was personal assistant, which meant the man was at Day's beck and call 24/7.

It was Chazz who'd found a boutique on short notice and acquired a new pair of shoes in Kellar's size. Chazz kept track of Day's schedule. He cooked. He was a personal shopper. A houseman. And he was also Day's long-time friend, almost a brother. He'd become irreplaceable.

"Send Kellar Kennedy some flowers," Day told him when they'd finished with the emails. "And knock it off with the solo eyebrow raise."

Chazz hid a grin while he tapped some keys on the keyboard. "Roses?"

"God, no. Not roses. I'm not in love with her."

Chazz glanced up and waited.

"Something... fun," Day said.

"Fun flowers. Can you be more specific?"

"I don't know. What's a fun flower? A happy flower?"

"Google fun flowers," Chazz acknowledged.

"Here we go. Flower meanings. Not love. Let's see." He paused to read for a moment. "Begonia. Beware. Butterfly weed. Let me go. Pink carnation. I'll never forget you?" He glanced at Day.

"Not carnations. They're boring. Something unique."

"Unique and fun. Got it." Chazz went back to perusing the sight. "Yellow Lily. Happy, gay, walking on air. Ivy. Affection, friendship, fidelity. That's not a flower, though."

"How about daisies? Innocence. Loyal love. I'll never tell."

"Yes! Daisies. Exactly. Non-romantic, but upbeat."

"Non-romantic loyal love. Got it. White or yellow?"

"For Pete's sake. I don't know. Both?"

"Okay. Hang on a minute. Card?"

"Does there have to be a card?"

"Up to you, dating expert." Chazz said with a smirk.

"I don't know what to say."

"Well, let's start with why you are sending her flowers."

"Because I—" Why *was* he sending her flowers? Because he'd enjoyed her company last night. She'd been entertaining and amusing. She hadn't cared if she had impressed him or not, and she didn't seem to have any expectations of him, or of their non-date. She probably never expected to hear from him again.

Maybe that's why he wanted to send her flowers. Because she wouldn't be expecting it. They'd be a surprise for her as much as she'd been a surprise to him.

"Just put this on the card, okay? 'It wasn't *that* bad.' Make sure you emphasize *that*."

Chazz started typing. "It. Wasn't. *That*. Bad. Anything

else?"

Day considered the question. Kellar would figure out what he meant, and she'd know the flowers were from him. "No."

"He sent me flowers, Age."

"Really?"

Kellar could hear her sister's surprised gasp over the phone.

Kellar was multi-tasking, prepping her social media posts while talking to her sister for the second time that day. Adrienne had called earlier when she had heard the news, and *could not believe* Kellar had met Dayman Mac-Day a second time—*and* gone to dinner with him. When the flowers arrived, Kellar decided to call her back and give her the details, hoping to distract Adrienne from her worries over her little girl.

"Daisies," Kellar said.

"Daisies," Adrienne repeated. "That's unusual."

"Right?"

"Was there a card?"

"Oh, yes. It said, 'It wasn't that bad.'"

Adrienne tried to stifle a giggle and failed. "That's funny."

"Yeah, the same way him saying I'm interesting is flattering."

"Oh, Kel. He must have read your blog this morning. He was teasing you."

"You think?"

"That's what it sounds like to me. You were pretty hard on yourself, even if it was in a joking way. What color are the daisies?"

"White and yellow. They're really pretty."

"Happy."

"Exactly."

"He wants you to be happy."

"I am happy."

"He sent you flowers that perfectly reflect your state of mind. I think he likes you."

"I don't think he *dis*likes me. The flowers don't mean anything, though, right? It's just a courtesy."

"That, and he must have been thinking of you."

"For about five seconds. Okay, Age-it, I have to go. Kiss Gracie for me."

Kellar ran her fingers across the daisies. She'd slept in and had been barely through her first cup of coffee while talking to her agent when the doorbell rang. She'd put Johanna on hold after she peered through the peephole.

Day had certainly managed to surprise her. She hadn't expected to hear from him again. Certainly, she hadn't expected flowers. But daisies? What was that supposed to mean? The card was obviously a tease. She'd known before she even opened it, they were from him. She just didn't know what the point of it all was. So he could extend his "perfect date" persona?

It hadn't been a date. Not really. Just an impromptu publicity stunt.

But hey, the flowers would provide her with more material for her blog.

"Dayman MacDay commented on your blog post," her assistant told her later that afternoon. Carol lived in Ogden, Utah. Kellar had never actually met her, but she didn't know what she'd do without her. The woman was a cyberspace and social media genius who kept her blog posts, website, calendar, newsletter, and everything else in Kellar's professional life running smoothly. They spoke on the phone daily, and occasionally did a Zoom meeting.

"He did not."

"Go look for yourself. Need me to bring it up for you?"

"No. Just tell me where it is."

"It's the forty-fourth comment."

"'You're better than you think you are?' What's that supposed to mean?"

"Given the context of your post, I assumed he was saying that you're better at dating than you think you are."

"Not likely. Maybe he didn't even post this. Maybe it was someone posing as him."

"I checked. It's genuine. It's his personal account."

"Huh." Kellar scanned through some of the other comments. Most were excited or supportive don't-be-so-hard-on-yourself responses from her followers about her date. Some commiserated on their own dating challenges. A few haters were jealous of her good fortune.

"Do you want me to respond?" Carol asked. Carol often responded to commenters posing as Kellar, thanking, cheering, or commiserating, whichever was appropriate.

"No. I'll take care of it."

They went on to discuss other business, but Kellar's mind stayed on the fact that Dayman MacDay had taken the time to post a comment on her blog. It didn't mean anything, just like the flowers. But again, the thought came that he was handing her priceless material.

Maybe she could drag out their contact? String his pseudo-interest along? Writing the book had drained her and she was close to running out of ideas. She desperately needed a new thread, but she'd be up front with him about it.

She hung up with Carol and looked at the daisies again. All day she'd had an idea to write about them. She itched to get to it.

But first a reply to his comment. She flexed her fingers, thought for a moment, then typed. *Thanks for giving me so much new material. I needed it.*

She started working on the blog. Three paragraphs in her phone pinged and a response to her reply appeared. *Happy to oblige.*

"Seriously?" Kellar said to herself, right before she typed the same one-word reaction back to him. He must have hit the notification button when he'd typed his original comment. Otherwise, they wouldn't be having this exchange via her blog's comments section.

Quid pro quo? was his next comment.

Wasn't he worried that this interaction between them was in a public forum? She could imagine the conversation about it buzzing on TMZ before the other entertainment shows picked up on it.

Kellar's brow furrowed. She typed a series of question marks.

She waited, but nothing happened. Typical. He'd lost interest, got distracted, got another call, had to leave. He left her hanging like most every man she'd ever wanted to count on did.

She still had those daisies, and she knew what she wanted to say about them. She started typing again.

Twenty minutes later, the caller ID lit up as her phone rang. Unknown caller. She let it go to voice mail. The phone pinged with a message and then started ringing again. The same number showed up. Another message. The ringing began again.

Kellar couldn't ignore it, but she was prepared to make the call short. On the off chance that it was important, she answered professionally. "Kellar Kennedy."

"Let's have dinner again. I have a proposition for you."

"Who is this?"

"It's Day. From last night."

Kellar was officially thrown. "How do I know this is really you and not some crank call?"

"Seriously? You're screening me?"

"I'm a single woman. Can't be too careful."

"How about if I tell you a secret only you and I would know?"

"Such as?"

His voice dropped to on-screen sexy intimacy. "I nipped your earlobe in the green room."

Kellar's mind immediately sped back to the way it felt to be atop Dayman MacDay. His breath against her ear. The flick of his tongue. When she didn't respond, his voice dipped even lower. "And I enjoyed it."

Kellar started to laugh and once she started, she couldn't stop. He was messing with her, and she was enjoying it.

When her giggles died down, he said, "So, how about it?"

"How about what?"

"Dinner."

"When?"

"Tonight?"

She glanced at her computer screen. "I'm kind of in the middle of something."

"After you finish."

"I have to hit the gym."

"There's no need to be coy. I hate coy. If you don't want to go to dinner, just say so."

He kept throwing her off balance. He didn't do or say

what she expected. *Blog material,* her subconscious reminded her. This was business. It wasn't personal. Plus, she was curious about that *quid pro quo* comment.

"If I didn't want to go, I would say so. I simply wasn't expecting a dinner invitation. I didn't plan for it. I have some work to finish and a date with the gym. That's to work off last night's dinner, by the way."

"I can think of other ways you can work it off."

"Oh, I bet."

"Hey, I didn't mean it like that. We could go bowling."

"Bowling?"

"Or dancing. Dancing's a good workout."

"You like to dance?"

Day hesitated. "Sometimes," he said.

"Translation: I don't really like to dance."

He chuckled. "Okay. You got me."

Kellar looked at what she'd written and did some quick calculations. Another half hour with the daisy blog, an hour at the gym, an hour to get ready. "How about eight o'clock? Too early?"

"That'll work."

"Want me to meet you?"

"I'll pick you up. Where are you?"

Kellar rattled off the address and went back to work, still thinking about their conversation and his invitation. It was all very odd. But she had to admit, it was intriguing. *He* was intriguing.

Chapter Eight

♥

Kellar surprised herself by not obsessing about another non-date dinner with Day. She'd had fun last night, but it had been decidedly un-romantic. Yes, she'd felt that buzz of electricity or chemistry or whatever it was between them, but it was one-sided.

She knew enough about Day to know she was most definitely not his type. She wasn't famous, she wasn't stunning. She'd never have a hit record or a million-dollar modelling career or win an Academy Award.

And that was okay. She didn't have to date Day to get material from their time together. She could enjoy his company, have some good food, engage in stimulating verbal sparring, and leave it at that.

After her shower, she perused her wardrobe. He hadn't told her to dress up, so she wasn't going to. Even the Hollywood elite went slumming, and she was pretty sure that's what would happen tonight. Day wouldn't want to be in the spotlight with her. It wouldn't be good for his reputation, and she could imagine the questions it would raise, most of which would be some version of, "What's he doing with *her*? *Again*?"

She stared at herself in the mirror. "Stop concerning yourself with what other people think," she lectured her reflection. "We are not practicing self-sabotage these days, remember? Go. Have a good time with a man whose company you enjoy."

Shored up by her self-talk, she chose a pair of dark denim slacks, a tank top, and a jacket. She applied minimal makeup and kept her hair simple by blowing it dry and taming it with a couple of swipes from a flat iron.

On her way to the door, she was glad she hadn't set herself the impossible task of trying to impress him.

But he could impress her without even trying, damn him. He wore black slacks and a crew-neck sweater in a shade of pewter that complemented his eyes. He'd pushed the sleeves of the sweater up to reveal strong wrists and forearms and a sleek watch that probably cost more than her car.

Too bad she wasn't his type because she *really* liked looking at him. And talking to him. And watching his movies. Being with him. Being on top of him. *No. Don't go there.*

"You look nice."

Kellar wrinkled her nose. "That's almost as good as 'interesting'."

"Day's Dating Rule Number One: Don't criticize a compliment." He smiled at her.

"God, I am bad at this, aren't I? And this isn't even a date. Okay, let me try. You look very nice."

"Thank you."

"You're welcome." A long pause ensued with him standing in the doorway and her looking at him.

"By the way, who said this isn't a date?" he asked.

"You said you had a proposition for me. I thought you meant a business proposition."

"Day's dating rule number five: Mix business with pleasure whenever possible."

"How many of these rules are there?"

"An infinite number. I make them up as I go along."

Kellar laughed.

"Are you ready?" he asked.

"Sorry. Come in, won't you? I just need to change purses."

He stepped inside, closed the door, and looked around. "Nice place."

Kellar removed the essentials, lip gloss, keys, wallet, tissues, breath mints, a pen and a mini pad of paper from her everyday bag to a smaller clutch. "Thanks. It suits me."

"Is this where the magic happens?"

She'd left the double doors to her office open, and he peeked inside waiting for an answer. "If you're referring to my work, yes."

His eyes twinkled. "What else would I be referring to?"

"My boudoir, I suppose, but you won't be seeing that."

"If you say so."

"I don't think it even needs to be said."

"Then why did you bring it up?"

"I—" She stuffed her phone into the already packed clutch but refused to take the bait. "I'm ready to go if you are."

"Sure."

He escorted her to a shiny black Porsche Carrera and opened the door for her. "Nice car," she said.

"Thanks."

Kellar thought she should pinch herself even though she wasn't on a date with Day. She thought of Justin Timberlake's hit, "Bringin' Sexy Back." Because, oh my God, the car, the man, the divine smell of his subtle cologne and the black leather interior oozed sex appeal.

Her non-date had just begun, and already she was having fun. She'd have fun if all they did was drive around. If she could just sit and look at him and watch his hands on the steering wheel and the gearshift.

Something bluesy played on the sound system, but it was turned low, providing the perfect amount of background music to cover the lack of conversation. She smiled as the familiar scenery went by. No one could see them through the tinted windows, but she could see out as it began to get dark.

"You're awfully quiet," Day noted.

"I thought it would be a refreshing change. You're not complaining, are you?"

"No. Do you like sushi?"

"Love it."

"Good."

And then Day remained quiet too, but it wasn't tense

or uncomfortable. At least Kellar didn't think it was. It was... peaceful.

I'm not on a date. I don't have to talk to him. And I don't care if he talks to me.

He took some twists and turns and streets she wasn't familiar with until she gave up trying to anticipate where they were going. Eventually, he pulled into a crumbling parking lot and killed the engine. He got out and came around to open her door.

A nondescript cinder block building painted a dark shade of coral with cream trim proclaimed itself to be Mai-Lee Sushi Bar. Day opened the coral-colored door, and Kellar walked into a dimly lit but crowded space. An Asian hostess greeted them and asked them to follow her.

Kellar caught glimpses of giant internally lit aquariums and small candle-lit tables with single spotlights hanging over each of them, so you could see your food, but you wouldn't have to look at your companion. She felt a bubble of laughter in her chest. Could Day have found a more out of the way place than this?

The hostess stopped at a table for two and pulled out a chair, which Kellar took. A server appeared the moment they were seated. Day ordered a Japanese beer, so Kellar did as well, along with a glass of water.

"I know this place isn't much to look at," Day said, "but they have the best sushi I've ever eaten."

Kellar let go of the giggle she'd been holding back. "What?"

"It reminds me of that *Sex and the City* episode when

Carrie can't figure out why Big keeps taking her to this out-of-the-way Chinese restaurant. She thinks it's because he doesn't want anyone he knows to see him with her."

"That is not why I brought you here. Geez."

Kellar reached over and patted Day's hand, hoping to remove the pained look from his face. "I never said it was. The reason Big keeps taking Carrie to the same restaurant is because he thinks they serve the best Chinese food in the city. The circumstances were similar, and I drew a correlation. That's all."

"Okay. And for the record, I would be proud to be seen with you anywhere, any time."

"Aww. It's sweet of you to say that."

"I'm not being sweet. I'm being honest. What is your problem, anyway? Do you have to question everything I say?"

"Gosh, you're touchy. Low blood sugar? All I meant was that we both know I'm not your type, so us being seen together isn't likely to generate any kind of speculation."

"We're together now," Day pointed out.

"Sure. At an out-of-the-way restaurant. I didn't notice any paparazzi lurking outside."

"No, but every man, woman, and child in this country has a cellphone with a camera. That's all it takes. Next thing you know, they let the hounds lose."

"Oh. Well, good thing the lighting's so bad in here then, huh?"

"Besides, how do you know you're not my type? Is your self-esteem so low that you think I couldn't possibly be attracted to you?"

Kellar gave his question a minute of thought. "Hmm. Maybe. Based on your past relationships I would have said your type is beautiful, leggy blondes.

"And how did those work out?" he asked with a grim smile.

Their beers arrived and Kellar let Day order for them again since he was familiar with the menu.

"One beer," she warned him. "Unless you want me to start blabbing like I did last night."

"Blab all you want. I enjoyed listening to you."

"You did not."

"See, there you go. Being argumentative. How deep are your trust issues? Do you believe anything I say?"

Kellar wasn't going to discuss her trust issues with Dayman MacDay. At least not on their second non-date.

"We hardly talked at all in the car. That was nice, wasn't it?"

"Exactly. And that's what makes this perfect."

"Care to expand on that?"

"There's no pressure here." He gestured between them. "We can just... be."

"I know. Isn't it great? I kept thinking how wonderful this isn't a date. I don't have to try to impress you. I don't have to care what you think or if you'll call me again or if I've completely turned you off. It's the absence of expectation. We can relax. Talk. Not talk. I like it."

Day grinned. "Me too. That's what I wanted to talk to you about."

"Oh. The quid pro quo thing?"

"Yes. I need a break from dating."

"You? But I thought you were seeing that actress."

"Which one?"

"I don't know. I can't remember her name. The young, strawberry blonde. Starring in that new Nicholas Sparks movie."

"Luna Jones?"

"If you say so."

"No. I'm not seeing anyone right now."

The server brought bowls of crunchy fried strips and sweet and sour dipping sauce. Kellar reached for some. "I have to tell you, since I met you, what? Twenty—" she reached for his wrist and turned his watch so she could see the time. "-eight hours since I met you, you've given me enough material for a week's worth of blogs. I hope you don't mind if I use it. I don't even have to use your name."

"Of course not. The press had a field day with our appearance last night. Did you see the photos from Shar-iffe?"

"Some of them."

"Last night started me thinking. And please don't tell me whether I had a good time or not. Dinner with you was a refreshing change for me."

"Because I actually ate?"

Day laughed. Kellar liked his laugh. A lot.

"You didn't just eat. You cleaned your plate."

"Hey, I had to. There are children starving in Africa."

"I know. I was going to overnight your leftovers. Except there weren't any."

"It's a Midwest thing. Where I come from it's a sin to waste good food."

Just then, a sampler platter of sushi arrived. They assured the server they needed nothing else, and dug in.

"I want to try one of everything," Kellar said. She popped one of the rolls into her mouth. Her eyes grew wide as she chewed. Day nodded knowingly. "Oh. My. God," she said as soon as she swallowed. "That's the best yellowtail I've ever had."

"Told you."

They devoured several more pieces before they slowed down and Day spoke. "About last night. The way you handled yourself on the show should do wonders for your book sales."

Kellar leaned forward in a conspiratorial manner. "That's exactly what I thought. And I have you to thank for it."

She looked over the remaining pieces of sushi before she chose one.

"It doesn't have to end there. I think we can be mutually beneficial to each other." Day took a drink of beer.

"In what way?"

"Did I mention I need a break from dating?"

"You did."

"There are a lot of events I'm expected to attend. Parties, charity gigs, the awards ceremonies this season. Premieres." He leaned forward and crossed his arms on the table. "I'm not a fan but showing up is part of the job. I'm especially not a fan of showing up alone. I hoped you might be interested in going to things like that with me. As a friend."

"But not as a date?"

He leaned forward. "Here's the way I figure it. The press will have a field day. We say we're just friends because it's the truth. They'll *assume* we're dating."

"They won't believe us. If anything, they'll speculate even more."

Day beamed at her. "Exactly. Win-win. Publicity for you. Enjoyable no-strings-attached companionship for me."

"No."

Day lifted an eyebrow. "No?"

"I can't."

"Can't? As in, 'I am incapable of being friends with Dayman MacDay?' Or as in, 'I don't want to.'?"

"As in it goes against my dating philosophy."

Day's brows knit to join his confused frown. "But it *wouldn't* be dating. That's the whole point."

Kellar sighed. "Look. You know how I became a dating expert, right? I started the blog because of my own dating disasters. Readers responded with their experiences and started asking for advice. Then I got into coaching. The blog took off and the next thing I knew, I had a syndicated column, a weekly podcast, and a book deal.

"Do you know the number of times this same scenario has come up from my readers over the years? *Hundreds*. A guy tells a woman he just wants to be friends. Maybe he does. Maybe he doesn't. The woman agrees. Sure, just friends. But eventually there's a shift on one side or the other. The guy wants sex, or the woman wants to start a romantic relationship. Something. Always. Happens." Kellar knew she needed to make her point.

"Then they come crying to me, asking why it didn't work. Bottom line? It never does. I've never seen a single case where it did, except maybe in a movie. Therefore, my stance is, don't do it. Just don't go there. You'll avoid a whole lot of heartache."

"I disagree with your core philosophy," Day said. "I believe a man and a woman can be friends without it going any further."

"Ah, yes," Kellar agreed. "I forgot the one caveat. If one or both of them are gay."

Day's frown came back. "You're saying you can't do this, even though it would help your book sales and boost your blog stats, because you've been advising your followers against it?"

"I don't want to be seen as a hypocrite." Kellar sat back in her chair and picked up her drink, glad Day understood.

"But you don't *know* it won't work from personal experience."

"Correct. But I've watched *When Harry Met Sally* a bunch of times."

"Refresh my memory. They end up together and happy at the end of the movie, don't they?"

"After making each other miserable for the last half of it."

"What good is a happy ending without a little misery to make you appreciate it?"

"Nice try."

Day leaned forward and stacked his forearms on the table. "How would your followers feel about you doing it as an experiment? You've been preaching to them that male/female friendships never work. But you can admit you've never actually tried it yourself. Now's your opportunity."

Kellar thought for a moment and began to see the possibilities. "Maybe... It seems like it *could* be a win/win. For both of us. I can blog about hanging out with you?"

"Of course."

"And you get to relax because there's no 'relationship' pressure," she said with air quotes.

"Please say yes. I'm already breathing easier than I have in years."

"Do you have any idea what it will do for my book sales if people think I'm your girlfriend?"

"I do."

"But I'd be using you."

"Quid pro quo," Day reminded her. "I'm using you, too. It's mutually beneficial."

"So now I'd be a dating expert. Who's horrible at dating. Who's not really dating The Sexiest Man Alive. But everyone thinks she is."

"It's real life, babe. You can't make this stuff up."

"Well," Kellar said, pretending to think about it. "I do like you."

"I like you, too."

"We can experiment with being friends. But if this blows up in my face, I'm out."

"I think it will work."

"I think you're wrong."

"What's the worst that could happen?"

When A Man Sends Flowers

♥

Who doesn't like getting flowers? If you're like most of us, it probably doesn't happen very often. But when it does, isn't it one of the best surprises ever?

It's too bad more men don't realize this. It's an inexpensive way to get a woman's attention. Men don't like to send flowers because they feel it's a waste of money because cut flowers don't last very long. They don't understand the appeal to women.

Clue: When the flowers you sent start to wilt, it's a reminder to bring your love a fresh bouquet.

Maybe your man sends you flowers on Valentine's Day or your birthday or anniversary. But does he ever send them when there's no reason at all? Don't you wish he would? A surprise bouquet shows not only that he's thinking of you, but that he thinks highly of you. He wants to please you.

It doesn't have to be a dozen roses. They don't have to be delivered, either. Anyone can stop at a florist or a super-

market or buy them on the street. We don't really care, do we? If he (or she) shows up with a bouquet, we label him as thoughtful and caring.

(Unless he's trying to get out of the doghouse. That's the one exception to whether we appreciate his flower-giving gesture!)

Do we care what kind of flowers we get? Probably not (barring allergies). It's the thought that counts.

Why just the other day, I received this lovely bouquet of daises from a male… acquaintance? admirer? friend? I'm not exactly sure how to categorize him. I was puzzled but delighted by the daises he sent.

"Why daisies?" was my first thought. But I've tried not to over-analyze it. Daisies are happy flowers, and receiving a bunch of them made me happy. Every time I look at them, I'm reminded of my new friend's thoughtfulness.

Guys, isn't that enough of a reason to give a girl flowers every now and again?

Chapter Nine

K ellar was ready to upload her blog post when her
phone rang. "Hi, Johanna," she said.

"You're guaranteed to make the *New York Times* and
USA Today bestseller lists. Congratulations."

"I am?"

"All because of your appearance on Jamie Falcon's
show and the dinner date he arranged with Dayman
MacDay. We gotta send him a thank you note."

"It wasn't a date."

She'd slept later than usual after she and Day had lingered over tea and a plate of tiny pastries last night. She
had a ton of questions, mostly about wardrobe expectations and logistics. He'd given her a glimpse into the
world of how things were done at his level of stardom.
She'd have a wardrobe stylist, the pick of dresses and jewelry from various designers. There'd be a hair stylist and
makeup artist. Everything would be coordinated ahead
of time. All she had to do was show up and smile. And
remember "who" she was wearing. Dress, shoes, jewelry.
His assistant, Chazz, would provide her with a schedule

of upcoming events.

They'd driven back to her place in another comfortable silence. "You don't have to walk me to the door," she'd said to Day. "This isn't a date."

"I know, but I want to make sure you're safely inside before I leave."

He kept his hands in his pockets and once she had the door unlocked, they said goodnight. And that was that. The end to another wonderful non-date.

"Doesn't matter, it *looked* like one," Johanna insisted. "Dinner at a trendy Hollywood hotspot with the hottest actor alive and the world's most eligible bachelor? Believe me, for a dating expert, you hit the jackpot."

"I figured I'd get some mileage out of it," Kellar conceded.

"Oh, honey, you got frequent-flyer, first-class-upgrade with a complementary bottle of *champagne* mileage out of it. I've been fielding calls all day. The *Today Show* wants you. *Tommy Cantone.* GregG. CNN. *Candy and Cooper.*"

"Seriously?"

"Hasn't Newcastle's publicity department contacted you?"

"Maybe. I haven't checked my email yet."

"Megan," Johanna said, referring to the head of her publisher's publicity department, "should be getting in touch. I don't have to tell you how important it is that you take advantage of every opportunity. Book selling is all marketing. And if you can arrange to be seen with

Dayman MacDay again, that wouldn't hurt."

"I'll see what I can do," Kellar said.

"The clip of you two on Jamie Falcon, the bit where he puts the heel back on your shoe, has gone viral on YouTube, by the way."

"It has?"

"Yes. A million hits already. Go watch it. And get to work on your next book."

"I am. I mean I will."

After the call, Kellar wandered into the kitchen to pour herself more coffee. She didn't know why she was so languid this morning. She should be more excited about the sales news and the personal appearance requests. It's just that it was all work, she supposed. Interesting, but work. And she'd been working a lot for a long time. It was finally paying off, but she wouldn't mind a break, either. She was tempted to play hooky today. Get in some retail therapy or go for a drive. Do a spa day.

Her laptop screen stared at her. She should at least check her email and post her blog.

Day pressed the doorbell and waited for Willow to answer. Even though he had a key, he preferred to use it only in an emergency, no matter how many times Willow assured him he could just walk in. She had free access to his place as well and had no compunction about coming and going as she pleased, especially if she was having one of her low periods where she wanted to hide from everyone.

The door swung open, and she drew him into a hug as soon as privacy was assured. Day loved Willow like the sister he never had. He'd sworn to protect her and relied on her unwavering loyalty to him. She was one of the few people he could be completely real with, and he was the same for her.

"What smells so good?" he asked, following her to the kitchen. He set the bottle of wine he'd brought on the island and peeked at the pans on the stove. Willow loved to cook and experiment with food. She had a knack for seasoning, and even when she ventured into uncharted culinary territory, her creations were tasty and satisfying.

"I'm trying something new with rutabagas." Willow lifted a lid and stirred the contents of one of the pots.

"Rutabagas, huh?" Day opened her fridge and took one of the bottles of beer she kept stocked there just for him. "Isn't that like the potato's ugly cousin?"

"Taste-wise yes. But they're more closely related to broccoli and brussels sprouts. They're low-cal and highly nutritious. Lots of Vitamin C."

She examined the wine. "Want to open this for me?" She fussed with a few things near the stove and checked on whatever was in the oven. More tantalizing aromas wafted out when she opened the door.

He got a corkscrew from the drawer, found a glass for her in the cabinet and poured.

Day took a seat at the counter and nursed his beer while Willow put the finishing touches on a salad and sipped her wine. They talked shop until she had two plates prepared to her liking. She carried them to the breakfast nook, a cozy space looking out over her pool and stunning garden.

Day tasted the food and complimented her on everything, then got down to why he was here. "I've had a brilliant idea,"

"Another one?" Willow teased. "That makes two so far this year!"

"I'm trying to beat my record." He finished his beer and got a glass of water before he continued. "Did you see that bit on Jamie's show last week?"

"How could I not? It was *everywhere*. Nice publicity stunt, by the way."

"It wasn't a stunt."

"What was it then?"

"A fortunate series of events that led to my brilliant idea."

"Wasn't very fortunate for that author. She was a disaster."

"Are you kidding? She worked that whole scenario to her advantage. Impressed the hell out of me."

Willow set her fork on her plate and gave Day her complete attention. "Impressed you, huh? Go on."

Day sketched the outline of his recent interactions with Kellar, including the arrangement they'd agreed to.

"An escort for awards season? No strings attached?

You're kidding, right? You could have asked me."

Day covered her hand with his and squeezed. "Come on, Wills. That wouldn't be good for you, and you know it."

She looked down at her plate and after a few seconds, nodded. "I know."

"I think this will be fun. I can relax. She doesn't expect anything more from me. I don't expect anything more from her."

Willow gazed out the window, a wistful expression on her face. "Expectations can change."

Day allowed her the moment of melancholy, even though he wanted a verbal pat on the back or applause. She turned back to him after a minute and gave him a forced smile. "I hope it works out the way you want it to, Day."

"Why wouldn't it?

"No reason. I look forward to meeting your dating expert. Maybe she can help me with my love life."

"We could get together this week," Day said. "Meet up for drinks at The Fig?" He named one of their favorite off-the-beaten-path haunts. "What's your week look like?"

"God, I haven't been there in ages. I'll have Bev check my schedule and let you know."

They went on to talk about other things, cleared the table and sat back down with slices of rutabaga spice cake and espresso.

Just before five, Kellar found The Fig in West Hollywood easily, negating Day's claim that it was a little-known celebrity gathering place. Already she'd spotted an aging super model and a recognizable character actor, probably lingering after a late lunch, or here early for happy hour.

The hostess led her through the charming and funky space to a 4-seat high-top in the bar. Day had texted he was running late, and Willow Thorne had not yet arrived. Kellar ordered a drink called the Mighty Maui from the specialty cocktail menu. The coconut, pineapple, and dark rum concoction promised to be something she could sip slowly. She wanted to stay on her toes around Willow.

She studied The Fig's unique furnishings and décor where hanging plants threatened to take over the view through the windows and second-hand stores must have made a huge contribution. The refinished chairs and tables, worked, though, as did what looked like antique Mexican tile. There was a certain warmth and kitschy elegance, and she wondered if that was the vibe they'd intended.

The staff seemed pretty laid back and while she watched the bartender prepare her drink her mind drifted, as it often did, to yet another blog idea. *Drinks With Day.* Or technically, *Drinks with Day and Friend. Day and Willow.*

She probably wouldn't write about this meet-up anyway. She had Day's permission to drop his name as much as she liked. But something told her the very private Willow Thorne wouldn't like it if her name came up on one of Kellar's blogs.

The drink proved to be tastier than she expected, and she relaxed a bit more after the first sip. She'd been downplaying her reaction to meeting with Willow ever since Day had suggested it. The two were long-time *friends*. His word. She was one of the few people he trusted. The other being Chazz. Willow knew about Day's arrangement with Kellar. So, in theory, Kellar had nothing to fear.

It should be interesting. That's what she kept telling herself. Because she liked studying people, analyzing the dynamic between them. Willow and Day made two interesting subjects, for sure.

"Kellar?"

So lost in thought was she, Kellar didn't notice Willow's approach until she felt a touch on her shoulder. "Lovely to meet you, Willow," she said.

"Likewise." Willow flashed her famous smile.

She took the seat across from Kellar. The server arrived in a flash to take her order. Kellar found herself a bit starstruck by Willow Thorne and couldn't help staring. "Forgive me," she said, before things got uncomfortable. "I'm sure there's some top-secret Hollywood trick that keeps you from aging at all, but honestly, you're radiant.

Glowing? I don't mean to gush. Chalk it up to jealousy."

A surprised laugh tinkled out of Willow's throat. "The tricks aren't top-secret. That much I can tell you. Just very, *very* expensive." Her drink arrived and once the server left, she said. "Thank you for the compliment. I hope you're not trying to butter me up."

Taken aback, Kellar wasn't sure if Willow was serious. "For what?"

"Oh, I don't know. An in with Day, maybe?"

Kellar took offense as she was sure Willow meant her to. "I didn't know I needed one."

"We've been friends for a long time, Day and me. We've always got each other's back. You'd do well to remember that." Willow took a nonchalant taste of her cocktail. "Hmm. Not bad." She offered Kellar a cool smile.

"I know I haven't been *friends* with Day for as long as you have, but trust me, he's got nothing to fear from me."

"That's just it, though. I *don't* trust you. And I don't trust this crazy arrangement you talked him into."

"Me?" Kellar squeaked. "I did no such thing as I'm sure he told you."

Suddenly Day swooped in and planted a kiss on Kellar's cheek and then on Willow's while Willow's eyes flashed warning signals at Kellar.

"How are two of my favorite ladies?" he asked, his delight evident.

"Happy as a couple of pigs in mud, isn't that right, Willow?"

Day laughed while Willow frowned. "I bet she's got a

hundred sayings from her Midwestern upbringing," Day informed Willow. "She uses them only when she's at a loss for anything else to say. Which is rare." He grinned at Kellar, and she smiled at him, happy to be a source of entertainment.

"Isn't that sweet?" Willow's insincerity was obvious, but Day didn't pick up on it. Or pretended not to.

Day ordered a beer. "Sorry, I'm late. What did I miss?"

"Willow's been warning me not to take advantage of you." Kellar patted Day's hand. "You're so lucky to have a friend like her looking out for you."

"That's Willow. She's the big sister I never had."

"She also seems to be under the impression that being awards season companions was my idea. Perhaps now's a good time to set her straight," Kellar said with a winning smile. If Willow thought she was going to intimidate her, she could think again. She'd done nothing to hurt Day, nor would she. She'd also hadn't done anything to warrant Willow's distrust and suspicion, but she wasn't going to defend herself against false accusations, either. Day could either straighten his good friend out, or they could part ways, agreement be damned.

Day looked at Willow. "I told you it was my idea. In fact, Kellar wanted nothing to do with it. I had to talk her into it."

"What I said earlier, Kellar? That was a test. I wanted to see how you'd react." The smile made another appearance. "Forgive me?"

Kellar shuddered internally. Willow's behavior reminded her so much of her father. The challenges he'd issue that too often felt like a test she might fail. Followed by apologies she eventually learned meant nothing.

"That depends," Kellar said. She concentrated on stirring her drink for a second with no plans to make this easier for Willow. She'd have to do more than turn on that award-winning, you gotta-love-me charm to make amends.

"On what?" Willow asked.

"How I did on the test."

Both Willow and Day laughed.

"She passed, right?" Day asked.

"With flying colors," Willow answered. But she didn't look happy about it.

"You do that a lot?" Kellar asked. "Test people the moment you meet them?"

Willow managed to look uncomfortable, but Kellar couldn't tell if she was acting or not. "Not everyone."

"I guess that makes me one of the privileged few, doesn't it?" She toasted Willow with her drink and swallowed some more of it. A few more minutes and she'd make her excuses. If she'd learned one thing from her father, it was that there wasn't room or time in her life to spend on someone like Willow who couldn't treat her decently. Even if she was one of Day's best friends. She hadn't forgiven Willow nor would she. She tucked that nugget into the mental file she kept of people she wanted nothing to do with.

Day sat back and looked from Willow to Kellar then at

his beer. "Well, this isn't going the way I hoped it would." His cell phone vibrated on the table. "I'm sorry. I need to take this. I'll make it quick, promise."

The minute he walked away, Kellar went on the offensive. "You've got some nerve, you know that?"

"I said I was sorry." Willow's lower lip stuck out just a bit.

"No, actually. You didn't. You said, 'forgive me' in a way that implied you hadn't done anything wrong."

"Fine. I'm not sorry anyway."

"Perfect. Because I have no intention of forgiving you."

"Fine."

"Fine."

The two were glaring at each other when Day returned.

Willow picked up her purse at the same time Kellar reached for her car keys.

"I have to go, Day," Willow said. "Kellar? It's been...enlightening."

"Willow, don't—"

She sent him a warning look, brushed a kiss on his cheek and left.

Kellar slid off her chair. "Great idea us all getting together. Let's not do it again, okay?"

"Kellar—"

She kept going, afraid if she stayed, she'd say something about Willow she'd live to regret. Day's long history with Willow meant that's where his loyalty would be. Day trusted Willow implicitly.

No matter how she might be beginning to wish otherwise, Kellar's arrangement with Day was temporary. Whether or not his friends liked or approved of her had no bearing on anything. Because after awards season, she'd become nothing more than a memory to him. That's what she'd signed on for. And that's how it would be.

Confounded, Day stared after the two women before he decided he might as well finish his beer.

He was used to Willow's games. Kellar was not. He'd sensed a weird tension between the two of them, but chose to ignore it, hoping it would pass. He didn't know exactly what had been said, but Kellar had apparently stood up for herself which must have surprised Willow who sometimes tended to steamroll right over people she didn't like.

Day had hoped the two women might become friends. Willow had been important to him for a long time. And Kellar was becoming more important than he'd ever expected her to be.

This whole "let's just be friends" thing was harder than he thought. Maybe Kellar was right. It rarely worked. And someone always got hurt.

Day called Kellar the next day to apologize for Willow's behavior at The Fig, confessing that although he didn't know exactly what had been said, he wanted to make amends.

"She should make her own amends," Kellar said.

Into the silence that followed, she added, "But I'm guessing she won't because she never does."

His lack of response told her she was right. "Look, Day, you and Willow go back a long way. You and I are temporary. You don't owe me anything. Neither does she. Let's move on, okay?"

"Maybe we won't be temporary," Day said.

"I'm pretty sure that's what we agreed to."

"Things could change."

Kellar became suspicious. "What things?"

"Anything. Everything. How about if we keep ourselves open to the possibilities?"

Kellar couldn't think of what to say to that or why Day was even suggesting it. They had an agreement. One she'd had trepidation about from the beginning for all the reasons she'd outlined when Day first proposed it. Was he already thinking they could be more than companions for a season? And where might that lead? Probably to more pain and heartbreak. At least for her. If she even let herself go there.

"Kellar? You still there?"

Run her internal warning system suggested. "Day, I've got to go. We'll talk soon, okay?"

Not for the first time did she ask herself why she'd agreed to this crazy plan. She should have known better and followed the advice she'd given countless others: It never works. Somebody always wants more.

The question was, what did Day want from her?

Chapter Ten

♥

Three days later, Kellar made her way into another green room and stopped short. Day looked up from the bottle of sparkling water he was pouring over ice and smiled. "This is a coincidence."

She eyed the glass he'd prepared. "Stay away from me with that or there could be serious consequences.

He chuckled and sauntered toward her, glass in hand. "You could spill it on me this time. How about it? Down the front of my shirt so it drips onto the crotch of my pants?"

She took a cautious step back and held up her hands. "No. I'm like a ticking time bomb here. I don't want to take any chances."

He stopped a few feet from her. "You look great. I like you in red."

"Not too bright?"

"It's perfect."

"How have you been?" she asked.

"Good. Hitting the New York talk shows this week. How about you?"

"Wait. Are we doing the same shows at the same time?"

"Maybe. Candy and Cooper?"

She nodded.

"*Viewpoint*?"

"Yes."

"McLaren?"

"Surely we're not scheduled for the same days."

"After our initial stunt? I wouldn't be surprised."

"Don't they clear it with you? I mean a celebrity of your stature..."

Day grinned. "The bookers schedule it with my people, and they send it to Chazz. He gives me a list and I usually ignore it. I prefer spontaneity."

"I prefer not to be blindsided by some movie star hiding in plain sight," Kellar half-joked.

"Liar. You milked every second of it while I encouraged you. But even if we are—"

"It doesn't matter."

"If we're asked—"

"We say we're just friends."

"And no one believes us."

Kellar grinned. "God, this is fun."

"I know, right? Let's stay at the same hotel. Really give them something to talk about."

"Oh. My publisher makes those arrangements. I'm sure it won't be anywhere grand like you're used to."

"I can stay wherever I want. The less grand the better. It will look like we're sneaking around."

"You're terrible."

"Hey, the paparazzi has made my life miserable for years. It's payback time."

She beamed at him. "Besides, we have nothing to hide."

"That's the beauty of our nonexistent relationship."

One of the assistants poked his head in the door. "Mr. MacDay? We're ready for you."

Day drank the water he'd poured and set the glass down. He squeezed Kellar's elbow. "I'll see you later."

"Right. See you."

She gave the table he'd set his glass on a wide berth and took a seat on the sofa in front of the television. She wondered why she'd been the lead guest on Jamie Falcon's show before. By rights, Day should be on first. Maybe Jamie's producers just wanted to hold the audience and tease them with Day's later appearance. Tommy Cantone's people weren't messing around. They led with the big guns. If it weren't for the sensation they'd created on Jamie Falcon's show, she wondered if anyone would stay tuned to see her spiel.

Of course, now everyone wanted know what would happen next. Including her.

She liked watching Day. The camera loved him from every angle. He had talk show banter down to a science. Tommy led him right into a funny story about the making of his latest film. Day was animated and got the timing on the punchline just right. The audience roared.

"He certainly knows how to work a room," she said to herself.

The assistant returned. "Miss Kennedy? This way, please."

She batted down the few butterflies as she followed the assistant down the corridor. Dayman MacDay would be a hard act to follow.

Tommy didn't waste any time once she was introduced and seated next to his desk. "So, you two know each other."

Kellar glanced over at Day. "Yes. We've met."

Tommy said. "You met on another network's late night talk show, didn't you? And now the whole world knows about it."

"I'm not sure the *whole* world knows, but yes. We met in the green room."

"Is it true he poured a bottle of water on you?"

Kellar giggled. "Not exactly."

"And then you tackled him? That's what I heard."

"I didn't exactly tackle you, did I?" She looked at Day then back at Tommy. "It wasn't a *fight* or anything. It was more like..."

"Unexpected slapstick comedy," Day interjected.

"Exactly. One accident led to another and the next thing you know I'd fallen on top of him."

"That must have been a hardship." Tommy winked at Day.

"It was actually one of the nicer experiences I've had in a green room." Day said with a smirk.

Kellar patted his hand. "Aren't you sweet?"

Tommy appeared perplexed. "Wait a minute. Are you

two dating?"

"No," they said at the same time.

"We're just friends," Kellar added.

"Hey, I saw the viral clip of the Cinderella moment you had on YouTube. I heard you two got pretty cozy over dinner too."

"That might have been the wine. I get very chatty when I'm tipsy."

"Let's talk about that when we come back. More with Dayman MacDay and dating expert Kellar Kennedy. Don't go away."

The commercial break flew by with makeup and hair touchups and a brief whispered conversation between Tommy and his producer.

"And we're back. So, Kellar, what kind of a guy do you usually go for?" Tommy asked.

"Being that I'm still single, not the right kind, apparently."

"Is that what you tell women? If they're still single, they're pursuing guys who are wrong for them?"

"I don't have to tell them. They already know. What I try to do is suggest ways they can stop wasting time on the wrong guys, so the right guy has a chance when he comes along."

"For example? What should they look for?"

"For starters, is he respectful? Does he suggest a late evening date in the middle of the work week? Is it the kind of date you're interested in? Did he even bother to find out what you're interested in? Is it all about him showing off who he is, or him finding out more about you?"

"So, if he invites you to the sumo wrestling championships on a Wednesday night after a couple of rounds of beer pong...?" Of course, this drew chuckles from the audience.

"It wouldn't be *my* ideal date."

"What about you, Day?"

Day mugged for the camera. "What about me?"

"Well, you're something of a dating expert yourself." Day leaned back and grinned as the audience laughed at Tommy's gentle ribbing. "If you were going to ask Kellar here out on a date, hypothetically of course, because we understand you're *just friends*." Tommy gave an exaggerated wink to the audience, which made them titter. "What kind of date would you plan?"

Day rubbed his jaw as he seemed to consider the question. Tommy circled his finger, encouraging Kellar to turn in Day's direction. "Go ahead. Let's roleplay for our audience so the guys can see how to do it right and the ladies can see what getting asked out on a decent date looks like."

"You're putting me on the spot here," Day warned Tommy and the audience. He leaned toward Kellar. He picked up her hand and stroked his thumb along the back of it. "I've got this house in Malibu. I'd love for you to see it. We can light a fire. Have some wine. Watch the sunset. Fire up the grill. Play... Scrabble?" The audience chuckled.

"That sounds lovely," Kellar said, and it did. She loved Scrabble. And Day's thumb rubbing the back of her hand sent tiny prickles of pleasure up her spine. "But I'd say no," she added, to laughs and gasps.

"You'd turn down a date with Dayman MacDay?" Tommy repeated. "Why?"

"Because, as delightful as his invitation sounds, a first date should always be somewhere public and neutral. Always proceed with caution. A couple needs to get to know each other before they move to a more private and personal setting."

"Ah, but technically this would be our second date," Day countered. "Or am I that forgettable?"

The audience oohed.

Jimmy tried to get the conversation back on course. "Okay, so let's say he's asking you out on a second date. How did he do?"

Kellar thought about it and smiled and turned her attention back to Day. "Well, it sounds like he wants to move our friendship to the next level, so in that case...I'd hold off the visit to his home in Malibu until the third date if there is one. Also, I prefer to play Monopoly, and I like my steak medium rare."

Like a hot potato, Day dropped her hand and looked at Tommy. "She seems kind of high maintenance. We could just grab some sushi and go bowling."

The audience roared.

"Let's go to dinner," Day suggested after the show.

"Together? Again?"

"I'll buy you another steak."

"I'm supposed to meet my agent and my publisher's VP of publicity."

Day gave her a devilish grin. "Even better."

"You are evil," Kellar breathed.

"And you love it."

"I do. They'll die if I show up with you."

"Just think of the publicity they'll both generate which means more book sales for you."

"As well as keeping other women away from you."

"I am sort of brilliant that way," Day admitted, his eyes twinkling. "Let's go."

Autograph seekers were gathered near the exit, behaving themselves under the watchful eyes of studio security. Day good-naturedly scribbled on whatever he was handed and Kellar found, much to her surprise, several of her books thrust forward for her to sign. Delighted, she scribbled and chatted, as they were herded steadily toward the curb. Day made a show of pausing before they got into the waiting limo, making sure the photographers lurking nearby had time for several shots of him handing Kellar into the car.

The restaurant was not well-known, but Day hoped their presence would trigger an X trend and the photogs would be waiting once they were ready to leave.

Megan's and Johanna's eyes grew as big as saucers when Kellar arrived with Day in tow. "I hope you don't mind. Day wanted to go to dinner, and I didn't think you'd object if he joined us."

"It's fine," Megan assured her. She scooted closer to Johanna along the semi-circular banquette.

"Fine," Johanna agreed. Kellar performed introductions and Day put on his usual charm, then helped Kellar out of her jacket and handed her into the booth, settling himself next to her.

Wait staff hustled over. The other diners buzzed in excitement. Cellphones popped out of purses and pockets, as expected. Day ignored it all. He turned to Kellar. "What would you like? Pinot grigio?"

Kellar laughed out loud at their inside joke. "That would be lovely."

He ordered the same brand of beer he'd had at Shariffe.

"Certainly, sir."

"Don't let me keep you from talking business," Day said to the three women. "Your secrets are safe with me. Pretend I'm not even here."

"How'd Tommy Cantone go?" Megan asked.

"Pretty well. He thinks Day should help me write my

next book."

That got everyone's attention, including Day's. "I don't recall him suggesting that."

"He didn't exactly. But he said we're both dating experts in our own ways."

"That is a brilliant idea!" Megan exclaimed. She focused on Day. "Any chance you'd be interested?"

Day leaned next to Kellar and pushed a lock of her hair out of the way so he could whisper in her ear. "You're devious."

Kellar grinned as little hairs stood up along her neck. She loved the warmth of his breath against her ear.

Johanna and Megan stared.

Their drinks arrived followed by appetizers. "So how about it, Day?" Megan asked. "What would you say to co-authoring a book with Kellar?"

"I don't think Kellar needs any help writing books. She's already proven that."

"Of course, but that's not my point. It's the *synergy* I'm talking about." She turned to Kellar. "What exactly did you have in mind?"

Absolutely nothing. But Kellar couldn't admit that. She'd been yanking Day's chain. She hadn't expected Megan to grab the chain and run with it. She'd have to make something up on the fly. "Day has dated a lot of women, but he hasn't found a lasting relationship."

"Haven't been looking for one," he muttered for her ears only.

"And I'm good at giving advice about dating."

"To everyone except yourself," he said in the same tone.

Kellar shot him a look. "So maybe we could combine our strengths and learn from each other's weaknesses."

"I don't have any dating weaknesses," Day said, loud enough for everyone at the table to hear. "I'm an expert, remember?"

"You're also an expert at breaking the hearts of the women you date."

"Are you saying you can teach him how to stop doing that?" Johanna asked.

Kellar looked at Day and seemed to give the question serious consideration. Only Day saw her wink at him. "I'd be willing to try."

"And what's he going to teach you?" Megan wondered.

"Yeah," Day said, "Since you're already such an expert." He was laughing at her. She should have minded, but this entire conversation was ludicrous. That Megan and Johanna seemed to be falling for it only added to the hilarity. Kellar leaned forward and motioned them to do the same. "He can teach me how to be a better date. Because I really, truly stink at dating."

"Kellar, come on. I told you, you're not that bad."

Johanna and Megan sat back, looking perplexed.

Megan looked at Johanna. "They're not serious. Are they?"

Johanna studied Kellar and Day. Kellar didn't even try to wipe the earnest expression off her face. "Probably not. Even though it'd have bestseller status before they even start it."

And just like that Kellar had the perfect idea for her next book.

"*The Un-gettables*?" Day asked as they headed to the hotel.

"Guys like you. Women, too, for that matter."

"I'm un-gettable?"

"You are."

"Maybe I just don't want to be got. Did you ever think of that?"

"Is that true?"

"It might be."

"Or... you just didn't want to be got by any of the many, many women you dated. So that begs the question, why did you date *those* particular women?"

"Are you planning to psychoanalyze my choices?"

Kellar grinned at him. "I might. But I think it'd be easier to interview the women."

Day groaned. "You don't want to do that."

"Why not? It's the only way to be fair. I could get your take on why those relationships didn't last, which apparently is because you didn't want them to. But I'd like to know if that's how the women saw it."

Day grew quiet. He looked out the window. "Not all of them," he said so softly Kellar almost didn't hear him.

"The book doesn't have to be about you, you know," Kellar said. "There are lots of un-gettable people out there I can interview and write about."

Day looked at her. "Maybe it would be the kindest thing you could do," he said. "For those women, I mean. Figure out why I chose them, why I let them think there might be a happy ending. Why I eventually broke their hearts."

"You think it would give them closure?"

"Or vindication. Something."

Maybe it will give me closure, too. Kellar had to admit the thought of figuring out the behavior of men like Day tantalized her. There were thousands of singles out there trying to figure out the same thing, wondering why their love interests left them.

Already she saw a vision of the book's layout. Using one of Day's prominent relationships as a connecting theme and then laying out the stories of everyday people, sprinkled in among the stories of a few other celebrity-types along with her analysis. She really didn't need Day's perspective. Not if she could get a candid interview with at least one of his exes.

Chapter Eleven

♥

As premieres went, this one wasn't that important. The only reason Day wanted to attend was because the director was a friend of sorts and someone he'd worked with. Day wasn't even in the movie, which meant the spotlight wouldn't be on him, or Kellar.

She'd forced smiles throughout the evening, hoping no one would notice her internal angst about the call she'd gotten from her mother earlier. Poppy wasn't expected to last through the night.

If Day noticed anything was wrong with her, he didn't comment on it. His publicist escorted them on the red carpet, directing Day to the entertainment reporters for quick sound bites. Kellar was perfectly happy to be relegated to the background.

They sat through the film, a fun but forgettable action/adventure peppered with explosions, and she was happy to climb back into the limousine.

"After party?" Day asked as their driver waited for a break in the traffic. "Yea or nay?"

Kellar dug her cell phone out of the purse she'd left

in the car. She put up a finger while she listened to the message her mother had left.

Tears surged into her eyes. "I'll have to skip the after party."

"What's wrong? Is it your grandmother?"

Kellar swallowed down the lump of emotion clogging her throat, not wanting to lose control in front of Day. "She passed a little while ago."

He slid an arm around her shoulders, drawing her close. "I'm so sorry."

She pulled away. "Don't, or I'll fall apart."

The limo pulled into the street.

Silence reigned for a time before Kellar spoke again. "I appreciate the sympathy." Day didn't look as though he believed her, but she went on. "I just need to be alone. I have to make a reservation and pack. Process this in my own way."

"Sure." He sounded even less convinced. "I'll have Chazz make your reservation. The limo can take you to the airport."

"You don't have to do that."

"I know. But I want to help. And since you won't cry on my shoulder..."

Let him do something for you.

That thought seemed like it came straight from Poppy.

"Okay. Thank you. That would be great."

He took her hand and she let him hold it during the rest of the drive. At her door he squeezed her shoulders and kissed her hair. "Chazz will text you with the flight information."

Kellar's lips trembled. "Thank you, Day."

Kellar blotted her tears as she packed a carryon. She'd only be in Indiana a couple of days. Three at the most. She'd become an expert at choosing clothes suitable for multiple occasions. She spoke to her mother again, and she called Adrienne. Her mother had made preliminary plans with the funeral home earlier in the day. The viewing was set for the day after tomorrow; the funeral and burial for the day after that.

Kellar surprised herself by not falling apart. Sadness at the loss of Poppy remained, but knowing she was at peace and no longer in pain brought comfort. Poppy, a believer if there ever was one, told Kellar long ago not to be sad, but to think of death as a reward. Kellar even found herself smiling as she got ready for bed, remembering all the words of wisdom her grandmother had shared, the way she'd helped shape Kellar's life. Gratitude crowded out the sadness.

"How's my famous daughter doing?" her mother asked once they were out of the airport traffic and on the way to Charlotteville.

Kellar gave her mother a sidelong glance. "I'm not exactly famous, Mom."

"Sure, you are. You're a bestselling author and you're dating a Hollywood actor."

"We're not dating, Mom. I told you."

Her mother kept her eyes on the road. "What would you call it then? Keeping company?"

The old-fashioned term got a laugh out of Kellar. "That's more accurate. But not in the romantic sense."

"Why not?"

"Because we're not. We're friends. We spend time with each other. We like each other."

"That could lead to more."

"It won't."

"Why not?"

Kellar knew her mother was merely expressing curiosity, but saying, "We have an arrangement," would only lead to more cross-examination.

"How's Gracie?"

"Sad about Poppy like everyone else. I worry that it's hitting a little too close to home for her."

Kellar remained quiet. Because of Gracie's condition, Adrienne had been forced to have the kind of conversations that no child her age should be subjected to.

"But she's a trooper, and she's still holding her own. We hold our breath every time she goes in for tests, but so far, so good. Her appetite isn't great, though, so if you can tempt her to eat, that will help. Bribe her if you have to.”

"Do you need help with the arrangements?"

Her mother shook her head. "I took the clothes Mom wanted to wear to the funeral home. I might need you to fetch and carry or find room in the fridge for food, but otherwise, we're set."

They spoke of other things for the rest of the drive, and Kellar was glad to finally see the house as they pulled into the driveway. It could use a new coat of paint, and some of the shrubbery needed to be trimmed, but between her mother and sister were doing an admirable job of keeping the place up.

Kellar felt the same sense of homecoming she got every time she walked into the house where she'd grown up. Her sister greeted her, and their hug went on for a long time.

"Now, where's that niece of mine?"

"Upstairs. She's supposed to be taking a nap, but I bet she's wide awake and saw you arrive from the window."

"I'm going up." Kellar shed her jacket and washed her hands at the sink before climbing the stairs. She tapped softly at the door to her old room and opened it a crack.

"KK!" her niece cried from the bed. Her arms shot up and Kellar noted how thin they were before she swooped in and gathered the child in her arms. She felt small and fragile which made Kellar be extra gentle even though Gracie squeezed her neck as hard as she could.

When they separated, Gracie scooted back against her pillows. There were dark circles beneath her eyes, but the eyes themselves sparkled with mischief.

"You're supposed to be taking a nap," Kellar informed the little girl.

"I'm not tired," Gracie insisted.

"Maybe we should read a book then."

"Yay!"

Kellar chose one from the stack of favorites on the nightstand, toed her shoes off and laid down. Gracie snuggled close to her and held the book open. Kellar started to read the familiar story. Gracie knew it by heart and turned the pages without being told.

The next thing Kellar knew, a small hand was patting her face. She woke to see Gracie's bright eyes close to hers.

"Who are you?" Kellar asked.

"Gracie!"

"Where am I?"

"In my bed!"

"What happened?"

"You fell asleep. Then I fell asleep."

"Oh. No." Kellar arranged her expression into one of mock horror. "Did we take a nap?"

"Yes!" Gracie shrieked, then went off into a peal of laughter. Kellar tickled her tummy, wishing she could bottle Gracie's laugh and take it home with her. She'd have to record it before she left.

Judging from the light coming in through the windows, Kellar guessed it was mid-afternoon. Her stomach rumbled, reminding her that she hadn't eaten all day. "Time for a snack."

They made their way down to the kitchen. Kellar wondered where her mother and sister were. Napping, she hoped, unless Gracie's voice had woken them. There were already a couple of casseroles in the fridge. Kellar by-passed those after locating a small deli tray. Someone had baked pumpkin bread as well as a cherry pie.

She and Gracie had a whispered conversation about what to eat and Kellar assembled a plate for them to share with child-sized bites of the various goodies.

At the funeral home the following evening, Kellar became vaguely aware of a rising murmur amongst the friends and family members gathered in small groups and sitting in the rows of chairs in the viewing room. She glanced around and saw Day enter, resplendent in a black suit and maroon tie. Behind him, Chazz, in a less impressive blue pinstripe, finished signing the guest book and followed.

What? How? Why? Not in a million years could she have predicted Day's presence here, and yet she welcomed it. Despite knowing most of the people around her, she'd been feeling very alone.

"Excuse me," Kellar said to two of Poppy's elderly friends. She strode toward him without questioning how glad she was to see him. She fell against him, and the moment his arms closed around her, she absorbed his warmth and strength, knowing it was exactly what she needed after the strain of the past couple of days.

Finally, she released him and looked up. "I can't believe you're here. I didn't know you were coming."

He tucked a strand of her hair back into place. "I left you a message, but maybe you didn't get it. Anyway, isn't that what friends are for? To be there in times of trouble."

She'd met Chazz only once before, but turned and gave him a brief hug as well. He allowed it while remaining stiff and uncomfortable. "Thank you for coming," she said, to which he replied, "Sure."

"Let me introduce you to..." Before they could move a step, some of the other mourners moved in for introductions. To Kellar's mortification, some asked to take selfies, which Day politely declined with, "Perhaps another time." Even so, Kellar was sure a few phone cameras were not so subtly in use.

Finally, she extricated him and escorted him to the front of the room. "Mom, Adrienne, this is Dayman MacDay. Day, this is my mother, Robin, and my sister, Adrienne."

"I'm sorry we're meeting under such sad circumstances," Day said. "My sympathies to you both. This is Chazz Prescott."

Chazz nodded to them. "I'm so sorry for your loss."

"It's a pleasure to meet you both," Robin said. "Thank you for coming."

She became distracted by more visitors pressing forward. Kellar pulled Day away from the receiving line.

"Excuse me," Chazz said. Kellar barely noticed when he stepped away.

"I haven't been checking my messages today," she said to Day.

"I wasn't even sure I should come because we're so newly acquainted, so if this is too awkward—"

"Of course not. It means a lot to me."

"Are you sure? Chazz thinks I'm overstepping. I hate to tell you how often he's right."

"I'm glad you're here."

Day took her hands in his and tilted his head. "Are you sure? I kept thinking if it was my grandma, you would be there for me if you could."

"Of course," she answered without hesitation. "And I can say with the utmost certainty, Poppy would be thrilled that you're here."

"Then we won't make a big deal out of it, okay?"

"Okay." She leaned up and kissed his cheek, squeezing his hands as she did so. "I should go back to the receiving line."

"I'll wait for you."

She rejoined her mother and sister trying to remember the last time anyone had been there just for her.

When she looked Day's way again, she saw him with Chazz in a corner, his back to the crowd. Chazz was studying his phone, tapping keys every now and again, while appearing to have a serious conversation with Day. This was most likely a ploy to keep autograph and selfie seekers at bay. It seemed to work. Although there was a small circle of hopefuls lurking a few feet away, it didn't appear anyone had the chutzpah to approach.

In another ten minutes, the viewing would be over. Kellar longed to be back in her childhood home, out of her high heels, curled up on the sofa with a cup of tea or a glass of wine, with only her mother and sister for company and Gracie sound asleep. Although, that wouldn't happen for a few more hours, as her aunts, uncles, cousins, and family friends would likely be there as well.

The funeral home director appeared with an announcement that the viewing had concluded. As those remaining made their way to the exit, Kellar approached Day and Chazz. "Come to my mom's house, won't you? We have a ton of food."

By the time Day and Chazz arrived at the house, all the relatives were there helping themselves to salads, casseroles, cakes, and pies dropped off by friends and neighbors. But they all did a double take as the two men began unloading their own contribution to the evening. They set out several bottles of wine and a case of beer, along with a bottle of top-shelf Irish whiskey.

Everyone who hadn't met Day, and even those who had, pressed forward to greet him. Kellar watched Chazz edge away from the crowd, even as Day seemed to embrace it, shaking hands and repeating names.

"He's something, isn't he?" Adrienne said, standing next to her.

"He is," Kellar said, aware of the note of pride in her voice.

Day uncapped the whiskey as Uncle Tony appeared from the dining room. He'd raided her mother's China hutch for the good crystal highball glasses.

"That beer looks pretty good to me," Adrienne commented. "You in?"

"No. But I'll have a glass of wine."

"Be right back." Kellar watched her sister wade into the fray. She said something to Day, who laughed. He poured a glass of white before he looked across the room at Kellar, raising the glass in a silent salute.

Her mother took up the position next to Kellar previously occupied by Adrienne. "Your friend is a hit."

"Wherever he goes, apparently," Kellar agreed.

"I'm surprised he's here," Robin said thoughtfully. "Though maybe I shouldn't be."

"No. It surprised me, too. I didn't know he was coming."

"Why do you think he did?" Robin seemed genuinely curious.

"Because that's what friends are for."

Adrienne returned and handed the wine to Kellar. "Mom, can I get you something? You must be dead on your feet."

"I'm fine," Robin lied. "But you're right about my feet.

I'm going to find a seat and stay there until everyone leaves."

Adrienne watched her go before she said, "Day's buddy doesn't look too happy."

Kellar saw Chazz slouched near the fireplace as if he wasn't sure what to do with himself. His gaze flickered to the two of them before he resumed glowering at his phone. Adrienne took a healthy swig of her beer. "I'm going to see if I can make him feel more at home."

"Good luck." In Kellar's limited experience with Chazz, she'd yet to see him fully relax. He always looked on guard, like he was Day's watch dog or something.

She drank some wine while her sister linked her arm through Chazz's and pulled him away from the corner.

"Uh oh," Kellar muttered to herself. Chazz wouldn't be able to tell her sister no, no matter what she had in mind. He reluctantly followed her to the buffet set up on the dining table. Adrienne handed him a paper plate as if he were a child, then pointed to the various dishes. When Chazz didn't object, she spooned some onto his plate, sipping on her beer as she went.

Kellar smiled, watching the two of them. If Chazz needed a bit of mothering, Adrienne could certainly provide it.

"There's that smile I was hoping to see." Kellar hadn't seen Day approach. He stood next to her with a highball glass in his hand filled with ice and a finger of whiskey. "By the way, I didn't mean to hog the spotlight over there, but I wasn't in a position to whip up funeral potatoes." He indicated the counter where his contributions were dwindling fast.

Kellar giggled, surprised he even knew what funeral potatoes were. "Did Chazz reprimand you again?"

"Well, I do pay him to be my conscience. I also ignore him a lot, even when he's right."

"I don't think you can help hogging the spotlight, being that it loves you so much. You never have to apologize for being who you are. But also, you're a wonderful diversion from the sadness everyone's feeling. And, I repeat, Poppy would be thrilled."

"Whew. Thanks. I feel better."

Kellar nodded toward the dining room. "Adrienne's making sure Chazz doesn't go hungry."

Day chuckled. "I wouldn't say he's a picky eater. But there are a lot of foods he avoids."

"Let me guess. Red meat. Carbs. Dairy."

"Also, gluten. Alcohol. Sugar."

Kellar leaned toward him conspiratorially. "Keep him away from the iced tea."

"He's a big boy. And I'm sure he's safe with your sister."

She saw the two of them head for the small sitting room off the entry hall. "Looks like." She turned back to Day. "Where are you staying, by the way? And for how long?"

"Not sure. Chazz was having trouble finding a hotel nearby. Seems there's a basketball tournament happening locally. But he'll work something out. He always does."

"Don't be ridiculous," Kellar told him. "You can stay at my grandmother's house."

"Shouldn't that be reserved for out-of-town family?"

"Most of Poppy's family lives around here. Let me ask my mother and double-check, just to be sure."

After Kellar disappeared into the living room, Day studied the family and friends gathered in groups, chatting, eating, drinking. The warmth of the house and the people in it wrapped around him.

Growing up on the road, there hadn't been too many family gatherings like this. His grandparents were already up there in years by the time he came along, and the few other relatives were far-flung.

But Kellar's family had a history. Ties to each other. A home. It made him miss his parents.

When she approached with a smile on her face, a brilliant idea began to take shape.

"It's settled," she said. "You and Chazz can stay at Poppy's."

Chapter Twelve

♥

An hour later, Day stepped out of the upstairs bathroom to discover a small face peering out of the room next door. The pretty brown eyes of a young girl gazed up at him, her complexion an unhealthy shade of bluish white.

He dropped down to her level without advancing further. "Hello, there."

She put a finger to her lips. "Sshhh."

"Oh. Sorry," he whispered. "Do we need to be quiet?"

"I'm supposed to be asleep."

Day grinned and kept his voice down. "Me too. I'm Day. What's your name?"

She glanced down the hallway before she answered. "Gracie."

"Nice to meet you, Gracie. Why can't you sleep? Too much noise?"

Her gaze dropped to the worn baby blanket she clutched to her chest. "Poppy died." Her eyes seemed even bigger than before, the dark circles beneath them more prominent.

"I know. I'm sorry. You must be sad."

"I might die."

She said it so matter-of-factly while she plucked at the blanket, Day was taken aback. This wasn't a conversation he was prepared to have with a child he'd just met. "It's a scary thing to think about, isn't it?"

She shook her head, her straight brown hair swinging back and forth. "Kids get sick. Kids die."

Day couldn't argue with that. He noticed a fading bruise on top of her hand. A healing puncture wound of the kind left after the removal of an IV line. Her fingers were long and slender, the flesh barely seeming to cover the bones beneath.

"Uh oh. Is somebody up past her bedtime?"

Kellar appeared at the top of the stairs, heading their way. Day stood and Gracie peered up at her.

"What's the matter, pumpkin? Couldn't sleep?"

Gracie's gaze swept in Day's direction.

Kellar pushed the door to her room open. "Want me to tuck you back in?"

"Can Day come too?"

Kellar glanced up at Day. "Sure, he can." She took Gracie's hand and led her back to bed. Day followed, his gaze taking in as much as he could of the bedroom's details as the single Cinderella nightlight allowed. Wallpaper straight out of the sixties with big floppy flowers on a faded yellow background. White painted furniture from another era. Posters of unicorns and dinosaurs and cartoon princesses. Shelves were stuffed with toys, books, puzzles, and games. Ruffled yellow curtains hung across the windows.

Gracie's bed was a white four poster with a sheer pink canopy draped from the ceiling across the headboard. The comforter and sheets featured Snow White and the Seven Dwarves.

Gracie crawled in and threw herself back onto the pillow. Kellar pulled the covers up to her chest before she pressed a kiss to her forehead.

"Sweet dreams, baby," she whispered.

Gracie clutched her blanket and reached past her with her other hand. "Day, too."

Kellar stepped back. Day bent and pressed his lips to Gracie's forehead. "It was nice meeting you, Miss Gracie. Have princess dreams."

Gracie gave him a shy smile.

When Kellar closed the door behind them, she said, "Looks like you've got yet another fan."

"What can I say? It's tough being irresistible." He turned serious as they reached the bottom of the stairs. "May I ask what's wrong with her?"

Kellar's face fell. "Leukemia," she said quietly. "They caught it early. So far, she's responding well to treatment. We're hoping for the best."

Day put his arm around her, and she allowed herself that moment of comfort and warmth and silent sympathy and understanding. But she warned herself not to get used to it.

In a quiet moment over coffee the next morning, Day outlined his plans with Kellar. "I'd like to be there for you at the funeral service today, but I think I should bow out of the burial at the cemetery and that Ladies Guild luncheon you mentioned. It's not exactly a secret, but the last thing I want to do is turn my trip here into a media event."

"I understand. But what will you and Chazz do the rest of the day?"

"Movie stuff. I want to get a feel for the area. I might use it in a film. Then I plan to head back to the airport with Chazz tomorrow morning," he said.

"Oh. You're leaving?"

"Chazz is. But I have an idea you might be interested in."

"Really? Do tell."

"Let's take a road trip."

She gave him what he thought of as her skeptical look. "A road trip to where?"

"To visit my parents in Pennsylvania."

"Your parents?" she echoed.

"It's a four-and-a-half-hour drive if we don't stop. But, of course, we are going to stop."

"At a truck stop? For breakfast?"

"At least one. Breakfast, lunch, dinner. Whatever you

want."

Kellar's face lit up at the prospect, then her expression fell. "I would but…"

"But?"

"I promised Adrienne, I'd go get tested tomorrow. To see if I'm compatible as a possible bone marrow donor for Gracie."

"I thought you said she's responding to treatment?"

"She is. But we need to be prepared. It might be difficult to find a good match for Gracie's blood type and the other factors that go into a transplant. Usually, a sibling has the best possibility of being a match, but she doesn't have any siblings. Adrienne and my mom have already been tested.

"I'll go with you. There's no reason I couldn't get tested. Chazz too."

"Day. You don't have to do that. And shouldn't you ask Chazz before you volunteer him?"

"Of course, but I know he'll want to help. After that, Chazz can head to the airport, and we'll take our road trip. I'll have you back in LA by Sunday."

"Day, I don't know—"

"Don't know what?" Adrienne appeared in the kitchen. She grabbed a mug and poured some coffee.

"I was just saying Chazz and I would like to join Kellar for bone marrow testing tomorrow," Day said before Kellar could answer. "And then Kellar and I are taking a road trip to Pennsylvania."

"I haven't agreed—" Kellar began, but her sister spoke

right over her objection.

"That sounds brilliant, Day. The more people who get tested the better our chances of finding a match. Even if you're not a match for Gracie, you might be for someone else. And as for the road trip? She'll love it, won't you, KK? Between you and me," she said, speaking once again to Day, "she needs a vacation. Even if it's just a couple of days."

"Could I speak to you for a moment in private?" Kellar took Adrienne by the elbow and steered her out of the kitchen, smiling brightly at Day over her shoulder. "We'll be right back." She firmly closed the door to the combination mudroom and laundry room. "What do you think you're doing?" she hissed. "He wants me to meet his parents! His *parents*!"

Adrienne took a sip of her coffee then cradled the mug in her hands. "So?"

"I can't meet his parents."

"Why not?"

"Because they'll think we're—we're—"

"You're what?"

"Dating!"

"Oh, come on now. I'm sure he's told them you're just friends."

"We tell the whole *world* we're just friends. Fat lot of good it does."

"I'm sure you're not the first of Day's 'friends' they've met, and he seems pretty tight with them.

"There! See? That's what I'm talking about!"

"What?"

"You didn't say friends, you said '*friends*' like you were making air quotes, like we're not really just friends. Even you believe it, and you don't even realize it!"

"I think you're getting paranoid, sis."

"Am I? Am I?"

"Yeah, you are. Look, you'll get a couple of days off and a fun road trip with a guy whose company you clearly enjoy. Meet some new people. You're back in LA before you know it. Let Day handle his parents. They're *his* parents, after all. Plus, think of the material this could generate. You can do a whole series on meeting the parents and extended family, how to avoid awkward moments, or how to deal with it when it happens."

"Hmm. Maybe you're right."

"I'm always right. I thought you'd figured that out by now." Adrienne smirked and drank some more coffee. "Are we done here?"

"Yes." Kellar hugged her sister. "Thank you for talking me down. This is all so weird. I don't know exactly how to handle it sometimes."

"You don't have to handle anything. Just go with the flow."

Kellar eyed her. "Have you *met* me? I don't know how." Another thought occurred to her. "You don't think maybe Day has an ulterior motive?"

"Like what?"

"I don't know..."

"I think his parents live within driving distance and

he's taking the opportunity to visit them, with the added bonus of having you as a traveling companion. He knows you like road trips, and he figured maybe you'd need a breather after Poppy's funeral. It's what a friend would do."

Kellar looked into Adrienne's eyes and saw that she was right.

Kellar rose early the next morning and went for a run. She'd missed it these past couple of days and her body told her so. Too much food, too much sitting, too much wine, and a less than buoyant state of mind. Running cleared her head like nothing else. Usually. But today it seemed her thoughts were churning as fast as her legs.

Day stood smack in the middle of those thoughts, and everything seemed to spiral out from there. Coming here to support her. Volunteering to be tested as a donor. What a difference his presence in her life had made.

Now meeting his parents. *His parents*!

She'd be lying if she said she wasn't looking forward to the road trip. And not just for the food. She decided to add another mile to her run, anticipating the extra calories she'd no doubt consume.

She'd forgotten how cold and damp the air could be this time of year. The sky was still overcast from a light rain earlier. Her running shoes slapped at the damp pavement and she upped her pace as she passed the high school.

That was the thing about coming home. A thousand memories assailed her every time, and not all of them pleasant.

For example, the day she learned her dad had left. She'd come home from school to find her mother and Adrienne clinging to each other, surrounded by crumpled tissues and untouched cups of tea. Seeing them like that, Kellar's stomach dropped like a stone.

Something inside Kellar died that day. She'd clung to the belief, the illusion, the pretense that she had a loving father. She thought of all the moments he'd missed. The birthdays and school events. The promises he made and broke. The number of times she'd forgiven him when he did something to try to make up for his absence. But had it ever been enough? If he'd truly cared, if his family was important to him, he'd have *been there*.

But he'd chosen not to be. She didn't know how she could be crushed by the news, and yet not really surprised. At the time, Kellar said what she was sure they were all thinking. "Maybe it's better this way." Over time she'd hardened her heart and faced the fact that her dad might never get help for his addiction and choose his family instead.

Maybe, she'd thought in retrospect, after being let down all those times, she'd always been waiting for the final shoe to drop. Once it did, she'd stopped hoping that her father, or any man for that matter, would ever be there for her.

Kellar passed the hamburger joint she'd worked at those last two years of high school, and the community college where Adrienne had begun taking classes the year before while working full time in a medical office. They'd pooled their money to cover the household expenses, and there had been precious little left at the end of each month. Which only made Kellar more determined to succeed. Struggling through that dark and difficult time drove her and shaped her into who she was today.

Kellar jogged through the few blocks of downtown, which always made her a little sad. Although some of the historic buildings had been preserved, many were abandoned now and boarded up. The old red brick structures were crumbling and some of the scrollwork had fallen away. The ancient sidewalks were cracked and uneven.

Abandoned. That's how Charlotteville made her feel. Although she always looked forward to seeing her family whenever she visited, she was always glad when it was time to leave.

By the time Kellar showered, dressed, and packed, Chazz and Day were ready to go. Chazz and Adrienne chatted in the kitchen while Day sat at the table next to Gracie, coloring books and crayons spread out in front of them. Her mom was exhausted last night, so she had said her goodbyes early and planned to sleep in.

Kellar didn't know what shocked her more. Chazz *chatting* or Day *coloring*. Somehow, she felt as though she'd stepped into an alternate universe.

Adrienne saw her first. "I called the hospital yesterday. They know all three of you are coming. They emailed the paperwork for Day and Chazz. I figured since you already completed yours, they could fill theirs out on the way if you drove. That way, it won't take too long for the cheek swabs."

Adrienne, in her usual organized fashion, had thought of everything. "Chazz can take an Uber from the clinic to the airport and you guys can head out straight away. Day can return the rental car at the Pittsburgh airport."

"Wow. Okay. I'm ready to go." She embraced her sister. "Thanks for everything. I love you."

"Love you too."

Gracie slid off her chair and Kellar swung her up and into her arms. Gracie wrapped her arms and legs around Keller while Kellar hugged the girl tight, reminded again how thin she was. "You know you are one of my favorite people in the whole world, right?" she whispered in her ear.

Gracie nodded, her silky hair tickling Kellar's cheek.

"I love you, baby. I'll talk to you soon, okay?"

Gracie nodded again and Kellar set her down.

Day said, "What about me? Do I get a hug?" He stooped to Gracie's level, and she put her arms around his neck. "Wow. That's a good hug. I'll see you around, okay?"

"And you'll come for my birthday like you said?"

"I said I would do my very best to be here. The future holds no guarantees, right?"

Gracie nodded as if she understood the hidden meaning of Day's words. Kellar filed away the snippet of conversation between them to think about later.

"Chazz isn't much of a hugger," Day informed Gracie. "You can just tell him goodbye."

Gracie looked up at Chazz. "Bye Chazz."

Chazz almost smiled. "Bye, kid." He held out his hand and Gracie slapped it.

"You realize I'm not authorized to drive your rental," Kellar reminded them as they stowed their luggage and Chazz handed her the key.

Day leaned close. "It's okay to break a rule every now and then. I won't tell if you don't." She got a whiff of his subtle cologne along with the scent of him underneath.

Chazz got in the back and Day took the passenger side. Kellar adjusted the seat and the mirrors and set off.

The appointment went smoothly enough, but before they could leave, the public relations director and chief administrator of the hospital asked for a few minutes with Day. Chazz left to catch his Uber to the airport while Kellar tried to hide her annoyance at the intrusion, but Day took it all in stride.

They asked if Day would consider doing a public service announcement and an interview about the importance of bone marrow donations for their website. Day agreed without hesitation. He gave them his publicist's number to arrange scheduling with them. After that, he walked Kellar to the car and got behind the wheel.

"You were awfully accommodating," she mused as they pulled out of the parking lot.

"It's a good cause," he pointed out. "I honestly never thought about it before I met Gracie. There must be a lot of kids that could be helped by more people getting tested and being willing to donate."

"I'm sure that's true."

"You seemed annoyed, though."

"Only at the intrusion. I don't know how you do it. Deal with the lack of privacy day in and day out, I mean. People always wanting something from you."

"Those same people buy tickets to my movies. Making successful movies is what gave me the financial freedom to make the kind of films I *want* to make. I'm grateful to them. If they want a picture or a handshake or a couple of minutes of my time, and I can accommodate them, I don't see a reason not to."

"You were sure a hit with my family."

"Nice people make it easy."

From there they segued into talking about family and Kellar shared a few colorful stories about hers until nearly an hour later.

Day pointed to a billboard advertising a truck stop with a 24-hour restaurant. "What do you think? Are you ready for breakfast? Or lunch?"

Kellar hadn't eaten anything all day. Possibly Day hadn't either. "I might be ready for both."

Chapter Thirteen

♥

The parking lot wasn't overly crowded. Once Day parked, he popped the trunk. He searched the side pocket of his black leather carry-on and found a pair of tortoiseshell glasses and a gray wool flat cap. He donned both and closed the trunk.

"What do you think?"

"Are you trying to hide from all those wonderful people who buy your movie tickets?"

"I'm trying to enjoy an uninterrupted meal with a friend."

"I can't believe how much it changes your look, but I don't know if it will guarantee you won't be recognized."

Day guided her toward the entrance. "All it needs to do is provide a modicum of uncertainty. I *might* be Dayman MacDay. But then again, maybe I just bear an uncanny resemblance to him. I mean, if you didn't know me, would *you* believe you saw me here?"

"Probably not. I saw a photo of Pamela Anderson without makeup recently. I'm not sure she'd be recognized immediately either."

No one seemed interested in their arrival. A sign near the cash register invited them to seat themselves. They found a clean booth near a window. The laminated menus were stuck behind a metal napkin holder with an attached basket holding packets of condiments.

Paper placemats were laid out on the table, along with utensils slotted into narrow wax paper bags.

Kellar picked up a slightly greasy menu and opened it. Her stomach growled and her mouth watered as she perused the offerings.

"Oh, my God. I want it all. A patty melt. Fries. Hashbrowns. Eggs over easy. Pancakes with blueberry compote and whipped cream from a can. Country fried steak. Biscuits and gravy."

Day laughed. Kellar looked up from the menu. A middle-aged waitress in a pink nylon uniform and a white apron set plastic glasses of water in front of them. "Coffee?"

"Sure," Day said, then looked to Kellar, who nodded in agreement.

"Cream?"

"Of course."

The waitress left.

"You know the coffee will be bad."

"But strong."

"What was so funny before?"

"You."

"I wasn't serious about ordering everything on the menu."

"I know, but it made me think of the one other time I brought a woman to a truck stop restaurant."

Kellar feigned offense. "You mean I'm not your first?"

"No, but you're by far the most enthusiastic."

The waitress plunked down two thick white mugs and poured coffee into them. She set a bowl with miniature sealed cups of cream between them. "You know what you want?"

"Oh, uh. Could we have a few more minutes? Your menu is so... diverse."

"Sure thing." She squeaked away on white non-skid sole shoes.

"*Diverse*?" Day chuckled as he reached for the cream.

"So much fat. So many carbs. We might have to divide and conquer." Kellar clarified. "Let's figure out what we want before she comes back. Then you can tell me about your previous truck stop date."

"It wasn't a date."

After they ordered with a plan to share, he launched into his story. "Her name was Brittany. Or Tiffany. Might have been Brandi with an i."

"I see she made quite an impression on you." Kellar sipped the black coffee, surprised to find it wasn't bad. She added half a pack of sweetener to it and sipped again. Better.

"It was years ago. There were a bunch of us working on the same project. I can't recall now how she and I ended up on the road together in the first place."

Kellar eyed him over the rim of her mug. "Charming."

"Anyway, she wasn't thrilled with our choice of pit stop eateries."

"Imagine that."

"She asked the waitress if the veggies in the Western omelet were organic."

"What did she say?"

"Something like 'Aren't all vegetables organic?'"

Kellar snorted. "Did she ask if the eggs were free range?"

"Of course."

"I can just see the waitress rolling her eyes."

"I don't think she even dignified the question with a response."

Kellar grinned and took a sip of coffee. She loved how they could get on a roll of conversation like this.

"She then asked if she could she get her omelet without the ham and egg whites only."

"Let me guess. The answers were no, no and no."

Day squinted. "Actually, they were willing to accommodate her. But I think they began to wonder what planet she was from."

"Was that the last time you suggested a truck stop meal to a woman?"

Day pretended to think before he answered. "It might be. Until I met you."

Kellar giggled. She could picture Day with his picky companion. Day being Day, he probably did his best to accommodate her.

"I suggested the fruit cup," he continued. "That was a

mistake."

"Canned?"

He nodded. "Fruit cocktail. Swimming in high fruc-
tose corn syrup. Tiffany/Brittany/Brandi refused to
touch it."

"Did she dump it over your head?"

"No. She simply complained the entire time the rest
of us were enjoying ourselves. Then asked me to find an
organic supermarket."

"You didn't."

"Trust me there were none within a hundred miles of
where we were."

"Was that the end of the relationship?"

"It wasn't a relationship. She was a production assistant or something on a music video I worked on out in
the desert. Didn't have a big budget. One-day shoot. She
ended up riding back to LA with me. I never saw her
again."

Kellar remembered the video. "For Riverside's White
Lotus single, right?"

"Yeah." Day's eyes lit up. "You remember them?"

"Just that one song. The video was fantastic. You. The
girl. The motorcycle in the desert."

"Too bad the band didn't last. They broke up right
after that album's release."

Their food arrived without notice or comment from the waitress. She set down the numerous plates along with an indecipherable, handwritten check, refilled their coffee, said, "Pay at the counter," and left.

Kellar cut into the country fried steak, slathered with thick white gravy, scooped up some hashbrowns, and put the forkful in her mouth. She closed her eyes and savored the bite. "Oh, my God. So good."

Day grinned at her. He poured syrup on his pancakes and cut a big bite. "You know one of the things I like best about you?"

Kellar glanced up from her next bite of steak, which she'd dipped in the runny egg yolk. "My appetite?"

"How much you enjoy everything."

"I don't enjoy *everything*. Funerals suck."

Day swallowed another bite of pancake. "Sure, but you notice and appreciate things others don't seem to. Small things. Like this, for example." He indicated the spread before them. "One of your best memories is a road trip with your family and a meal at a truck stop."

"Maybe that's because it's the only trip we took like that. Maybe it's because it was when my family was still—a family."

"Your family is still a family."

"Before my parents split up, I mean. The four of us."

Kellar concentrated on her food, hoping Day would take the hint and change the subject.

"Where's your dad?"

"I don't know," she said without looking at him.

"You don't stay in touch, huh?"

Now she did look up and something in her eyes told him he'd come perilously close to dangerous emotional territory.

"No. We don't. I don't talk to or about him. Ever. If I can avoid it."

Message received loud and clear. Day took another bite and changed the subject. "Something else I like? You're easygoing."

She sent him a look he interpreted as both grateful and amused. "Translation: Low maintenance."

"You say that like it's a bad thing."

"Not bad, necessarily. Boring, maybe."

"Now why would you say that?"

"I'm not going to provide you with a funny anecdote like Tiffany/Brittany/Brandi, am I? There's nothing amusing about the way I'm hoovering up everything from three plates. I'm forgettable, remember? Thus, my many no-show dates."

"Are you kidding? The first time we met we crashed onto a glass table and then you walked out onto a late-night talk show with more confidence than I've seen during the Academy Awards. I'm not about to forget you.

"I can't even remember Tiffany/Brittany/Brandi's

name. I ate a meal with her once, literally, and never saw her again. You? I'm not likely to ever forget. Whether you're the source of an amusing anecdote or not."

But you did forget me once. Kellar concentrated on her food, even though she was ready to push the plates away. Was now the time to ask him about that? She tried to reconcile the man who showed up at her grandmother's funeral with the man who stood her up in college. This Day seemed just as sincere as he had then. She wanted to believe he was, but she wasn't ready to trust her own judgment where he was concerned.

Day gazed at her as if he were memorizing her features. Disconcerted, she dabbed her lips with a napkin and pushed the plates away. "I think I've had enough."

"I don't think I'll ever get enough. Of being with you, that is."

Wings of panic fluttered in her chest. What did he mean by that? It almost sounded romantic. No! No! No! They were friends only. If she fell for him for real, he might break her heart again. She wasn't like those other women he'd had relationships with. The ones who'd taken the break-ups in stride and moved on without a backward glance. "I'm going to the restroom. Meet you outside?"

She didn't wait for his reply before she made her escape. Day couldn't have feelings for her. She refused to allow it. She had to stay strong. Keep their relationship exactly where it was. Friends. Companions. Convenient escort. She couldn't date Day, because even though she could face a live audience when not looking her best and turn it to her advantage, she had no confidence in herself when it came to dating.

Day had come a long way in the last ten years and so had she. On the outside, anyway. But inside lurked that girl who always expected to be let down.

Joking about her inadequacy helped her deal with her real fear of heartbreak. If she never let a relationship get to the point where she cared too much, it didn't hurt as badly when it ended. She could pretend to try and later chalk it up to one more guy she'd been wrong about.

It wasn't lost on her that she never claimed responsibility for those pseudo-relationships ending. Never admitted that fear and her own sense of inadequacy held her back. She couldn't. Not when she'd built her whole career on being the single girl who was still trying to get it right.

Day paid the bill and hit the restroom. When he left the restaurant, Kellar was pacing next to the car.

"You okay?" he asked, getting in. He tossed his hat and glasses onto the backseat.

"I ate too much. I enjoyed every bite, but now I feel like a five-mile hike is in order."

Day glanced at the dashboard clock. "Won't be able to do that until tomorrow. It will be dark by the time we get to my parents' place. Plus, I told my mom we'd stop for supplies on the way."

"Oh, good. They know we're coming. I'm glad you didn't plan to surprise them."

"If it was just me, maybe I would have."

She arched an eyebrow at him. "But I come with a warning label?"

He chuckled. "You should."

"What's that supposed to mean?" Kellar wasn't sure if she should be offended or flattered.

"It means I had no idea what I was getting in to when I propositioned you."

Offended it was. "Hey, we don't have a contract. You can get out of this any time you want."

"That's the thing." Day looked at her as he started the car. "I don't want to."

There it was again. That hint of *something*. Was he testing her to see how she reacted? If that's what he was doing, she refused to take the bait. They were friends. She planned to keep it that way. Even though she'd preached to her followers that it never worked. She'd make it work in this case or die trying.

"Are there hiking trails near your parents' place? Because I can tell you right now, I'm going to need a workout of some kind tomorrow."

"Their place backs up on a federal game reserve with all kinds of trails. There's also a state park only a couple of miles away. We'll get you your workout, don't you worry."

"Isn't there hunting on federal game reserves?"

"Mostly in the fall and winter. My dad will know. We could hike the trails in Malibu sometime, too."

"I'd like that. I've hiked a bit in the Santa Monicas, but it's been a while."

"How come?"

"Oh, you know. Work. Plus, it's not all that convenient to access from my place."

They went on to talk about other places they could hike. Day felt her out about camping in the mountains. He considered telling her about the land he'd recently acquired in Wyoming but held back. He wasn't sure why. Maybe he wanted to see where this friendship of theirs took them first.

The occasional lulls in conversation weren't uncomfortable. Before long a song on the radio, the passing scenery or a stray thought ready to be shared started them talking again.

They made one last pit stop to gas up and hit restrooms and pick up a few things at a grocery store. It was dinner time when Day pulled up in front of a log cabin on a wooded lot several miles from the last small town they'd passed through.

The outside lights were on to welcome them, casting a warm glow over the front porch with its Adirondack chairs and a padded glider. The door opened and his mom stepped out, followed by his dad.

Day caught his mom in a bear hug, smothering her acclamations of how glad she was to see him and how happy she was that they were there. He and his dad clasped each other, laughing.

Kellar inched her way around the car while Day finished greeting his parents before he drew her forward. "Mom, Dad, this is Kellar Kennedy. Kellar, these are my parents, Estelle and Ed."

"Pleased to meet you," Kellar said.

Estelle took her by surprise when she hugged her. "Welcome. Any friend of Day's is a friend of ours." She stepped back. "Come in, come in. Let's not stay out here in the cold and damp."

Kellar followed Estelle into the warmth of the house. Ed went to help Day with the luggage and the bags from the grocery store.

A fire burned cheerily in a stone fireplace. The interior featured lacquered wood, the décor a mix of native American and rustic farmhouse, including lots of bright cushions and more subdued knitted throws. A long island separated the kitchen from the main room. On the opposite side was a hallway that Kellar guessed led to bedrooms and bathrooms.

Kellar paused to admire the living space. "This is lovely."

"Thank you. It's comfortable and just enough for me and Ed. Now, what can I get you to drink? Day said white wine, but he didn't specify." Estelle went into the kitchen. "I have Chardonnay, pinot grigio and sauvignon blanc. The sauvignon blanc is from New Zealand."

"I'll try the sauvignon blanc, please."

"Oh, good. I wanted to try it, too."

She withdrew the bottle from the door of the refrigerator. "I don't even need Ed or Day to open it, either. How about that?" She unscrewed the lid before she got wine glasses down from the top shelf of the cabinet. She had to stretch to reach them. Kellar had a hard time picturing Estelle MacDay driving a big rig. She couldn't be more than five foot three of soft rounded curves. A mix of short messy curls and waves framed her face, and her blue eyes danced behind delicate tortoiseshell bifocals. She looked ready for her next adventure.

The men came in. Ed carried the grocery bags to the counter, while Day headed down the hall with their luggage.

"We're having that wine from New Zealand," Estelle informed her husband. "What about you and Day? Beer?"

"I don't hardly think so," Ed said. "Day brought a bottle of good Irish whiskey." He moved past her for some highball glasses which were lined up on the shelf below the wineglasses. He pulled out two and closed the cabinet, then nudged Estelle aside with his elbow. "Move over woman. Never stand between a man and his liquor."

Estelle rolled her eyes as she stepped aside. She poured wine and handed one of the glasses to Kellar. "Now what's all this?" She began to unload the bags just as Day returned. "Day, you didn't need to bring anything. I just went to the grocery day before yesterday."

Kellar slid onto one of the stools along the counter,

ready to enjoy the show.

"I know, Mom. But we're here kind of spur of the moment. I didn't want you to have to make another trip."

"I would have made do," she insisted. But she didn't seem displeased, either.

Ed set the highball glasses he'd filled with ice on the counter and reached for the bottle. He poured and slid one over to Day. They clinked glasses and sipped.

"Ah," Ed said. "That's the good stuff."

"Mom, what are you cooking? It's not your world-famous chicken tortilla soup, is it?"

"It is. And Mexican cornbread. We can eat any time, but I thought you'd want to unwind a bit first. Oh! What is this?" She withdrew a cake from the last grocery bag. "Chocolate Decadence." She eyed her son. "You're a bad influence on my diet."

"You can come hiking with us tomorrow, then. This one's already complained that she ate too much at brunch."

"Hiking? No thank you. I wouldn't be able to keep up and you'd have to carry me back. I'll just do some extra yoga tomorrow."

Chapter Fourteen

♥

They moved into the living room and Kellar sipped her wine enjoying the easy camaraderie between Day and his parents. She could tell from the conversation that he kept in close touch with them.

Estelle turned to Kellar. "My condolences on the loss of your grandmother, by the way. Were you close?"

"We were, yes."

"I always wished I'd known mine better, but it wasn't meant to be. I had a great aunt, Maxine, who was like a grandmother to me. She sure knew how to have fun. I still miss her sometimes."

After a few more minutes of small talk, Kellar set her glass aside and said, "Would it be alright if I freshened up before dinner?"

"Of course. The guest room is at the end of the hall," Estelle said. "Fresh towels in the bathroom."

Kellar passed a master suite on her right, a laundry/mud room on her left, then a bathroom, and finally the guest bedroom next to it. The view from the large window showed a vista of woods marching up a hilly slope and the winding road that she and Day had taken to get here. The room itself was simply furnished with red-and-black plaid comforters and curtains, and an area rug over the wood plank floors flecked with the same colors. Her luggage sat at the end of one of the twin beds. Day's at the end of the other.

"Hmm." No one had thought to mention they were sharing a bedroom. She lifted her carry-on onto the bed and unzipped it.

Day's unexpected voice behind her made her jump. "If the sleeping arrangements are a problem, I can always sleep on the couch." Day leaned one shoulder against the doorjamb, arms crossed.

"That depends," Kellar said, concentrating on locating her toiletries and hairbrush.

"On what?"

She glanced up. "Do you snore?"

He barked out a laugh as if that was not what he expected her to say. "I don't think so. But since I'm asleep, how would I know?"

"Someone else might have heard and mentioned it."

"No complaints so far."

Kellar set her hairbrush and zippered bag of toiletries on the bed. "We're friends, right? Relatively mature adults?"

"Relatively."

"Since we're not sharing a bed, it's not a problem."

"You're sure."

She eyed him, taking in his height and his muscular

frame. "Maybe you'd rather sleep on the couch. Your feet are going to hang off that tiny bed."

"We'll see. Besides, think of your blog headline."

She arched a brow at the delightful thought. "My night with Dayman MacDay?"

"You'll break the internet."

Kellar giggled, not entirely displeased by the possibility. Then she grew serious. "You're being awfully generous. I appreciate it."

He stepped closer, bent, and kissed her cheek. When he straightened, he looked into her eyes. "I've enjoyed every minute of it."

He left her alone with her thoughts, and part of her wished he hadn't. No matter how often she warned herself not to go there, they took her to the same dangerous places where her fantasies and memories held court.

What it would be like if this thing with Day was for real and not just an unusual platonic twist on the friends-with-benefits scenario. Day left her feeling unbalanced and even more unsure of herself lately. Was he already dropping hints about moving beyond friendship even though they'd agreed they wouldn't?

Words like, *I don't think I'll ever get enough of being with you* and *I've enjoyed every minute of it* fed that tiny butterfly of hope and led to daydreams that wouldn't go away no matter how much she chased them. They brought "what if" thoughts with them every time.

She needed to consider the possibility that Day's easy charm was the only reason he said things like that. Not that he wasn't sincere, but she might be reading more into the words than he intended.

If hope was a butterfly, intent on flitting through her psyche, then memories were a cockroach that moved too fast to be stomped on.

He stood you up. He made a date with you, then he bailed. He was with another woman. You weren't that important to him. He wasn't as interested as you thought he was. And he's not now. Didn't you learn anything the first time? Don't be a fool.

Kellar gave herself a mental shake and reminded herself that her previous history with Day was *ten years ago.* They'd both evolved. Hadn't they? She wanted to believe so, but often she felt like that same rejected, insecure young woman who'd walked home alone, always on the outside looking in, afraid she'd never find love.

She counseled herself to live in the moment. To take this time with Day for what it was. To enjoy it and stop trying to control it. Wherever it led, she assured herself she'd be able to handle it. With that, she brushed her hair, applied more lip balm, and returned to the others.

The aromas from Estelle's kitchen had intensified during Kellar's time in the bedroom. Even though she wasn't particularly hungry, she found herself looking forward to the meal surrounded by the warmth of the home and the people in it.

"Can I help?" she asked.

Estelle lifted the lid of a crock pot and began to stir the contents.

She looked up with a smile. "You certainly can. That cornbread's ready to come out of the oven. Oven mitts are in the drawer there." She lifted her chin to indicate which one.

Kellar set the round cast iron pan on top of the stove and turned off the oven.

"Someone raised you right," Estelle said as she removed bowls from an open shelf. "Can't say that about some of Day's other girlfriends."

"I'm not his girlfriend." Kellar felt compelled to correct her assumption immediately.

Estelle slid her a sideways glance. "Oh? That's what he says, too."

"It's true," Kellar insisted.

Estelle gave a knowing smile Kellar couldn't trust. "If you say so."

"I do."

"Want to slice that cornbread? Knives are there next to the stove. We'll just serve it in the pan."

Nice change of subject. Kellar selected a serrated knife and cut the cornbread into wedges. Estelle saw something between her and Day that spoke of more than friendship. But didn't everyone? Not just the public, but her family as well. She'd caught her sister, who knew her better than anyone, with that same smug expression on her face. As if she knew something Kellar didn't. And even though Robin voiced acceptance of Kellar's explanation, underneath she'd sensed her mother's skepticism.

Were they wrong? Did she feel more for Day than mere

friendship? If she believed she could pull off a romantic relationship that *wouldn't* end with getting her heart broken, wouldn't she pursue him?

Ugh. Kellar did not want to have this conversation with herself. She didn't want to examine her feelings, her motivations, her expectations too closely. Great attitude for someone with an advanced psychology degree. But if she didn't, they'd just keep coming up until she dealt with them.

But that didn't mean she had to do it this evening.

The dining table accommodated four, and Kellar found herself seated between Day and Ed and across from Estelle.

The three of them had their hands linked, and Kellar realized both Day and Ed were holding their hands out to her. Embarrassed at the lack of warning, she took their hands while Ed offered a brief prayer of thanks for the food, fellowship, and family. Day squeezed her hand before he let go.

"Don't you like the soup?" Estelle asked after the others had begun to eat. "I can make you something else."

Kellar looked up from stirring the contents of her bowl. "Oh, no. I was waiting for it to cool a bit. Day and I stopped for a late lunch, and I think I'm still full from that."

"Kellar loves truck stops," Day said. "And road trips."

Estelle beamed. "Well, she'll fit right in with us, won't she?" Without waiting for an answer, she leaned toward Kellar. "You probably know, we raised this one on the road. Visited plenty of truck stops along the way."

"I do know," Kellar said, trying some of the soup. "It sounds like a fascinating life. This is delicious, by the way."

Estelle looked pleased. "Well, I don't know about *fascinating*, but it was different. By the time Day came along, we'd pretty much given up on starting a family. Ed and I were doing long hauls together. Figured it'd be just the two of us. A baby didn't change things all that much. They don't take up much space and we already had an expanded sleeper cab."

"I can't imagine how you made it work," Kellar said.

Estelle and Ed exchanged glances. "We just did. We already had our driving shifts worked out. Once he arrived, we adapted them to Day's schedule."

Day reached for more cornbread. "She's saying I ruled the roost."

She patted his hand. "Only because we wanted it that way."

"My laptop was my best friend until I was twelve."

"You're welcome." Estelle chuckled.

"After that they settled down," Day said, putting air quotes around the last two words. "And I started middle school."

"Did you want to go to school?" Kellar asked. "Were you nervous?"

It was Ed's turn to laugh. "This one? Nervous? Not a chance. Walked in like he owned the place. After a couple of weeks, he did."

"The teachers loved him," Estelle said, pride evident in her voice. "He made friends easily. Started playing baseball."

"And this was in Pittsburgh?"

"Right. We lived there until Day finished high school. Then off he went to California."

Kellar had been wondering about those days. "Forgive my curiosity, but what did you think of that?"

Estelle cocked her head as if no one had ever asked her the question before. "Well, he loved movies. After he got into the performing arts high school, we knew he'd do something with acting. Theatre or film. Directing, even. I can't say we were surprised."

"You supported his decision."

"We wanted him to be happy."

"You gotta love them, right?" Day's question was purely rhetorical. "Do I have the best parents or what?"

"They're pretty special," Kellar agreed. She realized she couldn't eat another bite of the delicious soup and put her spoon down.

"What about your parents?" Estelle asked. "They're in Indiana, is that right?"

"My mom is. She's a trauma nurse."

"And your dad?"

"He left when I was fifteen. We don't stay in touch."

"Oh."

Rather than have Estelle poke an old wound, Kellar brightened. "My sister is there. And my niece, Gracie. She's six. I'm close to them."

"Oh, lovely. You've got yourself a built-in girls' club."
Estelle turned to Day. "Speaking of siblings, how's
Chazz? I thought he'd come with you."

"He needed to get back."

"I hope he can make it next time," Estelle said. "More
soup, anyone?"

"Wait," Kellar said. "You and Chazz are related?"

"No, no," Estelle said, before Day could answer. "But
Chazz is like a son to us."

"Oh?"

"I'll explain it to you later," Day said, pushing his chair
back to help his mother clear the table. "I'll do the dishes,
Mom." He followed her to the kitchen.

Exhausted, Kellar excused herself early. No one seemed
to mind. After a shower, she donned an ancient gray
long-sleeved tee, worn thin by numerous wearing and
washings, and a pair of baggy flannel pajama bottoms.
Day was not going to be impressed or seduced or even
interested in what she wore to bed and that was just fine
with her.

Seriously. It was.

She checked her phone and plugged it in to charge,
before she settled down in the bed, tucking the pillow
under head. The bedside light wasn't too bright, so she
left it on.

Day tapped on the door and poked his head in. Seeing her already under the covers, he pushed the door open and came in. He went to his luggage and dug through his clothes. "I'm going to grab a shower. You can turn the light off if you want. I won't need it to find the bed."

"It's okay."

He disappeared. Kellar closed her eyes, but sleep didn't come as quickly as she thought it would. When Day came back, she saw his outfit was surprisingly similar to hers. She chuckled. "We have practically the same pajamas." She stuck a leg out so he could see the plaid.

"Which proves we both have excellent taste when it comes to sleeping attire," said Day. "You sure you're okay with sharing a room?"

"Promise you don't snore?"

He swatted her covered foot, before he turned out the light and got into bed. "What about you? I didn't even ask if you snored."

"Guess you'll find out." She knew the smile came through in her voice. "Hey, tell me about Chazz."

Day sighed.

"I'm just curious. He's so...engimatic."

He didn't say anything. The minutes stretched. Kellar puzzled over his silence, but decided it wasn't important. He wasn't required to share every detail of his life just because they were friends.

Day's quiet voice filled the darkness. "He was a friend from when we settled in Pittsburgh. A couple years younger than me. When we moved in, he was the first to come around. We lived in a rental back then. Middle-class neighborhood. Decent, but nothing fancy. Dad was still driving, but mom gave it up to stay with me. My parents wanted somewhere conveniently located for dad, and it was in a good school district.

"After we moved in, this kid named Charlie showed up every morning wanting to play. Scrawny as can be, shaggy strawberry blond hair, and a face full of freckles. All his clothes were faded, worn, or torn and either too big or too small.

"It was a couple of weeks before school started, and I didn't know anyone else. I'd never had a friend around my own age before, so I guess I was as desperate as he was.

"Mom sort of adopted him from the minute she met him. I didn't know it back then, but she'd made it her business to find out about his family and where he lived. His parents were crap. Unemployed addicts who did God-knows-what to pay the rent. Chazz was an after-thought to them. They barely cared if he ate or had clothes or went to school.

"If he was around at mealtime, which he always seemed to be, she invited him to eat with us. When she took me for a haircut, Chazz went with us. She'd always say it was two for one day at the barbershop so he could get a haircut."

"Which she paid for."

"When I got new school clothes—"

"Chazz got your hand-me-downs."

"She never presented it like that, though. She'd tell him

there were clothes I'd outgrown, and she didn't know what to do with and asked if he knew anyone who would like them. He'd tell her he did, and he'd show up the next day wearing them. It was like a game they played."

"He must have adored your mom."

"Still does." Day paused before he spoke again. "Even after I made other friends, he'd come around whether I was there or not. He'd help my mom with chores. She'd make him a snack or invite him to stay for dinner."

Kellar felt the press of tears in the back of her eyes. "She rescued him."

"She loved him," Day said simply.

"Then what?"

"I graduated and moved to LA. My parents moved here. I think it was hard on Chazz that they left. Hard for my mom, too. And my dad. He cared about Chazz, too, of course. He just wasn't there as much day to day. Anyway, my mom told Chazz how to reach her if he ever needed her.

"Mom wrote to him a few times. Birthday and Christmas cards. Like that. But she never heard back until five years ago. He'd been in and out of trouble. Drugs, mostly. A couple of legal snafus. He got busted again and was offered rehab. Again. But he had to have a sponsor. Someone who would take him in when he finished. Who'd make sure he went to meetings and stayed clean. If he didn't, he'd stand trial for the charges and probably end up in prison."

"So, he called your mom."

"She was probably the only person in his life who gave a shit about him."

"You did. Your dad did."

"Not like my mom. She called me and told me the whole thing. She wanted to be there for him. So did Dad, but they were looking at retirement."

"She asked you to help."

"Yeah. He and I hadn't been close in years, but I remembered this ten-year-old kid showing up at my door looking to be my friend."

"And now it's your turn to be his friend."

"I flew back to Pittsburgh. Met with him. Told him how it would be. He could start over in LA, live with me for a bit. I'd help him find him a job. He could reinvent himself. But he was only getting one chance. If he blew it, I'd cut him loose."

"What did your parents think about that?"

"They were on board with the tough love. Although I'll be honest. I don't know if my mom ever could have turned her back on him."

"It doesn't seem like she had to."

"Nope. I give Chazz a lot of credit. He's more than my PA. I don't know what I'd do without him. He's involved in my production company, my business interests, even my personal life."

"Didn't you say he's also a writer?"

"He's working on a novel. He's smarter than I ever gave him credit for, plus he's street savvy. He's got good instincts."

"About people?"

"People. Business. Even food."

"Well, he's not *my* biggest fan. What does that tell you?"

"He's also protective."

"He doesn't need to be with me. I can't hurt you."

Day didn't answer. Maybe he'd fallen asleep. Or maybe he didn't want to respond.

Kellar slept soundly until two a.m. She woke, stifling a groan and got out of bed.

With its usual perfect timing, her period had started. She tiptoed into the bathroom and left the light on so she could search quietly in her overnight bag for what she needed. Except what she needed wasn't there. Oh. No. She was *always* prepared for such emergencies with at least one tampon in the zippered compartment of her purse. Except she apparently hadn't transferred everything into the purse she'd brought on this trip.

No point in lamenting her lack of supplies now. The fact remained she had nothing. Nada. Zero. She contemplated her options. Estelle was well past the age where she'd have anything that could help.

A quick check beneath the bathroom sink and the narrow linen closet confirmed her fears. Except Estelle probably used the master bathroom and not this one. If she had supplies for say, bladder leakage, they could prove to be duo purpose, at least temporarily. Kellar plunked back down on the toilet.

Sure. She could just knock on her hosts' bedroom door at two in the morning and ask Day's mother if she had an unreliable bladder.

Oh, my God. Beyond embarrassing.

Plan B. Take the car and drive to the nearest store. At two a.m. In unfamiliar territory. On winding roads. In the dark. And where were the keys? Not being an authorized driver was the least of her worries. She'd have to wake Day. Explain. Oh, God. More embarrassment.

He's your friend. He's an adult. He'll understand.

True.

There was a tap on the door so soft she could barely hear it. "Kellar?" Day's whisper was just as soft. "Are you okay?"

"No!" she hissed, keeping her voice down.

She layered toilet tissue and placed it in her panties before she stood and yanked up her pajama bottoms. She cracked the door open. "I need the car keys."

Day stared at her uncomprehendingly, his hair mussed, his eyes sleepy. "Car keys?"

"I need to go to the nearest store. Or pharmacy. Or whatever's open."

"Now?" His incredulity raised his voice a notch.

"Sshhh!"

He glanced at the closed door of his parents' room. "What do you need so bad it can't wait until morning?"

"Take a wild guess."

His brow puckered. "A sudden craving for a slushie?"

"Just give me the keys, okay? The less you know, the better."

He crossed his arms, cocked a hip, and gave her a stubborn look. "Forget it. You're not going anywhere alone."

"Day… please." Desperation seeped into her voice. "I'll be fine."

"Tell me what's going on."

"A recurring monthly female plumbing issue for which I am not prepared."

Kellar could have laughed at the look of befuddlement on his face if the situation hadn't been so uncomfortable for her. Then realization dawned on him.

"I'll get dressed. There's a gas station that's open twenty-four hours out on the highway—"

"You don't have to. Just give me the keys—"

"Not a chance."

Kellar leaned against the bathroom doorjamb until he reappeared, wide awake, fully dressed, keys in hand.

"I'm perfectly capable of driving myself to the store and back," she informed him.

"Of course, you are. But this trip was my idea and you're my guest, so let me do this for you."

Kellar gave him a weak smile. "I'll go with you. Just give me a minute to get dressed."

"There's no need. I'm a grown man. I'm pretty sure I'm capable of purchasing feminine hygiene products all on my own."

"Get whatever they have. I'm in no position to be picky."

"Got it." He started down the hall.

"Day?" she called after him.

He stopped and turned around.

"Wear your hat and glasses. Otherwise, they'll sell the security video to TMZ."

He gave her a thumbs up and turned away, but looked back when she called his name again.

"Thanks."

He tossed the key fob in the air, caught it, and grinned at her. "What are friends for?"

By the time Kellar woke up the next morning, her phone told her it was after nine. Day's bed was empty, the covers arranged in a reasonable facsimile of a properly made bed. She yawned and stretched and closed her eyes again, snuggling down beneath the comforter with no reason to get up. Until they left for the airport late this afternoon, the day stretched out in front of her.

Day had returned from the convenience store around three. She suspected he'd chosen one of each product they had. By the time she crawled back into bed, he was already asleep. And she hadn't heard him leave the room this morning. *He's quiet as a ninja.*

She wondered if there was coffee. *Please, God, let there*

be coffee. She should probably get up and find out if she was so desperate. And she would. Right after a few more minutes of luxuriating. But a tap on the door prevented that.

"Come in."

Day came in. "I brought you coffee."

Kellar shot upright and held out her hand. "Gimme."

He handed a steaming mug to her with a grin.

She took a grateful sip. "It's like you read my mind."

Day dropped onto his bed and stretched his legs out in front of him.

"Did I miss breakfast?" Kellar asked. She hadn't eaten much the night before, and now she was starving.

"Mom kept it pretty simple. I think there's some bacon left. We had toast and eggs. Easy enough to make more."

Kellar set the coffee on the nightstand and pushed the pillows against the headboard so she could sit more comfortably. She retrieved the coffee and lifted the curtain to look outside. "How's the weather? It looks kind of gray out there."

"About forty. Supposed to rain later. Too cold for a hike?"

"Oh, we're hiking. After everything I ate yesterday and how little I've worked out the past few days? Plus sitting on a plane later for what, four hours? I need to hike. I *have* to hike."

Day held his hands up defensively. "Okay. Okay. We'll go whenever you're ready."

She eased back into the pillows and sipped at her coffee.

"But first I'm going to enjoy this."

A Night Spent with Day

♥

Isn't it always a bit awkward the first time you spend the night with someone? Or maybe the whole time isn't awkward, just certain moments.

He took me to a beautiful, homey cabin in the wilds of Western Pennsylvania with the promise of a home-cooked meal, chaperones, and a hike in the forest the next day.

This place was cozy, but with all the amenities.

After a satisfying meal and a glass or two of wine, we got the preliminaries out of the way, which mostly involved a discussion of whether either of us snores.

Turns out we wear almost identical PJs. How adorable is that?

Midnight confessions were made, as one does at a sleepover as I recall from childhood. And all went well until about two a.m. when a shortage of supplies threw a wrench into the works. An embarrassing situation followed but was handled with the kind of understanding and grace we all hope for but never expect.

The morning after need not be awkward, even if the night before was. A gentle tap on the door and the offering of coffee in bed goes a long way toward easing into the day after...

Kellar reread what she'd written and knew she couldn't post it, even though it was all true. It was too personal and way too open to interpretation. Besides, she wanted to keep some of the interactions she had with Day to herself. She wanted to cherish the sweet and funny moments only the two of them knew about. Her followers and the press were allowed to *believe* they knew everything there was to know and were only seeking confirmation, but she and Day knew the truth. And she liked sharing a secret with him. Well, and with Adrienne. And Chazz. And Willow.

It wasn't a secret anyway, was it since they'd been honest with everyone? She and Day were friends. Nothing more.

Chapter Fifteen

♥

Kellar stared at herself in the mirror. She'd never felt so glamorous in her life. The glittering red gown plunged, hugged, flattered, and flowed. Her hair had been coaxed into soft finger waves and arranged over one shoulder.

Because the gown was so stunning, her jewelry was kept simple so as not to detract from it. A silver cuff on one wrist and sparkling earrings.

Chazz stood behind her, his chin in his hand. The wardrobe stylist, makeup artist, and hairdresser clustered around him, holding their collective breaths, awaiting his determination.

"Turn."

Kellar did so carefully on the delicate heels she wore.

"Walk," Chazz said.

She took several steps in his direction. His expression didn't change.

"The earrings?" Dani, the wardrobe stylist, asked. The two seemed to have a code where only sentence fragments were necessary.

"Maybe," Chazz said. They stepped away together to peruse the jewelry case which held other possibilities.

"Can I have my water, please?" Kellar asked Sasha, who'd done her makeup.

She stepped forward and offered a straw. "Remember how I showed you to sip? That lip stain is supposed to last for six hours no matter what you do. But I know you're going to be chewing it off before you leave the red carpet.

"I'll try not to. Really, I will."

"Uh huh." Sasha was clearly not convinced.

The hairdresser checked her phone. "I've got to go. Sage Martinez is having a meltdown. Chazz, are we good?" she asked over her shoulder.

"Yeah, go on. Thanks, Shelby."

He and Dani returned with more earring choices. Dani held one up to Kellar's ear. Chazz shook his head. He nodded yes to the second choice, and Dani quickly swapped them out.

Chazz looked Kellar over once more. "She's as good as she's going to get, I think."

Kellar's eyes narrowed. What was his problem, anyway? She was stunning and everyone in the room knew it. Except him, apparently.

"Day's waiting. Let's go."

Chazz led the way out of the room. Dani and Sasha stayed behind to pack their gear.

Kellar loved listening to the dress rustle as she moved. She was beyond excited for her first ever red-carpet event—the Golden Globes.

Day was in the hotel suite's living room, staring out at the expanse of palm trees and swimming pools below. He set aside a glass half filled with ice and amber liquid when he heard their approach.

"She's ready," Chazz said, then headed for the kitchen.

Kellar frowned after him. She turned back to Day to find him staring at her. She stood still for his inspection, waiting for compliments.

"You look good."

She stared at him. "Good? That's all I get after three hours of prep? A 'she's ready' and a 'you look good.' I find that unacceptable."

A smile twitched at the corners of Day's mouth. "Very, *very* good. How's that?"

"No. I am stunning. Gorgeous. Glamorous. Killer. Pick any adjective you want, but it better be a step up from 'good' or I'm not going."

"Really? I thought we had a deal."

"Is it really so hard for you to give a genuine compliment?"

"'Very good' is a genuine compliment."

"Well, I need more."

Day sighed. "Sorry. I'm a bit out of practice. The women I've dated—" He stopped himself short.

"Go on. The women you've dated.... what?"

"Were impossible to compliment, so I stopped trying."

"Impossible to compliment? Who were these creatures? Please elaborate."

"Remember when I tried to compliment you the night

we went for sushi? You deflected it. Downplayed it. I called you on it."

"I remember."

"Good. Now multiply that reaction times a hundred. That's the kind of reaction I'd get in the past. Nothing was ever good enough, right enough, perfect enough. But I was a man so how could I ever figure that out? The dress didn't fit properly, the lip color was all wrong, the hair didn't work with the dress, why hadn't she chosen different jewelry. The list of what was wrong was endless and it all got thrown in my face."

"I wouldn't throw it in your face," Kellar said.

"Are you sure?"

"Positive."

"Here's the other thing I've learned about compliments. This especially applies to movies, but it translates to almost everything else. The more effusive the words, the less impact they have. Possibly, the less sincere they are. The less genuine. Because using such exaggerated terms often covers up a more honest assessment."

"I get it. Excessively flowery phrasing bad. Simple words good. But I still need you to pick one of those effusive words. I need to hear it."

Day grinned and took her hand. "I need to get the full effect." He spun her slowly around until she faced him once again.

"Okay. Here goes." Taking his time, he allowed his gaze to sweep over her from head to toe and back. "You're simply stunning."

Kellar beamed. "Thank you."

"Finally," Day said, "I've found a woman who knows how to accept a compliment."

Or maybe just one who desperately needs one.

Kellar was beginning to see why so many Hollywood relationships were doomed to fail. How could anyone just relax and be themselves? They were constantly judged, photographed, and picked apart. Striving for perfection became endless because, of course, perfection was impossible.

With the help of Day, Dani, and the limo driver, Kellar managed to get herself and her dress into the back seat without mishap. So far, so good. The hotel was only a few blocks from the theatre. Hardly enough time for her dress to wrinkle.

The line of limos moved fairly quickly as celebrity couples arrived one after the other and were hustled toward the press booths all along the carpet.

"Ready?" Day asked when their turn came.

"Ready." She wasn't, but she had no choice. Butterflies batted around in her stomach. She tried to remember the instructions she'd been given. Everything had been orchestrated to perfection, but she wasn't confident she wouldn't screw things up somehow.

The moment the door opened and Day got out, she was to slide across the seat right behind him. His hand would be there, waiting for her to grasp. There would be a moment, a pause, where he would wait to make sure she was upright, that her skirt was falling as it should. She'd give him a nod to signal all was well, and they'd hit the red carpet. Day's publicist would meet them there and lead the way.

The limo slid to a stop. The door opened. Kellar did a quick run-through of everything she'd memorized. Who she was wearing: dress, shoes, jewelry. Slide, take Day's hand, stand, nod. And smile. The most important thing she had to remember. Smile. Smile. Smile.

And don't chew off the lip color.

Day got out and a roar went up from the crowd of fans and spectators. While he waved with one hand, he extended the other toward her. She moved close enough to grasp his hand.

But at that moment he turned, inadvertently tugging on her hand. He wasn't supposed to do that. He threw off the rhythm of her slide across the seat, yanking her slightly sideways. Her feet came off the floor as she slid further to the edge of the seat. He turned back then, to help her out. She got one foot out, then the other, but her heel caught on the lining of her dress. She looked up at Day and hesitated, just as he lifted her hand. She went with it, trying to shake her leg so that the heel of her shoe would get unstuck from her dress, but it didn't work.

She nudged Day with her hip before she turned toward him. He still had hold of her hand. He hadn't yet stepped up onto the curb, which was just inches away, before she stumbled against him. Something inside the dress ripped. Day's feet hit the edge of the curb as her weight slammed into him. He fell awkwardly onto the red carpet with her on top of him, still holding her hand.

Amid the gasps, camera clicks and flashes, they stared at each other in stunned surprise. Ignoring the cacophony of shouted questions, his gaze dipped to her décolletage then back to her eyes. He gave her a wolfish grin.

"I've ruined you," she gasped.

"With my reputation? Hardly."

"Oh, God," she moaned.

"Kiss me," Day hissed.

"What?" She stared at him.

"Trust me. We can play this. Just kiss me!"

She realized he planned to spin this disaster the same way they'd spun the first one. She slammed her mouth down on his, lip stain be damned, and put everything she had into the kiss. Dayman MacDay wasn't the only one who could act.

Except she wasn't acting. When she felt the brush of his tongue against her lips, she opened to him, took his tongue inside of her mouth and sucked it as if she'd never get enough. The hand that wasn't still holding hers wandered up to her hair, messing up those perfect finger waves.

When their lips parted, Day stared up into her eyes. "Ready?"

Heat pooled low in her belly, even though that wasn't what he meant. "Oh, yeah."

He grinned and something behind his eyes told her he knew exactly what she was feeling.

Someone grasped her elbow, and somehow, she got

to her feet. Her traitorous heel came free of the fabric. When Day stood, the crowd cheered his recovery with hoots, hollers, and whistles. Kellar twisted around, trying to see the back of her dress. Day assured her it was intact. She could feel the ripped lining trailing where it shouldn't be, but it didn't show, and thankfully didn't snag on her shoe.

Day's publicist had emerged from somewhere and helped her brush the back of Day's tux. The woman spent the entire time giving Day a rundown of the stops he'd have to make and who he'd be talking to. While she spoke the crowd of spectators, reporters, and photographers created frenzied noise and activity as they jockeyed for position and attention.

"Got it," Day told her. Kellar couldn't tell if he was just humoring her or not.

She made a few minor adjustments to her dress, smoothed her hair, and smiled as she tucked her hand in the crook of Day's elbow. The crowd shouted encouragement. Cameras clicked and whirred, and the two of them finally started down the red carpet.

"What is wrong with me?" Kellar said out of the side of her mouth, keeping her smile pasted in place.

"Nothing as far as I can tell," Day answered, continuing to smile and wave. "But if you wanted to climb back on top of me all you had to do was ask."

She slapped his chest, relieved that his quick thinking had rescued her from another ridiculous situation. She'd been vaguely aware of the people who'd hovered close, not quite sure how to help. But mostly awareness focused on Day beneath her, her weight deliciously on top of him again. And judging by his perusal of her cleavage, he hadn't minded one bit.

Even though she'd eventually regained her senses and became painfully aware of the flash of cameras, of the crowd catcalling and cheering, of everyone staring, this was *not* how she wanted her first red carpet appearance to be portrayed.

Chapter Sixteen

♥

Kellar supposed a time might come when she'd be so jaded that attending an after party wouldn't interest her, but it hadn't happened yet. Of course, this was only the third one she'd been to, but she kind of loved celebrity watching.

She lost count of the number of famous people she'd met, actors, actresses, directors, and producers as well as musicians and cinematographers.

After each party she made notes about the event, the people, the food, what she wore, and any other details she might need for future reference.

She'd heard, "I loved your book" so often she'd begun to doubt that any of the partygoers had actually read it. No one told her they thought the book was good, and after Day's speech before the Golden Globes, that would have meant more to her. Those who gushed about her book probably only wanted to stay in Day's good graces, because no one knew when there might be a role available in one of his upcoming films. Especially now that he had formed his own production company.

Even though she knew it would be a logistical nightmare, Kellar set her glass of champagne aside and excused herself to visit the ladies' room. At least this swank Beverly Hills hotel had the forethought to include plenty of floor space and extra-large stalls in their restrooms.

The minute Kellar walked in she saw Willow Thorne touching up her lip color in front of one of the sinks. Their eyes met. Kellar smiled and said, "Hello, Willow." They'd met for a second time at another event a few weeks ago.

Willow gave her a cool nod, the corners of her mouth doing something that passed for a one-second smile before she returned her attention to her reflection.

This wasn't surprising. From the first, Kellar knew she and Willow were never going to be friends. She didn't get the sense that it was because Willow was jealous, however. She'd even broached the subject with Day.

"Willow and I have been friends for a long time," he'd told her. "She's protective, that's all. Aren't you protective of your friends?"

"You don't need protection from me, though. She's aware of the nature of our relationship."

"Of course."

"But she doesn't believe you?"

Day lay back against the limo's plush seat and closed his eyes. "It's more complicated than that."

"Complicated? How? Because you were once involved with her?"

He opened one eye and patted her hand. "No. Just give

it time. Willow will come around."

"I can't wait," Kellar said, not bothering to hide her irritation at Day's inadequate explanation. "Then we can all be *just friends*."

"Exactly."

After their first encounter, Kellar spent hours researching Willow Thorne. For someone at her level of fame, she rarely granted interviews. When she did, her personal life was off limits.

Most photographs of her came from awards show red carpets, publicity shots for the films she'd been in, and magazine features. The occasional paparazzi shot appeared, usually of her leaving the gym or a restaurant alone or with a companion. Several times the companion was Day, but nothing about those pictures suggested they were involved.

All of Willow's romantic relationships were so short-lived as to be over almost before they became official.

Kellar had no reason to doubt Day's word regarding Willow. Still, in her head was the image of the two of them sitting so close together in that restaurant, while she, Kellar, walked home alone.

Maybe, Kellar mused, Willow wanted more from Day but was afraid of ruining their friendship. That, at least, Kellar could understand.

Something about Day and Willow's relationship didn't add up. But for the life of her, Kellar couldn't figure out what.

When she returned to the ballroom, she got a fresh glass of champagne from a circulating waiter and spotted Day and Willow standing at one of the high tables with their heads together. Wow. Déjà vu all over again. The music was loud enough they could have shouted at each other without fear of being overheard.

Before Kellar reached them, Willow spotted her. Deciding it was pointless to waste a smile on her, Kellar kept her expression neutral. Willow's suspicious gaze assessed her, nothing more. Day said something to Willow when he saw Kellar approach, and the woman melted away into the crowd.

Kellar finished three sets of bicep curls and began on overhead triceps extensions, concentrating on her form.

In the mirror she saw a woman who'd seemed to be watching her earlier approach.

"Wow, you're really dedicated, huh? I think I've seen you here every day this week."

Kellar eyed the blonde, certain she'd never seen her in this gym before, even though she seemed vaguely familiar. Her makeup looked camera ready, and not one hair was out of place.

"Have we met?" Kellar didn't appreciate the interruption and continued to focus on her arms.

The mirrored walls reflected several of the woman's

surgically enhanced features, including a pair of manufactured C-cups.

"Not exactly. I'm Jeanine Hartman."

The name rang a warning bell. "Entertainment reporter, right?" Kellar kept her tone neutral, not allowing her distaste to come through.

Jeanine smiled, appearing pleased to be recognized. "That's right. For StarCelebs," she replied, naming both the show and its trash-filled online magazine. "And you're Kellar Kennedy. Dayman MacDay's latest girlfriend."

Kellar sighed internally. She couldn't fault a reporter for attempting to do her job, even if the job often required manufacturing salacious tidbits and furthering rumors about Hollywood players. "Day and I are friends. We aren't dating."

Jeanine's smile turned predatory for half a second before she caught herself. "Of course. I understand that's the official line you two are feeding the press. I thought an expert would have better judgment."

Even though Jeanine wore a high-end workout ensemble, she showed no interest in the dumbbells, the machines, or yoga area, and didn't have a single bead of sweat on her.

Kellar refused to cut her own exercise routine short because of this obnoxious reporter. However, she planned to mention the unpleasant encounter to the manager so it wouldn't happen again.

"When Day and I were seeing each other—" Jeanine

began, thus catching Kellar's attention.

"Wait. You and Day? *Dated*?"

Jeanine's eyes turned into ice chips. "Briefly."

"When was this?" Kellar had never seen or heard mention of a relationship between Day and this *reporter*.

"A few years ago." Jeanine clearly didn't like being interrupted.

Kellar didn't believe her. But why would this woman want her to think she'd dated Day? Kellar kept her mouth shut, switched to a slightly heavier set of weights, and began military presses.

"As I was saying, when we were seeing each other, I quickly learned that Day can't be trusted. In case you don't already know, he's a player and a hound dog, plain and simple. You might want to get out now before you take a hard fall like I did."

Kellar concentrated on her straining muscles. She didn't owe Jeanine Hartman a response or anything else. Jeanine stayed a while and watched her, arms akimbo, fingers drumming until Kellar set the weights back on the rack. She grabbed her towel and headed for the locker room, still ignoring the ill-mannered reporter. She'd probably made an enemy, and hoped the way she'd handled this encounter wouldn't come back to bite her in the ass.

A few days later Kellar and Day were seated at Gloria's, which Day insisted offered some of the best Mexican food in LA. They'd sampled the margaritas and were digging into the warm tortilla chips, queso, and salsa.

"Do you know Jeanine Hartman?"

"Way to ruin the start of a perfectly good evening," Day groused.

Kellar grinned. "I take that as a yes." Unperturbed, she munched on a chip, savoring the salt and the warm cheese.

"Before this goes any further, tell me why you're asking."

"She interrupted my workout the other day to tell me that you were a player and not to be trusted. She wanted to warn me before you dumped me like you did her."

Day snorted. "I never dumped her."

"I know."

"I never even went out with her."

"I figured as much."

"She might be mentally unstable."

"You don't say."

Day leaned closer and lowered his voice. "She's kind of been stalking me for a while now."

"Kind of?"

"Not like breaking into my house or cutting out magazine letters to create crazy notes of devotion. More like she shows up at the same parties and tries to corner me, or I'll be shopping or something and she just *happens* to be in the same store. Stuff like that."

"You can't make her stop?" Kellar nibbled another chip.

"Not when her father is Kerry Hartman."

"Who's Kerry Hartman?"

"Head of Kaleidoscope Studios. Responsible for a third of the blockbusters made in the last ten years."

"In other words, somebody you don't want to piss off?"

The server arrived with steaming plates. After she left, Kellar picked up her fork. "Wow. This looks delicious. I don't know where to start." She cut into the chicken enchilada.

Day glanced around at the dimly lit dining room. No one appeared to be paying them much attention. It probably helped that they were in a corner booth and Day's back was to most of the tables.

"The story goes, Jeanine couldn't cut it as an actress, so she turned to interviewing those who could. The show she works for is produced under the Kaleidoscope umbrella, which means it's connected to her father. She can't be fired no matter how outrageous or inappropriate her behavior is. She gets just enough airtime to keep everyone happy. That's between her stints in rehab, of course."

"Oh." Kellar had tasted everything on her plate and debated where to start with second bites. "Why is she under the impression that she dated you?"

Day winced. "Because I behaved stupidly." He addressed his own meal for a minute before he said, "This was years ago. You hear me? *Years*. Not long after I arrived in LA. Somehow, I got invited to this music exec's New Year's Eve party.

"I'd never seen anything so wild. Booze, drugs, people stripping and jumping into the pool. Some crazy stuff going on. "I didn't bring a date and Jeanine sort of latched onto me."

"Let me guess," Kellar said. "You didn't object."

Day gave her a guilty look. "I was young and dumb. Naïve, too. And Jeanine—"

"Is okay looking." Kellar grinned and got a glower in return.

"I'm baring my soul here," Day informed her. "Cut a guy some slack."

She held up a hand. "Please continue."

"We found an out of the way chaise lounge with a tiny bit of privacy, but thank God things didn't go any further than they did."

Kellar pushed her plate away. "What do you mean?"

"I wasn't exactly sober, but I didn't realize Jeanine was hammered until she passed out."

Day drank some water while Kellar waited for the conclusion.

"I tucked a couple of beach towels around her and left her in the very capable hands of a female security guard."

"That's it?"

Day nodded. "That's it."

"That doesn't explain why she thinks she dated you."

"Like I said, she's overly familiar every time our paths cross. I escape as best I can without offending her. She seems fixated on me, and it's embarrassing. That's why I said I think she's mentally unstable."

"You're not wrong. In addition to her stints in rehab, she's been hospitalized for psychiatric evaluation a couple of times."

"How'd you find that out?"

"Did a minimal amount of digging. It's not exactly a secret."

Day went back to looking grim. "There are no secrets in Hollywood."

"She's not dangerous."

"Not in the physical sense, anyway. She reminds me of a small dog who nips at heels. For some reason she wants to make me pay for whatever she thinks I did to her. She wants revenge, or something."

"Do you think she ever hassled your girlfriends?"

"Not that I'm aware of."

The server brought the check and Day handed over a credit card.

But those relationships were with mega stars who perhaps had less to fear from Jeanine's father. By comparison, Kellar was a nobody. Perhaps that's why Jeanine sought her out.

"Well, I'm not your girlfriend, so I shouldn't be worried, should I?"

"I don't think so. Just be cautious around her."

"So, tell me about your dating life." Comedienne turned talk show host Helen Fontaine fixed Kellar with her friendly yet intense blue eyes.

"There's actually not much to tell," Kellar began.

"Really? Because we have pictures." A photo of her atop Day at the Golden Globes, her lips sealed to his, popped up on the screen behind them.

"For instance, what was going on here?"

Kellar pretended to study the photo, although in truth she'd seen it from hundreds of angles already. "I... tripped?"

The audience laughed. "Of course, you did," agreed Helen. "And what about here?" Up came a shot of Day-man trying to repair the heel of her shoe on the Jamie Falcon show. "And here?" Next was a shot of the two of them entering Shariffe.

"Honestly? I think a certain talk show host wanted to try his hand at matchmaking. He offered to buy us dinner, so we played along. I know how it looks," Kellar admitted. "But we're just friends."

The audience let their disbelief be known.

"I heard you were also spotted together at a sushi restaurant." Fontaine did a Groucho Marx imitation, wiggling her eyebrows and pretending to hold a cigar.

"What?" Kellar asked, all innocence. "Two friends can't eat sushi together?"

"You say sushi and I say there's something fishy going on."

"Is this an interview or an interrogation? What's next? Thumb screws?"

"No, we'll jump right to water boarding. Come on. Spill," Fontaine joked.

Kellar put on her serious face. "I know how it looks. It *looks* like we're dating, but the truth is, Dayman and I are friends. We hang out. We go to awards shows. We get sushi. But we're not in a romantic relationship."

"Please return to Exhibit A," Helen ordered. Back came the shot of the kiss. "Let me ask the audience. If this looks romantic, make some noise." The audience roared. "Those of you who think it's just a friendly kiss, let's hear from you." Nothing.

Helen gave Kellar a falsely friendly smile. "Care to revise your statement?"

Kellar turned to the audience. "If you tripped and fell and found yourself on top of Dayman MacDay, wouldn't *you* take advantage of the situation? I'm only human!" The audience went wild.

Helen turned to them, pretending dismay at their support of Kellar's version of events. "Traitors," she admonished with a smile. She held up a copy of Kellar's book. "Kellar's book is Those Who *Can*, Date. Buy it, people, so you too can pretend to be *just friends* with a guy like Dayman MacDay." The audience applauded as the segment ended.

Chapter Seventeen

♥

"You've done it!" Carol exclaimed during their next Zoom meeting. "It's entertainment news official. You two are now officially known as DayK."

"Seriously?" Kellar thought back to that first meeting in Jamie Falcon's green room when she thought she'd killed Day. *DayK* had not been one of the nicknames she'd come up with.

"It was bound to happen sooner or later." Her assistant could barely contain her glee.

Carol was right. Kellar and Day knew up front that they'd be labeled as a couple and that no one, especially not the press, would believe they were only friends. The more they denied it, the more they believed what they wanted to believe. It worked. They were both getting what they wanted. Sales of Kellar's book skyrocketed, her blog and podcast numbers were through the roof. She had more interview offers, endorsements, and book deals than she, Johanna, and Carol could easily manage.

Day surely had no complaints, either. He was under no obligation to spend time with her other than the agreed-upon events, which left him free to concentrate on the movie he was working on, the first for his production company.

This was not to say that he didn't find pockets of free time, during which he came up with fun ideas of things to do. They'd gone bowling one afternoon and for burgers, fries and milkshakes afterward. One Sunday they'd sailed with friends of his who owned a special effects design firm. Flying under the radar, they'd slipped into the back of a jazz club one evening and a comedy club another time.

Nothing had changed, as far as Kellar could tell. They enjoyed each other's company. They truly had become friends. Every once in a while, Day made an off-hand remark about his interest in her as more than a friend, but if she ignored his comments, he didn't pursue it.

She'd turned the dating idea every which way and still couldn't see a scenario where they could be more that wouldn't end up with her heart broken and Day leaving her life forever. She hadn't realized what was missing until he'd entered—well, technically, re-entered her life—but it was this. Exactly what they had. She didn't want to lose it.

Her entire life, Adrienne had been Kellar's best friend, although, of course, she'd had other female friends. She'd never clicked with them the way she did with Day, and they never quite understood her the way her sister did. Day could identify with her work ethic, her drive, her ambition, because he was the same way. Other men, in her experience, were not quite so understanding.

She and Carol concluded their business and disconnected from Zoom. Kellar immediately went back to brooding. *Why can't friendship be enough?* She'd certainly fantasized about having more with Day. Dating him. Letting him sweep her off her feet. Falling madly in love with him. Making DayK a real thing.

But she always hit a wall in those fantasies because, try as she might, she couldn't see the two of them lasting. She always pictured herself sitting at a bar filled with anticipation and excitement, only for Day to no-show. Just like before.

You're not the same person you were ten years ago. Neither is he.

In her head, she knew that. She could rationalize it all she wanted, but in her heart, she couldn't trust what her head told her. She couldn't trust herself. And she couldn't completely trust Day.

The psychologist in her laid that at her father's door. And yes, she should be old and wise and mature enough to *get over it.*

But the men in her life always, *always* bailed on her eventually. And if the first man who's supposed to love you more than anything, your own father, does it, why shouldn't you believe every other man who comes along will do the same?

Kellar had been round and round with all the arguments in her head, but she still hadn't convinced herself. Admitting to her own cowardice and fear was easier than finding out what would happen if she dated Day.

She had to be realistic. Day's proposition had only included the current awards season, which would only last until the Oscars at the end of April, early summer if you included the Cannes Film Festival. Not needing a cover any longer, Day might drop her like a hot potato.

If he did, she would miss him. They had fun together, and she'd discovered fun was something that had been missing in her life. She might hear from him occasionally, but nothing more. These thoughts made her even more reluctant to become too attached.

At the desk in his home office, Day flipped through the latest draft of *Poker Face*. Something was still missing, but for the life of him, Day couldn't figure out what it was. Neither, apparently, could the screenwriter. Even Chazz, who often had brilliant moments of creative insight, was stumped.

Day had begun to question the wisdom of acquiring the rights to Rory MacAlister's life story. He'd been so intrigued by the man's desperation. Day wanted to explore how an ordinary guy, a family man, a man with a successful career, decided one day to chuck it all and become a full-time gambler.

Day understood that an out-of-control gambler had a disease, the same way an alcoholic or drug addict did.

But the screenplay lacked the drilling down aspect Day was looking for. He wasn't sure the script, as it was currently written, went far enough to show the pain and destruction a man like Rory left in his wake. Further, he also wanted to show how *unaware* a man like Rory was about how his behavior affected anyone else, including his family.

There had to be a way to portray the blindness, the corrupting nature of obsession, the destruction. But they weren't there yet. Not by a long shot.

Day glanced at the folder Chazz tossed on his desk. "What's that?"

"Information about your *friend*, Kellar Kennedy."

Day turned his attention back to the computer screen. "Kind of late for you to vet her."

"I wasn't. I was doing more research on Rory. I thought I might find something to kickstart that script." He nodded toward the pages on the desk. "As near as I can figure out, he started using the name Rory McAlister about a year ago. Probably trying to outrun debt collectors. McAlister is actually his middle name."

Day gave Chazz his full attention.

"Did he change it legally?"

"I can't find any evidence of that if he did."

"If he didn't, you know what this means, right?"

"The contract he signed as Rory McAlister is meaningless."

"But the attorneys would have verified his identity."

Chazz shrugged. "It's not that hard to get a decent fake

I.D. ”

"What's this got to do with Kellar?" As if he sensed everything Chazz was about to tell him, he said, "Don't tell me."

"Rory McAlister Kennedy is her father."

Day sat back in his chair and took a moment to digest that bit of information. "Unbelievable."

"Do you think you should tell her?"

Day frowned. "I don't know. She never talks about him. It's almost like he doesn't exist.

Chazz took a seat across from Day. "You two are friends, right? If the situation was reversed, how would you feel?"

"What are you getting at?"

"She's more than a friend to you. Or she could be."

Day stared at Chazz, unwilling to admit how much of that statement might be true.

"If you don't level with her, this whole thing with Rory could blow up in your face."

"Rory and I signed a confidentiality and non-disclosure agreement. In fact, I think you were there when he insisted he didn't want any member of his family to know he'd sold his story. Probably because he owes them all money. Come on, Chazz. You've been around the business long enough to know what happens when things slip. This town runs on rumors and gossip and a desperate entertainment press on the trail of the next big story. You don't expect me to blab about my business to Rory's daughter when she has absolutely no stake in the outcome of the project, do you?"

Chazz said nothing. He offered what Day referred to as the sphinx face. Knowing and silent.

Day leaned back in his chair. "Look, I'm pretty sure this thing with Kellar is only for the short-term. We have a deal for the duration of the awards season. That's it. I don't see any reason to tell her."

"It won't look good down the road if you don't."

"You're worried about the optics?"

Chazz frowned.

"She and I don't talk a lot about work. That's one of the things I like about her. She's not in the business. It's refreshing."

"Maybe that's what you needed all along. To be with someone outside the business."

"I'm not 'with' Kellar. I enjoy her company, okay? That's it. She's not interested in anything more. I'm not sure I am, either."

Chazz gave him a doubt-filled look. "You went to her grandmother's funeral, for Pete's sake. If you aren't interested, then what was that all about?"

Good thing Chazz didn't know he'd also gone out in the middle of the night to buy tampons for Kellar.

In the face of Day's silence, Chazz turned sulky. "I'm just saying that's more than 'enjoying her company' is all."

"Maybe I don't have it all figured out yet. This relationship with her is new territory for me. For both of us. I can tell you this, though. She's not in contact with her father.

She won't talk about him. I'm thinking maybe it would be best for everyone if we leave this tidbit of information where it is. If it somehow comes out later, we can deal with it then."

"Fine." Chazz stood. "If that's the way you want to go."

Chazz tended to hover like a mother hen at times. He looked out for Day's best interests, but sometimes he went to extremes.

"The weird thing is—"

Chazz waited.

"I feel like I've met her before," Day admitted.

"In LA?"

"No. I don't think so."

Chazz frowned. "She's only been in two places. Indiana and LA."

"*Falling Forward* was shot in Indiana."

"You could have met her then."

"If I did why wouldn't she mention it?"

"That was what? Ten years ago? Maybe she doesn't remember."

"Maybe." Day wasn't convinced.

"Does it matter?"

"No." Day didn't want to explain to Chazz the occasional sense of déjà vu he got when he was with Kellar. It was nothing persistent, but sometimes it hit him. The tilt of her head or a sudden smile. Something she said. He'd get that distant ping of memory. But he couldn't remember any specifics.

"Hey, see if any of your research can give us a different

take on this, would you?" He handed the latest version of the screenplay to Chazz.

Once Chazz left, Day used his forefinger to slide the folder closer, as if to keep himself distanced from the evidence. He flicked past the first few pages until he came to a bio of Kellar Kennedy.

Dating expert. Blogger. Columnist. Podcaster. Author.

Date of birth. Marital status. Alma maters.

Family. Sister: Adrienne Kennedy Cunningham. Mother: Robin Carmichael Kennedy. Father: *Rory McAlister Kennedy.*

Day's attention turned to the schools she'd attended, and one in particular. Indiana University East. Richmond, Indiana.

Something echoed far back in his brain. *Richmond. Indiana.* Wasn't that the name of the college town where his first movie was shot? It would be easy to check. Once his career took off, he'd been to so many places, been interviewed by so many reporters, most of the details were blurry. He could always look it up.

He wanted to believe the information Chazz had dug up changed nothing. No matter what Chazz thought, his relationship with Kellar and his relationship with her father were two separate and unrelated things.

But a second opinion never hurt.

His mom picked up immediately. "Hi, sweetheart. How are you?"

"I'm good, Mom. Is Dad around too? I want to run

something by you."

"Ed, it's Day." After a moment, she came back. "Okay, he's here. You're on speaker."

They exchanged greetings before he plunged into an explanation of why he'd called. His parents were the only outsiders he ever discussed his relationships or his career with. Anything he told them would go no further. They never held back and always told him the truth, whether it was good or bad. After he laid everything out, all he heard was silence, which meant they were taking in what he'd told them and formulating their responses.

His mother spoke first. "Do I understand correctly? You and Kellar are friends, nothing more?"

"Correct."

"What if it turns into more?" his dad asked.

Day hesitated. "I guess that would change things," he admitted.

"Do you think it could?" his mom asked. "Turn into more, I mean."

Day had to be honest. "It could. But she's not interested in anything more, so I'd say it's unlikely."

"Then why does Chazz think you should tell her now?"

"Because he's seeing something between me and Kellar that isn't there. At least it's not there yet."

More silence from their end. His parents had spent so long in each other's pockets they often knew what the other was thinking.

"If you were dating her," his dad said, "I'd say you should tell her. But you're not, so I don't think you need to."

"I agree," his mom chimed in. "But if your friendship with her turns into something more, tell her immediately. At that point, she deserves to know."

Day breathed a sigh of relief, having his own instincts confirmed. He spoke a bit longer with them before they hung up.

He hadn't mentioned to his parents that in Rory's daughter he now had a source. She could tell him what it was like having Rory as a father. How his behavior had affected her. All he had to do was get her talk about it.

He'd have to move fast. The awards season would end. And possibly so would Day's relationship with Kellar. He shied away from the thought that she wouldn't be in his life any longer. He liked her. They had fun together. There was something between them he didn't want to lose even if he didn't know exactly what it was. Something beyond friendship. Soul mate? He almost laughed at the thought. He'd never believed in such a thing before. But maybe…if Kellar ever stopped deflecting the hints he'd been dropping. If she ever gave him a chance to prove that friendship could successfully develop into something more.

Anyway, his parents had agreed he didn't owe her any explanations *right now.*

No matter what Chazz said.

Willow leaned halfway across the table to emphasize her point. "She can ruin you."

She and Day were seated at one of their favorite spots, a Mexican café not from Day's production office. Mid-morning, the place was nearly empty, which is how Day liked it. The food was authentic, and they did something to their huevos rancheros that had Day hooked. Day chuckled at his friend's overly dramatic tone and forked up another bite before he addressed Willow's statement.

"Ruin me, how?"

Willow pushed a few bites of food around on her plate. "Emotionally."

"Do I need to explain this for the thousandth time?" Day asked in exasperation. "We're just friends. The same as us."

Day didn't understand Willow's discomfort with Kellar. When he'd explained their arrangement, she hadn't been exactly enthusiastic. But her initial suspicion had become something close to animosity after he'd introduced them.

"It's not the same, and you know it," Willow said narrowing her eyes. "You like her."

"I do like her. Maybe if you'd give her half a chance you'd like her, too."

Willow muttered something Day didn't hear. "Spit it out, Willow. I've got a meeting in half an hour."

"I've never seen you like this," Willow said. "Even when you were supposedly in 'love', I don't think you liked those other women the way you like Kellar."

"What are you talking about? Of course, I liked them."

Willow shook her head slowly. "Kellar gets you. And, I think, you get her. You have fun together and you've never gone near a bedroom." She held up a hand to forestall Day's protest. "I know. I know. That isn't an option right now. But don't tell me you're unaware of the chemistry between you. She lights up around you."

"She does?"

"And you—"

"What am I doing? Glowing like I'm radioactive?"

Willow glowered. "Acting like a bumbling idiot. Or like you're besotted."

"Oh, come on, Wills. Besotted? Are you serious?"

"Besotted's the wrong word. Delighted. That's the right word. Like a kid on his birthday who hasn't opened his presents yet but knows he's getting everything he wants."

Day grinned at her description. "You paint quite a picture."

"Look me in the eye and tell me you don't want something more with her than friendship."

Flummoxed, Day focused on his food. Willow continued, keeping her voice down. "I don't think she trusts you, though. There's something she's holding back."

I'm holding back with her, too. His lie of omission had begun to weigh on him. He was beginning to think Chazz was right. He should tell Kellar about Rory, the movie. Everything. Also, that he was starting to have feelings beyond friendship for her. And let the chips fall where they may. Irritated with himself, with Willow, with the whole situation he'd created he said, "So what? This is an arrangement, not a relationship. She doesn't need to trust me a hundred percent." Except…he wanted her to. He wanted to be the one guy who didn't let her down. And if they were ever able to level with each other, he promised himself he would be.

Willow flapped her hand at him. "Dayman Raymond MacDay." Willow had the uncanny ability to sound just like his mother on those few occasions when she'd been irritated beyond reason with him. "You're my best friend. I don't want to see you get hurt. Not by her."

Day looked at the check and leaned back to access his pocket. "I'll be careful," he promised. "Now, can we talk about you?"

Willow allowed him to change the subject, but she wasn't happy about it. She was one of the most intuitive people he knew, so if she sensed something about him where Kellar was concerned, he could have just owned up to it. Maybe he wasn't ready to discuss Kellar's resistance to his interest.

Thoughts of what Willow said dogged him the rest of the day, in between meetings and phone calls and the million other things demanding his attention.

Apparently, everyone close to him saw something between him and Kellar. Something that hadn't happened yet, but in their minds was a foregone conclusion. Maybe it was time to admit that he'd been sensing the same thing on a wavelength he refused to tune into. Suddenly it all seemed too big, like a potential relationship with a capital R. Something he couldn't walk away from. Didn't want to walk away from. But didn't know how to get from where he was to where he wanted to be. Or thought he wanted to be.

He did some deep breathing which always seemed to help him focus and calm his mind. It wasn't like he had to move his relationship with Kellar forward immediately. He could take it slow. Let it progress organically.

He usually enjoyed the drive home, even in heavy traffic, but when he finally arrived, he went straight to the fridge for a beer to try and unwind.

Chazz gave a non-judgmental glance before he returned his attention to stirring the contents of a wok.

Day took a seat at the island, concentrated on the beer, and tried not to brood. "Smells good." Chazz's culinary skills never ceased to amaze him. He had a way with seasoning that made the simple ingredients he used sing.

Chazz scooped organic wild rice onto two plates and spooned the stir-fried vegetables over it. He slid grilled shrimp off a skewer onto Day's plate and tofu onto his before he took the seat adjacent to Day.

Day got another beer from the refrigerator and mineral water for Chazz.

After a few bites, Chazz said, "Tough day?"

Day smiled. He and Chazz often behaved like an old married couple. Chazz didn't pry, but if Day wanted to talk, he lent an ear, offering feedback only if requested. *Usually.*

"What's your opinion of Kellar?"

Chazz shifted his attention to his food, rearranging it with his fork. Only an idiot would be blind to his discomfort with the subject.

"You don't like her."

Chazz looked up. "That's not it."

Day waited Chazz out until he finally spoke again. "It's how much *you* like her."

Amazing, Day thought, how his two closest friends saw things about him, while he'd been knowingly downplaying his interest in Kellar.

Day motioned with his fingers. "Let's have it." He drank beer while Chazz talked.

"You start this friendship with her, which I get. It serves a purpose and benefits both of you. Typical celebrity BS. But you're different when you're around her."

Day started to eat again. "Different how?"

"You're not on guard as much, for one thing."

Day supposed that could be true. He knew he relaxed when he was with Kellar, became more himself. But hadn't he done that in his other relationships? In a moment of insight, he realized the answer was no. In some way he'd always remained "on" with them. Why?

Was it because of the lack of expectations? He and Kellar weren't dating. They were barely performing. They didn't have to impress each other. Didn't have to put on a false persona because of an overhanging concern that the person you were with wanted the star, not the man. They already being real with each other. At least, Day thought they were.

Chazz interrupted his thoughts. "I think you're attached to her in a way that goes beyond friendship. I'm not sure she feels the same way."

"You're afraid I might get hurt?"

Chazz nodded.

Day wondered if he was that out of touch with his own feelings. He knew he enjoyed Kellar's company, but he hadn't realized how much he dropped his public façade when he was with her. He wondered if that was the first time he'd done so since he'd made it in Hollywood.

"Maybe I need therapy," he muttered to himself. Practically everyone he knew swore by it. He'd always thought of himself as grounded, above the psychobabble. But he supposed he could see the value in an objective sounding board.

Kellar's a psychologist.

He sat back from the counter at that reminder. Could she be playing mind games? Getting him to fall for her while all the time holding herself back?

He thought his instincts about people were pretty good. That his ability to read them had sharpened since he'd been in LA. But maybe he'd been fooled more often than he liked to think.

The entire day had been messing with his head. He pushed back from the counter. "I'm going for a run."

He rarely ran right after a meal or in the evenings, preferring early-morning workouts, but he had to get out. Out of the house and out of his own head. Miles of sandy beach and physically pushing himself were sure to calm his agitation.

He started out at a slow jog and practiced some mindfulness techniques he'd picked up over the years. Letting his thoughts float free, allowing them to come and go without getting attached to any of them.

When he made the turnaround, he let himself think about Kellar. He liked being with her. He liked the lack of expectation placed on him. She had a great work ethic and a strong connection to her family. Her intelligence, humor, and ambition attracted him. He looked forward to seeing her, felt buoyed when she opened the door and welcomed him into her space. When he teased her, she knew it and gave as good as she got. All of that explained why he made excuses to see her more often.

Kellar shut him down every time he sent out a feeler about his interest in moving their relationship out of the friends only zone either by ignoring his words or pretending to misunderstand his meaning. But was that because she wasn't interested? Or was she determined to prove a point?

He slowed to a walk as he approached his house. On the bottom step of the deck, he sat and checked the time. A bit late, but his parents would still be up. He hit the number for his dad's cell.

When he picked up, Day went right to the heart of his call. "Dad, how'd you know you were in love with Mom? How'd you know she was the one?"

"Is this about Kellar?"

"Yes." He didn't have a reason to skirt around the truth with his father.

Ed ruminated before he spoke. "Well, I guess it was that I always felt better about myself when I was with her."

When Day didn't respond, Ed went on. "The more I was around her, the more I liked being around her. And then I didn't *not* want to be around her. Plus, she was pretty and funny and smart. We laughed at the same jokes. But, bottom line, I liked who I was when I was with her."

"Didn't you like who you were when you weren't with her?"

"I guess I did, but I never thought about it much before I met her. I only remember how I felt after I met her. Like I didn't want to be without her. I didn't want those feelings to go away."

Day sat with that for a minute. A lump of emotion filled his chest. "I ever tell you what a good father you are?"

Ed laughed. "Every morning with my coffee," he said, referring to the "Best Dad Ever" mug Day had given him for Father's Day when he was twelve.

"Thanks, Dad."

"You bet."

One thing rang true in his mind as he went up the stairs to get ready for bed. A trite phrase, a cliché, but still appropriate.

It's easier to ask for forgiveness than for permission.

Chapter Eighteen

♥

Standing half-dressed in the middle of her walk-in closet, Kellar was almost a hundred percent certain she heard a knock on the front door. "You're early," she muttered. "And *I'm* running late."

She perused her wardrobe, trying to decide what to pair with black jeans and hair that refused to cooperate.

Something loose and flowy? She fingered a boho top. She'd only need a tank or a camisole under it. Or something more fitted? She plucked the tailored pinstriped shirt from its hanger. Maybe with the right heels...

She shrugged into the shirt and tried out the look in front of her full-length mirror.

Another knock.

Dammit, why did he have to be so early? She needed more time. Time to pick the right shoes and a pair of earrings. Time to decide if she wanted to wear this shirt after all. Time to do *something* about her hair disaster.

Day would just have to wait.

She arrived at the door in bare feet with a couple of bottom buttons undone. "You're early. I'm not..." Her speech died away as she stared at the man outside her door. *"Dad?"*

Rory Kennedy's smile was exactly as she remembered it. His eyes lit with pleasure. Except it was pleasure at her reaction, not from seeing one of his daughters again. After what, five years? Not since Grandpa Kennedy's funeral.

"How's my second-best girl?" he asked with a grin, extending his arms.

Second best, she wanted to say, realizing that's how she still thought of herself. Because of him. Her own father. Who'd hung her with that term of *endearment*. Because he'd already dubbed Adrienne as his "best girl" by the time Kellar came along. All she could ever be was second best.

Did he really think he deserved a hug? After he'd gambled away everything they had and divorced her mother? After he'd started another family, maybe more than one for all she knew. She'd barely ever heard from him. And when she did, it always began with him acting like a doting father and ended with him asking to borrow money.

Kellar stood her ground. He dropped his arms, and his smile slipped a notch. He didn't look like he was down on his luck. In fact, based on his appearance alone, she'd have guessed him to be doing fairly well. There were a few strands of silver in his reddish-brown hair that hadn't been there before. She'd seen enough high-end salon styling to know that's what helped him achieve the look of a distinguished gentleman. His shirt sported a discreet Polo logo, his slacks held a perfect crease, and his leather loafers gleamed. "What do you want?"

His smile faltered a bit more, before he rescued it. "I came to see my second-best—"

She held up a hand to stop him from saying it again. "No. Don't call me that. Do you have any idea how being told I'm *second* best has made me feel my entire life?"

"Honey, I didn't mean—"

"What do you want?" she asked again, trying to un-clench her jaw.

"I just wanted to see you, that's all. I had business in LA. Since I was in the area—"

It was all Kellar could do not to laugh in his face. She could only imagine the kind of business he had. Either a meeting with or avoidance of a loan shark. Or maybe buying into a high stakes game.

"I haven't seen or heard from you in five years," she reminded him. "Why now?"

The door to the unit next to hers opened and her neighbor stepped out and paused while she locked her door. She glanced their way.

Kellar gave her a half wave. "Hi, Cindy."

"Hey." Cindy smiled and gave Rory a once-over before she headed toward her car.

"Could I maybe come in?" Rory asked. "I thought we could sit down and talk for a little while."

Kellar found she didn't have it in her to turn her back on her father completely. Even though he'd done a good job of turning his back on her, her sister, her mother, and his only grandchild. She stepped back, waved him inside, and closed the door. He followed her into the living room.

She dropped into a chair. "Have a seat."

He took the sofa. After glancing around, he said, "Nice place."

"Thank you."

"How have you been?"

"I'm well, thank you."

Kellar's stomach knotted. She felt the same way every time she saw him since he'd walked out on them, a mixture of anger, hope, disappointment, frustration, sadness, and love. She'd spent years wishing he was different, wanting him to have an epiphany, regret what he'd done, and beg to come back.

Even though he wouldn't change, she still wanted to believe in him. She wanted him to fix the heart he'd broken the day he walked out.

Rory, apparently, felt none of the things that were fighting for top spot inside her. He relaxed against the cushions like he belonged there and started to speak. Telling her about his life in Vegas, his latest game, how much he'd won, which tournaments he'd entered.

"How's Mildred?" Kellar interrupted.

He looked momentarily confused. "Meredith, do you mean?"

"Right, Meredith."

Kellar forgave herself for getting the woman's name wrong. She'd only met her once, at the funeral.

"We're no longer together," Rory said. "You know how it is."

Kellar tried to hold back her sarcasm. "Yes, I certainly do." How it was, was that once he left her mother, her father couldn't stick with one woman. She occasionally received updates about him and his current relationships from the cousins, aunts, and uncles on his side of the family. But he didn't need to know that.

"So anyway, as I was saying about this high stakes tournament, the entry fee is a hundred K. I'm having a bit of a cash flow issue at the moment, so I thought—"

"*That's* why you're here?" Keller spluttered in outrage, though she shouldn't be surprised.

"I figured, hey, you're doing pretty well, maybe you'd like to invest in your old man. I even saw your book in the airport. I think it's great, honey. You're on the talk shows, you've got an actor boyfriend. And not just any actor. Dayman MacDay. He's in the top ten of the Forbes five hundred—"

Kellar stood. "Get out."

"I met him. Did he tell you? I always pay my investors back, you know. With interest, of course."

"Get. Out."

This time he heard her. "What?"

"This can't be the first time a woman's said that to you. Get. Out."

Rory gained his feet. "What's wrong, honey?"

"Don't call me that. I'm *not* your honey."

"You're not honey. And you're not my second best—"

Kellar slapped him across the face hard enough to leave a red mark on his cheek. He reached up to touch it, eyes glittering, a wounded expression on his face. Kellar never realized until that moment how much she'd longed to lash out at him. Or how good it would feel.

"What was that for?" he asked, rubbing his cheek.

"If you can't figure it out after all these years, it's not my problem." She went to the door and held it open.

He sauntered toward her, hands in his pockets, like a little boy who'd been caught and thought charm might get him out of trouble.

"I guess I deserved that," he said. "I won't hold it against you." He lifted a brow.

Kellar jerked her head toward the threshold. The moment he was on the other side, she slammed the door as hard as she could and twisted the deadbolt. Her hands shook as she went into the kitchen and opened the cabinet door to her liquor supply. Ah, there. She took down a bottle of blended whiskey and a highball glass, poured a finger, and knocked it back.

Too much adrenaline. Too many emotions to process all at once. A surprise visit from her father was just... too much. She splashed a bit more whiskey into the glass and swallowed it in one gulp. The alcohol helped. She felt slightly calmer, if a little tipsy.

There came another knock on the door. If that was him again, if he tried to smarm and charm his way back into her life, she'd, well, she didn't know what she'd do. But it would be more than a slap.

Through the peephole she saw that it was not her father. Cautiously she opened the door, but Rory was gone. Day offered his trademark smile and looked absolutely delicious in a gray polo shirt and black slacks. The minute he stepped inside, she locked her arms around him.

He didn't have to be told what she needed. He held her the way she held him. She laid her head on his shoulder and sighed. Why did she have to like him so much? She liked everything about him. She breathed in his scent, a mix of citrus and spice. Was Day the only person she ever truly relaxed around? It felt that way sometimes. He expected nothing from her except *her*. And right now, she needed that more than anything. Not to be made to feel second best. Not to be used or manipulated. Not to be disappointed by someone who was supposed to love her unconditionally. Just accepted for herself.

One of Day's hands cupped the back of her head. He kissed her hair. Just the slightest press of his lips. That tiny gesture of caring gave her so much comfort right now.

"Tough day?"

She nodded against his shoulder, loving the feel of the soft cotton blend of his shirt against her face.

"You started drinking without me?"

Kellar smiled and nodded again.

"Whiskey?"

Another nod.

"Can I have some?"

She straightened so she could look into his eyes. "You're the best man."

"Is someone getting married?"

"Unh uh. You're the best man I've ever met. The best man in my life."

Day peered at her. "How much did you have to drink?"

Kellar straightened, cupped his jaw, and pressed a kiss on his cheek. He followed her to the kitchen. She poured him a drink and herself another. They both sipped before she said, "My father was just here."

Day waited a beat. "And I'm guessing comparisons are being made."

"There is no comparison."

Day took a sip of his whiskey. "In the interest of full disclosure, he waylaid me in the parking lot."

"Oh, my God. I can't believe him. Did he ask if you had a spare hundred grand to loan him?"

Day chuckled. "No, not this time. Why would he?"

Kellar plunked her elbows on the counter and buried her fingers in her hair. She shook her head. "I honest to God cannot believe this is happening."

When she felt Day's touch on her back, she straightened and tried for a smile. But her gaze skittered away. She picked up her glass and drained it, then grabbed the bottle and strode to the sofa, where she plopped down and poured out some more.

"Better go easy on that," Day warned.

She pushed the bottle in his direction and settled back against the cushions. "I'm done after this. I just..."

Day took the chair across from her and waited.

"I haven't seen my dad in five years. And then he shows up, reminds me I'm second best, and asks to borrow a hundred grand."

"Second best? What's that all about?"

Kellar looked at him. "Funny that's what you pick up on."

"Gone for five years and wants to borrow money? I understand both of those," Day clarified. "'Second best' is a mystery."

Kellar studied the amber liquid in her glass. "Adrienne came first. He called her his best girl. By the time I came along, there was nothing left for me but being his second-best girl."

"Ouch."

Her gaze rose to meet his. "I don't think I realized how much it hurt me to hear that from him my whole childhood until he said it again just now. *Second best.* I told him to never call me that again."

Day gave her an encouraging smile. "Good for you."

She smiled back. "And I slapped him. God, that felt good."

"I bet." He eyed her glass for a moment before bringing his attention back to her. "When I met him just now, he reminded me we've met before."

Kellar stared at him. "You've met my father? You know who he is, and you never told me?"

"I met him in Vegas over a year ago. I didn't know you then and I didn't know he was your father. He used the name Rory McAlister, not Rory Kennedy, so I never made the connection."

Kellar thought about it. "I guess that makes sense. McAlister's his middle name. How did you two meet?"

"I was there for the kickoff for Jamie Falcon's vodka brand. Your father literally ran into me, and we got to talking."

Kellar waited, as if sensing there was more Day needed or wanted to say.

"He's actually the inspiration for the film I'm making."

"My father inspired you? I find that hard to believe."

"I'll explain. Still feel like dinner?"

"Sushi?"

"Perfect."

Kellar stood and took a moment to steady herself. "Give me five minutes." In her room, she stripped off the shirt and donned a camisole and the boho top she'd been considering before, trying to wrap her head around the fact that Day and Rory were already acquainted. She honestly didn't see how her father could inspire anything other than devastation and disappointment. She clipped her hair up, leaving a few strands loose around her face, and slid her feet into comfortable lug sole sandals.

The pressure she'd felt earlier over choosing an outfit disappeared. Day wanted her company over a meal and what she wore didn't matter. If they were photographed together, they would look exactly like what they were. *Friends.*

Mai-Lee's was more crowded than the last time they were here, and Kellar wondered if it had anything to do with their previous visit. All it took was a few cell phone pics of celebrity sightings posted on Instagram or X for the place to enter the trending restaurant zeitgeist. They waited only briefly for a table in the corner furthest from the entrance, and without really intending to, duplicated their order from the prior visit.

While they waited, Day said, "So tell me about your father."

"I'd really rather not." Hadn't Day picked up on that?

"I get it. But obviously I'm interested in the story. How he left. Why he left. How it made you and your mom, and your sister feel."

"Really, Day? How do you think it made us feel? Devastated. Abandoned. Hurt. Angry. Name a painful emotion, we probably experienced it."

"I was hoping you'd say that."

Kellar stared at Day. "What?"

"I'm not looking to glorify gambling," he said. "When I said your father inspired me, I didn't say I found him *inspiring*. His story inspired me to make a film about the way these addicts are clueless how their behavior hurts others. Especially their families."

"Oh."

"Him showing up and saying those things to you just now is a perfect example. Hearing *your* side will help me add depth to the characters and show them for what and who they are. It might also help me figure out what makes you tick."

"Your film isn't glorifying gambling?"

"Of course not."

Kellar drank some of her beer to fortify herself. After she set the glass back down, she answered Day's earlier question. "I'd just turned fifteen."

"Walk me through it. Did he leave for work one day and never come home?"

She shifted uncomfortably. "God, I really don't want to talk about him."

"I don't want to talk about him, either. I want to know how his behavior impacted *you*."

Suspicion narrowed her eyes. "Why? It can't just be about the movie."

Day grinned. "Only you, Kellar, could take a friend's interest in you and need a reason for it."

Kellar peered into her beer.

"You rag on guys because they don't listen," Day went on. "They don't ask women about themselves or if they do, they don't hear the answers. I know, I know. This isn't a date. We're not dating. But I am interested. And I do listen."

"Is this another of Day's dating tips? If a guy asks you about childhood trauma, don't be reluctant to share the details?"

Day held up his hands, palms out. "No, of course not. Sorry I pushed."

She studied him.

The fact that he backed off so quickly made her rethink her decision not to talk about her father. Was he using reverse psychology on her? To what end? It's not like he would use anything she told him against her. What had she said to him earlier? He was the best man in her life. And surprisingly, she'd begun to trust him.

"Are you going to use what I say as fodder for your film?"

"In the interest of full disclosure, I can't promise not to. Or to incorporate some aspects of what you tell me."

Kellar sat back and regarded Day with a slight frown. What was he really after? They'd agreed to use each other from the outset, but was he using her now in a different way? "How long have you known I'm Rory's daughter?"

"Not long. Chazz discovered it while doing research." Day leaned closer. "Kellar, look. I've already got the gambler's perspective. I've interviewed quite a few of them, not just your father. But that's only part of the story I want to tell. I need to understand, *everyone* needs to understand, how this kind of addiction affects those in their circle. The trail of devastation they leave in their wake."

Kellar looked down at her beer, trailing her thumb through the condensation on the glass.

"It might help someone else," Day said gently. "To know what you went through. *Are* going through. How you not only survived but flourished."

She looked back up at him. She rarely thought of herself as a survivor. Or flourishing. She attributed her success to working her ass off and keeping her nose to the grindstone. Subconsciously, she strove to be the best at everything she did instead of *second best*.

"It might also help you to talk about it, but I understand if you'd rather not."

Again, she noticed the lack of pressure being with Day inspired. "I'll tell you. But after I do, the subject will be off limits. Understood?"

Day hesitated before he agreed. "If that's what you want."

Kellar took a fortifying drink of beer.

"Dad traveled a lot. He was in commercial equipment sales, and he was good at it. When I was fifteen, he won a trip to Vegas for having the highest sales in the region. He and mom were supposed to go for a long weekend, but I came down with the worst case of the flu I've ever had. Even though Poppy and Adrienne were there to take care of me, Mom wouldn't leave. Dad went without her. He called the following Monday and said he wasn't coming back."

"Just like that?"

"It wasn't, but that's how it felt to me. I didn't know the extent of what was going on with him until later, but he always gambled. When he was on the road for work, he stopped at the Indian casinos or the riverboats. That's why he and mom used to fight about money. Once he got to Vegas, that was it for him. For us."

Their sushi platter arrived but she wasn't sure she could eat. Instead, she drank some more of the beer.

Day's appetite appeared unaffected. Kellar watched as he doused a couple of rolls in soy sauce and dabbed them with wasabi. He looked up from his plate. "Go on. I'm listening."

Kellar sighed. "Dad decided to stay in Vegas to gamble full time. Mom worked her ass off to keep the house, to make things as normal as possible for us, but she was so sad." Kellar transferred one of the rolls to her plate. She picked at the edges of it with her chopsticks. "We were all sad."

She blinked at the lobster and avocado roll, as she took herself back to that awful time. All the feelings she didn't know how to deal with. She didn't want to go back there.

Her head came up and she smiled at Day. "But we picked ourselves up and went on, the three of us, without him."

"You never heard from him?"

Kellar made herself swallow the sushi because she needed something in her stomach besides alcohol. "He'd call occasionally. He sent Mom money when he had it. But it wasn't regular."

She told him about how she refused to speak to Rory when he called. She never opened the Christmas gifts he sent that first year and initially wanted nothing to do with the birthday check. But she needed money to order a yearbook, so she reluctantly signed it over and her mother deposited it. No one was surprised when the check bounced. Somehow, the yearbook order went through anyway. Kellar later discovered Poppy had paid for it.

"You were really blindsided when he left. Did you feel like you didn't know him at all?"

Kellar thought about it. "Well, when you're a kid, you expect your parents to be there. If they abandon you, it sticks with you, you know? I think his leaving forced me to drop whatever illusions I'd had about him. I'd always known I couldn't trust him a hundred percent. Him leaving proved I was right."

"Probably made it hard for you to trust other people too."

"Everybody's got baggage courtesy of their family. Except for you," she amended. "With your wonderful parents and ideal childhood."

"Yeah, you'd think I wouldn't have any baggage, but weirdly, it works both ways, I think."

"How so?" Kellar took another piece of sushi.

"For one thing, I think I've been searching for what my parents have. The kind of relationship that just works, you know? Remember that old line, 'you complete me'?" Like that. Because that's the example I grew up with.

"And not having a lot of baggage? I think it's held me back in some ways. Especially career-wise."

"How so?" Kellar repeated, finding the conversation fascinating.

"When you don't have to overcome a lot of difficulties

early in life, you expect everything to be easy. I think I'd have more range as an actor if I'd had more challenges. I don't take a lot of dramatic roles. I stick to romcoms or action/adventure because you don't usually have to go as deeply into a character. I know my limits."

"You've thought a lot about this, haven't you?"

"I like to think I'm aware of my strengths and weaknesses. If I don't think I can do a role justice, I pass. I'm going to find playing the role of a gambler extremely challenging. I want the audience to understand why he is the way he is."

"Well, let me help you. He showed up for Adrienne's wedding at the last minute. She'd already asked Grandpa to walk her down the aisle. The last time I saw my dad was at my grandfather's funeral, his father's. By then he had remarried and had a couple of kids with his new wife. But he told me yesterday they've split up."

Kellar now found it easier to concentrate on eating, so she selected another roll.

"Do you have a relationship with them? Your half-siblings, I mean?"

"Haven't met them."

"Are there others? Ex-wives or half-siblings?"

"I don't know. I hope not. I wouldn't wish him as a father or a husband on anyone."

"What about when you were younger? Before he left? How was he as a father then?"

Despite her better judgment, Kellar finished her beer. And when the server appeared, she ordered another. "He was actually one of those fun dads. He'd take us on what he called adventures. Miniature golf, a movie, the bookstore. Little things that he treated as bigger than life. Or we'd go to an animal shelter to visit the puppies and kittens. A stable for horseback rides. Things like that.

"But looking back, you could see the signs, even then. Everything was a bet with him. 'I bet you can't climb that tree. I bet you can't get straight A's. I bet you can't clean your plate in fifteen minutes.' There had to be a challenge or a dare or else it wasn't fun for him. It's like that's how he broke up the monotony of life. He did it to make the routine more interesting."

"And did you clean your plate and get straight A's?"

"Most of the time. He'd grudgingly pay me off with ice cream or dollar bills when he lost. But it was never enough, you know? It wasn't enough to make him stay. *We* weren't enough."

"What happened if he won? Did he make you pay up?"

"Sure. Not with money, because we didn't have any. Usually, it would be something to make his life easier. Washing the car or mowing the grass. Weeding the garden. Sweeping the garage."

She concentrated on picking her roll apart. "He'd be so gleeful when he won. Gloating. Telling us how he knew we couldn't do whatever the challenge was."

Kellar's head came up. "I started to hate those bets and after a while I refused to play. "I filled a couple of notebooks with my teenage angst after he left. 'Dear Diary, Daddy doesn't love me...' That kind of stuff." Kellar tried for a self-deprecating tone but missed by a mile. She sat back and twirled her second beer around in circles, trying to gauge Day's reaction. He appeared deep in thought. She sipped at her beer, waiting for his response.

"Do you still have them? The notebooks?"

Like a lot of writers, Kellar hung onto almost everything she'd written, never knowing when she might be able to use it or wanting to see how far she'd come. "Yes. Why?" As soon as she asked, she knew the answer. "You want to gather more insight for your film?"

"Always. But I don't expect you to share them with me. That's your private stuff."

Surprising herself, she waved away his concern. "It's ancient history. You're welcome to look at them. If you promise to guard them with your life."

"I promise." Day hesitated before he said, "You don't share your story very often, do you?"

"You're the first."

"What makes me the exception?"

A smile tugged at her lips at the serious tone of Day's question. "Maybe because you wouldn't leave it alone?"

"Or maybe I really am interested. In you."

His focused gaze wouldn't let her look away. His words once again indicated a desire to move beyond friendship, causing fear to war with excitement deep in her gut. Why *had* she told him her story? Sure. Maybe her story would help someone else realize they're not alone. But the simple answer was that she trusted Day. How was that possible when she found it hard to trust any man?

Day had somehow managed to slip past her defenses through this friendship he'd started. The lack of expectations allowed her to relax. Knowing Day expected nothing from her meant she could be more fully herself around him. And like it or not, her family history was part of who she was.

"Or maybe it's the fact that I trust you," she told him quietly. Even saying the words scared her. Trust made her vulnerable, took her one step closer to opening herself up to being hurt.

Everything about Day seemed to soften, especially his eyes. "I trust you, too." Day held up his glass and waited for her to do the same. "I know the awards season is almost over, but I still want to see you. What do you say? Friends forever?"

"Friends forever," Kellar agreed, clinking her glass against his, trying to shut down that little warning voice inside encouraging her not to believe a word he said.

<h1 style="text-align:center">Chapter Nineteen</h1>

♥

Back at Kellar's place, Day followed her into the spare bedroom and watched her rummage through the closet. Although there was a bed in the room, it appeared she used the space mostly for storage. One shelf held books and photo albums.

He could hear her shifting things around in the closet. "Need any help?"

"No. I'm pretty sure I can find the box they're in."

"Mind if I look at your pictures?"

She stuck her head out and he held up one of the albums. "Knock yourself out."

He sat on the bed and opened the cover. Turning the pages slowly, he watched both Kellar and Adrienne grow from little girls to adolescence. Robin and Rory were in some of the photos, making them look like a happy family of four. Day studied them to see if he could pinpoint a moment in time when the life and the family Rory had created stopped being enough for him. Was there a hint of his dissatisfaction? A sign or a look on his face that said, "Pretty soon I'm going to ditch all of this for something better."

If there was, Day couldn't find it. Maybe Rory wore a mask the entire time. Or maybe his decision to make a life for himself in Vegas, alone, was inspired more by opportunity than anything else.

Kellar backed out of the closet holding a purple spiral-bound notebook. "I guess I wasn't as traumatized as I thought. There was only one notebook." She held it out to him.

He didn't take it immediately but looked up at her. "You're sure you want me to see it?"

"It's ancient history, Day. But I'd like it back when you're done with it."

"Of course. Mind if I borrow this album as well?"

"As long as you promise to take good care of it. I don't have duplicates of those pictures."

"I promise." He bent and kissed her cheek. "I'll call you."

After dropping Kellar off Day got back in his car, set the notebook and album aside, and phoned Chazz.

"See if you can get ahold of Rory Kennedy. I'm pretty sure he's here in LA. If he is, tell him I want to see him at the production office tomorrow at ten."

He disconnected and drove while he thought about what Kellar had told him. He'd kept his excitement from her, because little did she know, her experience as Rory's daughter provided what had been the missing link in the script.

What better way to demonstrate his main character's complete cluelessness about the destruction he'd left in his wake than to showcase his daughter's pain? He'd look over whatever she'd written in the notebooks for idea seeds, but he wasn't even sure he needed them.

Being told you're second best your whole life wasn't the worst thing that could happen to a kid, not by a long shot. But for this story, this film, it was everything. Kellar had never recovered from Rory's desertion. It explained so much about what she believed about men. Men bailed. Men couldn't be trusted. Men lied. Men made promises they didn't keep. She still hadn't dealt with the pain she'd experienced at fifteen. Until she did, she'd never be able to move forward in a relationship with him or anyone else.

Day's position in relation to Kellar was more precarious now than it had ever been. The legal restrictions prevented him from sharing the specific details about his deal with Rory. If they went their separate ways as planned, his connection to her father wouldn't matter.

Except now he didn't want to go his separate way. He'd dropped a few hints, sure, but he hadn't told Kellar how he felt. Yet. He was still figuring out why this thing with Kellar was hitting differently, and now everything felt ten times more complicated.

Could he pursue her romantically without coming completely clean about his history with her father? How, after he'd just promised he would never bring up her father in the future? This wasn't a secret he could keep forever. Especially not now that he'd found the key to the whole production. He'd already seen the scenes in his head. Knew just what he needed.

If he were dating Kellar, if they were in a relationship when the movie was released, she'd know. Then she'd think what? That he'd lifted a lot of things from her family's situation and put it out there for the whole world to see. And she'd be right. But he couldn't realistically portray a character inspired by Rory and tell the story of his addiction without showing what happened to his family.

Kellar claimed it was ancient history and she wouldn't be affected if he used what she'd told him or what she'd written in her notebook. He wanted to believe her, but maybe she wasn't even aware how tightly she held onto her own baggage.

At least he'd taken the opportunity earlier to come partially clean with her. She'd just admitted he'd earned her trust. He understood now what a big thing that was. And if he told her the rest of it?

Tomorrow, say? Or the next time he saw her? He wasn't sure how she'd react. She might terminate their relationship permanently. He'd then be free to make the film his way, but without her in his life. He didn't consider that an option.

She'd hate knowing that he'd paid Rory for his story. Day wasn't feeling too good about that now, either. He'd been pretty callous about it at the time, honestly not caring what Rory did with the money. But, of course, he'd gambled it all away, probably by the next day. Why else would he try to hit Kellar up for a "loan?"

Naively, he'd thought he was helping Rory out of a bad situation. But he understood the highs and lows of a gambling addict much better now. Possibly all he'd done was make a bad situation worse. While Kellar appeared not to have much sympathy for her father, she wouldn't take kindly to what she might perceive as Day taking advantage of him at an especially low point of his addiction.

He had to find a way to make his movie his way *and* make it the best damn way he knew how, all while continuing to build a bond with Kellar. He'd negotiated his way through sticky situations before. But none so important as this.

The next morning, Day told Chazz what had happened over breakfast. He concluded the recap with, "And there's no need to say I told you so."

Chazz's mouth quirked in satisfaction. Day threw his spoon at him.

By the time Rory arrived at the office, Day had already contacted the screenwriter and discussed the changes he wanted to make. Rory strolled in like he owned the place, looking prosperous and well rested. Day had seen through Rory from the first. But although he'd had numerous follow-up interviews with Rory, he just hadn't looked deep enough to realize how despicable the man was. Or how low he could go.

"Nice digs you've got here," Rory said, looking around. "Kind of bare bones. What do they call that? Minimalist?" He offered Day an ingratiating smile.

Day had purposely instructed the interior designer he'd hired to keep things as simple as possible. The less clutter and color, the fewer distractions. He found the offices soothing. If he needed stimulation, all he had to do was step out the door and be swallowed up by the sights, sounds and bright lights that were LA.

"You tried to borrow money from Kellar."

"She told you about that, huh?" Rory's lack of concern irritated Day.

"Seriously? You haven't seen her in five years, and you show up at her door and ask her for a hundred Gs?"

"What's it to you? She's my daughter. It's between her and me."

"And me."

Rory cocked his head and stared at Day, lips pursed. "Yeah? I hoped you'd see it that way. She threw me out on my ear. But *you* called me. You want to invest, is that it? It's a private game, invitation only—"

"Hell no, I don't want to *invest*. I want you to think about how you treat people. Specifically, your youngest daughter."

"I don't get it," Rory said. "Why am I here?"

"You're here because I'm pissed off. Stay away from Kellar. Don't go near her. Don't call her. Don't ask her for money or anything else."

Rory sat forward on his seat. He stabbed his finger in

Day's direction. "You may have paid for my story, but you don't get to tell me what to do, who I can or can't have contact with. I'm Kellar's father."

"You're so much worse, both as a father and a human being, than I ever gave you credit for."

Day's words appeared to have no effect on Rory. He sat back and tilted his head to one side, studying Day. "She doesn't know about our deal, does she?"

When Day didn't answer, he continued. "You're afraid I might let something slip, is that it?"

"You signed a confidentiality agreement. You were the one who didn't want your family to know. You let 'something slip,' I'll sue your ass six ways to Sunday. You thought you were down on your luck the day I met you? I can make it ten times worse."

Rory grinned. "First rule of money. You can't squeeze it out of turnip. Now it seems to me, you've got more to lose than I do by Kellar finding out about your association with her old man. I could tell her, and you could go ahead and sue me. I got nothing and you'll get nothing. Except a lot of negative publicity and lawyer bills. Unless you want to make it worth my while to keep my mouth shut."

"That's your plan? You try and shake down your own daughter and when that doesn't work, you think you can blackmail me? Why don't you try apologizing to her?"

Rory snorted. "She's never going to forgive me. I figured that out a long time ago. She thinks I did her wrong. Her, her mom, her sister. Kellar hasn't had two decent words to say to me in the last fifteen years."

"Then why'd you show up at her place?"

Rory shrugged. "Like I told her, she might still invest in her old man. I figure she's sitting on a pile of money, just like you."

"The way I see it, she doesn't owe you anything."

"Yeah?" Rory thought for a moment. "The way *I* see it her boyfriend made a deal with her old man that he conveniently forgot to tell her about. In fact, her boyfriend's making a movie based on her dear old dad's life."

"I'm not her boyfriend," Day said tightly.

"You sure act like one." Rory's nasty streak made an appearance. "I'll tell you one thing," he said, adding silk to his tone, "I'm not as sharp as I used to be. I have this what do you call it?" He snapped his fingers a couple of times. "Short term memory loss. I forget what I say to people. I forget when I'm not supposed to tell people certain things. I make a slip of the tongue every now and again—"

"Is that a threat?" Day managed to keep his tone even.

"Nope. It's a fact." Rory stood. "I think we're done here."

"Sit down. I've got a proposition for you."

Once Rory resumed his seat, Day relaxed, swiveling his chair slightly, his fingertips pressed into a triangle as he thought about the best way to achieve his goal. "How important is this tournament?"

"A million to the winner. Biggest tournament I've ever been in."

"But you're not in yet."

Rory shifted in his seat, adjusted the crease in his slacks, and waited. Day gave him credit. Rory could be patient when he thought there might be something in it for him.

"If you can't get the money for this tournament any other way, will you go see your buddy, the loan shark?"

"I'll get the money."

Day recognized Rory's false confidence for what it was. "From whom? Your own daughter threw you out when you asked for a loan. I imagine everyone else in your family knows better than to lend you a dime. If any of them even have the kind of money we're talking about. Which I highly doubt."

Rory started to rise. "I'm done with the lectures."

"Sit down." Day's voice was deadly quiet. "I'm not done."

Rory sat and stared. Day could tell he didn't like being told what to do, but Day had money. Rory needed money.

Day pulled his chair up to his desk and got down to business. "Tell you what. You figure out the financing for the buy-in. If you win, you repay your investors and everything's good. But if you lose—"

"I won't lose."

Day ignored him. "*If* you lose, you come see me. I'll pay off your debt if you want. But then I *own* you. You understand? You'll have a choice, just like you did the first time we met. Broken kneecaps or we do things my way."

Rory glowered at him while he thought about the offer.

Day wasn't sure what conclusion he came to before he got up and walked out without another word.

"Great. Now he's got me doing it," he muttered to himself, realizing the gamble he'd just taken.

Chazz tapped on the door of Day's home office. "Got a minute?"

Day looked up from the revised script he'd been poring over for what felt like the thousandth time during the past week. Happy for the break, he motioned Chazz forward. "What's up?"

Chazz took one of the chairs facing the desk. "You know that test we took when we were in Indiana? Turns out I'm a match."

Day set the script aside. "For Gracie?"

"No. Some other kid. From what Adrienne says, the treatment Gracie had is working. For now, anyway."

"I didn't realize you'd stayed in touch with her."

Chazz ducked his head. "Yeah."

Day couldn't decide whether to question him about this or let it go. As far as he knew, Chazz had been living like a monk the entire time he'd been in LA. Not for lack of opportunity, either. Day loved Chazz like a brother, but he'd be the first to admit he didn't know a whole lot about what made him tick.

"Are you... interested in Adrienne?"

Chazz awkwardly shifted in his seat. "I don't know. I mean, yeah."

"Those are two different answers," Day said, not bothering to hide his amusement. He turned to the small fridge hidden in the credenza behind his desk and took out a beer for himself and a flavored seltzer for Chazz. "So, which is it?"

Chazz settled a bit once he took a drink. "She's nice, you know? Funny. Not fake."

Perhaps without realizing it, Chazz had also just described Kellar. Day could understand his attraction.

"You talk to her often?"

"Text mostly, but yeah."

"Facetime?"

"When we can."

"Long distance relationships can be kind of tough."

Chazz drank some more. "I don't know if it's a relationship yet or not, but I don't plan on staying in LA forever anyway."

Day gasped in mock horror. "You'd leave me? And move to some place like Indiana?"

"I don't know. It could happen. The thing is, if I go do this bone marrow thing, there's a couple of days of recovery. Adrienne said I could stay with them."

"When are you going?"

"In the next day or two. I can still work from my laptop while I'm gone."

"No. Call Renee." She was the temp they used when necessary. "Bring her up to speed before you go and leave your work laptop here."

"You sure?"

"Chazz, how much time have you taken off since you've been working for me?"

Chazz looked at him as if he didn't understand the question.

"Have you taken a vacation?"

"No. I mean, not unless you count the places I go with you."

"Where you're still working, right?"

"Yeah, but Day, working for you isn't like...*work*. It's—"

Day waved off his objections. "Take a week. Hell, take two. Go to Indiana. Save a kid's life. Let Adrienne fuss over you. Pretend you're on vacation."

"If you say so, boss." Chazz gave one of his rare grins that took Day back to his memories of Chazz as that hopeful child looking for a safe place to land.

Julie Lightner turned out to be the easiest of Day's exes to interview. Her publicist actually returned Kellar's phone call after the first message. A second call came to confirm the time and place for a meeting: Julie's home in the Hollywood Hills the following week.

Kellar hadn't committed to writing the book she had in mind, and she certainly hadn't expected interviewing any of Dayman's exes would be easy. But here she was, having negotiated the winding driveway, ready to knock on Julie Lightner's door. Before she could, the actress herself opened it and flashed her famous you-now-have-permission-to-fall-in-love-with-me smile.

"Kellar?"

Starstruck, Kellar could only nod.

"Come in. Come in. I've got us set up near the pool."

A barefoot Julie wore cut off denim shorts and a loose white tee shirt. Next to her, Kellar felt decidedly overdressed in her sensible slacks, jacket, and flats.

"Maria made home-made lemonade before she left. Would you like some?"

"Sure. Thanks."

Julie poured from an insulated pitcher into a matching glass. "Sit," she said. "Anywhere you want. Make yourself comfortable. I'm so excited to meet you."

"You're excited to meet *me*?"

"You're surprised? I loved your book. You've been all over the talks lately. So, what's up with you and Dayman? I think he's smitten.

Kellar chuckled. Was she for real? "First of all, I'm the one who's star struck. I've been a fan of yours for a long time."

"Aren't you sweet?"

"Secondly," Kellar hated that she sounded like a fussy second-grade teacher reading off a list. "Day and I are just friends."

Julie looked at her expectantly. "Well, of course that's

the *official* story."

Kellar leaned forward. "It's true. We are just friends. We're not romantically involved. At all."

"Okay. Okay. If you say so." Julie lifted her glass as if saluting Kellar and took a sip.

Kellar drank some lemonade, stalling. She didn't want to get off on the wrong foot. Not dating Dayman was harder than she thought it would be.

"That's actually what I wanted to talk to you about, Miss Lightner—"

"Oh, God. Please, call me Julie. I'm not planning to call you 'Miss Kennedy.' I hope that's all right with you."

"I prefer 'Kellar', thanks."

"You want to talk to me about Day?"

"And any of the other relationships you've had that you'd care to share." Kellar took a recording device from her bag. "You're okay with me recording our conversation?"

Julie waved her hand. "Of course."

Kellar positioned the recorder between them and said, "I'm not quite certain of the angle I'm taking, but the book's going to be about un-gettables." Kellar set a notebook on her lap and took a pen from her bag.

Julie's eyes lit up. "Really? I love that! Un-gettables." She chortled. "That certainly describes Day."

"Does it?"

The humor vanished from Julie's expression. "Oh. I don't know. I probably shouldn't have said that."

"Why not? If you believe it's true?"

"Yes, but I'm not sure it is true." She leaned forward, her gaze intent. "I mean, look at George Clooney."

Kellar nodded at the example. She had an idea where Julie was going with this.

"George said he'd never get married again. He dated *a lot*. For *years*. Wouldn't he be considered the ultimate un-gettable?"

"I suppose he would." Kellar doubted she'd ever get the chance to interview *him*.

"Then he met Amal and *poof*." Julie snapped her fingers. "He's married with a couple of kids."

"Are you saying there's no such thing as un-gettable?"

"Maybe I'm considered un-gettable. Or I was, anyway. I've had my share of relationships, but none of them permanent." Julie's winning smile returned. "I'm saying un-gettable only lasts until somebody wants to be got."

Filing away Julie's suggestion about herself, Kellar scribbled on her pad. She liked that quote and planned to use it. "So up until now, as far as we know, Day didn't want to be got. And that was true during your relationship with him?"

"Don't get me wrong. I was crazy about him." Julie became thoughtful. "We had fun together. The thing about dating actors, and especially actors who date other actors, is it can be hard to know when someone *isn't* acting. We're so used to being on. Not just in front of the camera. But in public, and even in private. When you're young and the whole Hollywood thing is new to you, fame is new to you, fans and paparazzi and all of that, you feel you always have to be on, you know what I mean? You're out in public, maybe you're even trying to be private, but you're always aware of how you present yourself, what you wear, what you say. So that part of your life becomes acting, too.

"Where do you turn it off? *How* do you turn it off? I think that's why so many actors seek relationships with people outside of the business, or at least with people who aren't actors."

"The way Julia Roberts and Matt Damon did."

"Those relationships seem to be working, don't they?"

"But there are some successful marriages where both parties are actors," Kellar pointed out.

"Oh, sure. It does happen. Not usually between mega stars, though. Ever notice how often those seem to crash and burn?"

Kellar thought of a couple of high-profile couples who were currently in the midst of messy divorces. "Yes, now that you mention it. But I don't know if the statistics are any higher than average. Do you think the problem there has to do with a power struggle of sorts?"

"Sometimes it has more to do with ego. Big ones. Fragile ones. Someone's not getting theirs stroked enough. Someone else isn't getting built up enough." Julie shrugged to indicate she didn't have all the answers.

"Was that a factor in your relationship with Day?"

Julie took a moment to consider. "No. I don't think ego had as much to do with it as how often we were both working on location. The time we spent apart caused us to drift apart. We tried to revive it a couple of times, but I guess you could say our relationship died of natural causes."

"Earlier you said you thought the word un-gettable described Day perfectly. Would you care to elaborate?"

Julie shook her hair back as she relaxed into her cushioned chair. That same charming smile appeared. "As I suggested earlier, I've changed my mind on that. Men like Day aren't un-gettable. It may take them awhile to settle down, and sure, some of them never do. But if they find that one person, *the one*, then everything changes. You know what I'm saying? That's it. They're done looking. They're done dating."

"So, it's a matter of just not having found the right person?"

"It's kind of like shopping, isn't it?" Julie laughed. "I mean, isn't that what we're doing? Trying on relationships with different people. Seeing what suits, what's the best fit. Did you ever fall in love with an outfit, but after you've worn it a couple of times you realize it doesn't fit quite right, or it doesn't look as good on you as you thought it did back in the store?"

"The clothes buried in the back of my closet will attest to that."

"And were you ever drawn to something you were *sure* you wouldn't like?"

"But then you try it on and it looks fantastic?"

Julie giggled. "Exactly! I've resisted my stylist's choices more than once, but, as it turns out, she knows more about what works for me than I do."

Kellar sipped her lemonade, enjoying the tangy sweetness, and glanced at her notes while she considered where to go next in the interview. She set the tumbler back on the table and paused to consider her surroundings. Julie's home didn't appear to be as ostentatious or overly large as she'd expected. She'd created a comfortable space for herself, both indoors and out from what Kellar could see.

Flowering vines nearly covered the wall surrounding the backyard and strategic planting areas sported more greenery and blooming plants. A pool built more for entertainment than swimming laps connected to a spa, where water overflowed a rock wall creating a soothing non-stop burble. Wicker resin furniture with deep cushions along with an outdoor kitchen completed the space.

Seeing it for the first time sparked a thought she put into words. "Do you think a third party sometimes sees us more clearly than we ourselves do?"

Julie tilted her head. "Well, it's certainly true of a stylist." Her famous smile flashed again. "But, yes, I suppose, if you're asking about people, a third party might see things more clearly than we do. I mean, they're not caught up in our histories and fears and insecurities the way we are, right? I've had enough therapy to understand that all our baggage travels with us into every new relationship. A third party isn't privy to all of that."

"So, something that looks all wrong to us might in fact be the perfect fit, we just can't see it."

It wasn't a question, more of a revelation on Kellar's

part, but Julie clapped her hands and said, "Exactly!"

A man appeared from inside the house, two cylindrical tubes under one arm. He gave Kellar a brief, apologetic glance, before he focused on Julie. "Sorry to interrupt. I'm heading back out."

Julie held out her hand. "Come meet Kellar."

He stepped forward, taking her hand. "Kellar Kennedy, meet Joshua Chang. Josh, this is the dating expert that's been all over the news lately."

Josh smiled, dimples appearing in his cheeks. "Nice to meet you."

"Nice to meet you."

"I'll be right back," Julie said as still holding Josh's hand, she followed him into the house.

Kellar had a clear view of the two of them. They stopped at the front door for a passionate embrace before Josh left. If Kellar had to guess, she'd put Joshua Chang at about ten years Julie's senior, although it was hard to tell.

Julie returned to her seat with the look of a cat who'd gobbled an entire plate of tuna.

Kellar wasn't sure whether to ask about Josh or leave it alone. Her curiosity must have conveyed itself to Julie before she could decide, because Julie said, "Are we done? Can we be off the record now?"

"Of course." Kellar turned off the recorder.

"I did some remodeling on the house last year. Josh was the contractor."

Kellar waited.

"He came by with the plans one day and it was just him and me, going over them in the kitchen I wanted him to renovate." Julie closed her eyes for a second. "One minute we were discussing where to relocate the fridge and the next we were tearing each other's clothes off."

"Wow." Kellar couldn't help but be a little envious. No one had torn her clothes off in a long time.

"It's crazy. He's got no interest in the movie business or any of that. But at the same time, he's super supportive of my career. I don't want to make our relationship public, because I'm afraid that might ruin everything, you know?"

"Your secret's safe with me."

"I knew it would be," Julie said. "I sensed I could trust you." Julie thought for a moment. "His wife died three years ago, and his kids are almost grown. He says he didn't think he'd find anyone else. He wasn't even looking. Neither was I, not really."

"I wonder if that's part of the key," Kellar said. "When you stop looking or you, I don't know, kind of give up hope of finding what you're looking for. Maybe you don't even know anymore what you're looking for."

"Maybe it's because the expectations get in the way."

Kellar nodded. "And then, suddenly, there it is. The thing you didn't know you wanted, but now you can't live without?"

Julie beamed. "We're probably getting married later this year."

"Oh, that's fantastic. I'm happy for you."

"Thank you. It's like we can't believe we found each other. We want to hang on and make it permanent."

During the drive home, Kellar couldn't help but feel a little envious of Julie and Josh's relationship. They'd found each other after what sounded like some major heartbreak for both.

Kellar's thoughts turned to Day. He was the closest she'd come to meeting what she thought of as her perfect match. But theirs was more a friendship than a love match.

Kellar studied the outline for *The Un-Gettables*. At least she'd just written the beginnings of an outline. The interview with Julie Lightner had helped kick start Kellar's brain and as she transcribed the recording, she began to see how she could lay out the book.

There were so many reasons why lasting love was so elusive for so many people. Many could be traced back to childhood trauma resulting in an inability to properly deal with emotions as an adult.

"I'm proof of that," she muttered as she added some notes about trust and fear of commitment. Her need to say something that hadn't been said a hundred times before made her want to not just offer case studies, but practical solutions for readers.

The sights and sounds of her favorite coffee place became a kind of white noise once she got in the writing zone. This morning she'd snagged her favorite corner table, which allowed her to keep her back to the customers but offered a view of the prep lane to her right and the parking lot and street to her left.

If she needed a break from the screen or a few minutes of thinking time, she could focus on one or the other until she went back to the keyboard.

She scanned through the outline, stopping to make a few notes here and there. Her coffee was long gone, and her butt was numb from two hours sitting on the wood seat. Plus, she had to pee. Time to wrap things up and head home.

"Fancy meeting you here!"

Jeanine Hartman slid into the seat opposite her at the small table.

"Excuse me. I'm working." Kellar fumed on the inside, but she focused on her laptop screen, hoping the other woman would take the hint.

With a manicured fingernail, Jeanine tapped the side of the empty ceramic mug Kellar had pushed aside. "You're getting ready to leave, though, right? Which means you have time to talk to me."

"But why would I want to?"

"Because I know a few things about your boyfriend that you should know."

"I don't have a boyfriend," Kellar gritted out, already tired of trying not to let her irritation show.

"Oh, please. Anyone can see he's mad about you. Go

look at some of those red-carpet photos. He's got *stars* in his eyes." Even though Jeanine delivered this bit of news with venom, Kellar wondered if it could be true.

She closed her laptop and began stuffing it into its case.

"What's going on with Day and your father?"

Kellar wasn't quick enough to mask her surprise. "What?"

"They're pretty chummy, aren't they?"

"What makes you say that?"

"They met for at least an hour at Day's office."

"When was this?" Kellar asked, curious even though she didn't want to be.

Jeanine arched her eyebrows. "Day didn't tell you?"

Kellar had to scramble not to give away any more than she already had. "I just wondered which meeting you were referring to."

"So, you know they're working together?"

"Don't you have any *real* work to do?" Kellar pushed her chair back and gathered her things.

"I'm what they call a roving reporter. I find something juicy, then put a story together for the air."

"Don't you mean you conjure a story out of thin air? Look, Jeanine. I'm sorry for whatever childhood trauma you experienced that turned you into an obnoxious, obsessive adult. But you are sniffing around the wrong tree. I'm going to ask you nicely to stop harassing me. The next time? I won't be so polite."

Kellar stood and headed for the door.

"If you're such good friends, why don't you ask him

what they're doing together?" Jeanine called after her.

Kellar got into her car and slammed the door, annoyed that Jeanine got the last word. She rammed the key into the ignition and warned herself to calm down as she revved the engine.

"She just wants to make trouble," she muttered to herself as she backed out of the parking space. She could ask Day about it, though. All she had to do was bring up another Jeanine sighting and he'd be all over it. He'd want to know everything.

Unless he has something to hide.

What could he want to hide? He'd admitted he'd met her father in Vegas after they bumped into each other in the parking lot after Rory's visit to her. She knew the film he was making was about a gambler. Her father was a gambler. Day had interviewed him. She couldn't see how there was more to it. But Jeanine apparently thought she was on to something.

Once home, Kellar plunged back into work mode, barely taking a break until the phone rang around six.

"Hello, handsome." She smiled when she said it, enjoying the playfulness of her relationship with Day.

"Hi there, beautiful," he said. "What's shaking?"

"You tell me. I've been working all day."

"Me too. I miss you."

As much as she liked hearing Day's voice, her thoughts turned serious. "Day?"

"Yes?"

"I saw Jeanine Hartman again."

"And?" She knew she didn't imagine the wariness in his tone.

"She asked what was going on between you and my father." When Day didn't respond, she added, "Jeanine said you and him are chummy."

"Chummy?"

"That's the word she used."

"It isn't accurate."

"Did you meet with him, though? At your office?"

"Yes."

"Oh." Kellar realized she'd been expecting him to tell her everything Jeanine had said was a figment of her twisted imagination.

"It was after he came to see you. Since I knew he was in town, I asked for a meeting."

"Why?"

"Because I saw how much his visit upset you. I told him to leave you alone."

"You did?"

"You probably think I was out of line."

For a moment she found herself unable to speak, choked up with emotion. "I... didn't say that." When had a man ever had her back? Ever shown he wanted to defend her? Support her?

"Are you mad at me?"

"No." Kellar laughed, though she felt close to crying.

"Kellar, I'm not really at liberty to discuss everything about this—"

A beep on her cell interrupted them. "Day? Sorry.

That's Johanna calling. My publisher was supposed to make an offer today. Can we talk tomorrow?"

"Sure. No problem."

Chapter Twenty

♥

Kellar concentrated on the trail ahead of her, wondering where it would lead. Much like she was beginning to wonder where her relationship with Day might lead. Awards season ended with the Oscars last Sunday.

Day hadn't won any awards. Stars of action/adventure films rarely did. But Day attended to show support for those who were nominated. Kellar had reveled at being with him and dressed in the most glamorous outfit she'd worn yet, an Oscar de la Renta gown in silver and turquoise that she'd absolutely loved. And when the awards were over, they'd hit one after-party after another before finally crashing back at his place—in separate rooms, of course.

Even though the official reason for them spending time together had ended, they'd agreed there was no reason to terminate their arrangement. Their hike today in Malibu Canyon had been Day's idea.

The last few months had been a whirl of non-stop activity and travel, and Kellar was more than ready to get back into a more normal routine, even though it would only be for a week or two. She had interviews lined up with a few more celebrities who'd dated "un-gettables," although none of these were Day's exes. But that was okay, she really didn't want to focus on any one individual. She'd also found male subjects who were willing to tell their stories. She really wanted a well-rounded look at the experiences of both men and women before she began an analysis of the so-called un-gettables and those who were attracted to them.

"Hold up a minute. I want to show you something."

Kellar looked over her shoulder as she stepped to the top of the hill. Dayman was only a couple of strides behind her. She turned back to the sweeping view of canyon and ocean. She couldn't imagine what Day wanted to show her. It was all right here, as far as she was concerned. "God, this is gorgeous." She sighed as he stepped up next to her.

"Yes. It is."

She glanced up at him sideways to see his gaze on her, not the view.

"Very funny."

"No one's laughing."

Kellar's heart found a new rhythm as Day slid a hand along her jaw, his fingers gliding beneath her hair, caressing her ear. Then the other hand followed suit. She couldn't exactly see his eyes behind his sunglasses, nor could he see the panic fighting with excitement in hers. He bent his head and Kellar's eyelids closed. His lips touched hers, warm and firm, in an assured kiss. How could she not kiss him back when it was something she'd fantasized about for so long? When it was the exact kind of kiss that not only met but exceeded the one in her imagination?

Even it if meant that everything would change between them, that it might mean the end of their friendship, Kellar couldn't resist. The man knew how to kiss.

Day smelled of sunshine and sweat, trail dust and man. Her fingers dug into his shirt, either to pull him close or to push him away. Or maybe just to keep her balance because his kiss was seriously throwing her off kilter.

When it ended, he bent his head to hers. "Do you know how long I've wanted to do that?"

"Why didn't you?"

He brushed his fingers through her hair. "Because we're friends. And you were so sure if we went beyond friendship it would ruin everything."

"You shouldn't listen to me."

"I've been dropping hints for a while now."

"I know."

"And you've been ignoring them."

"I wasn't sure ..." If she'd acknowledged them, she'd have had to *do* something about them. Respond to them in some way. And she hadn't been ready to do that. Was she now?

"It's almost like you wanted to be right. To prove your point about all the advice you've given your followers. Men and women can't be friends."

She poked a finger into his chest and smiled up at him. "Seems like *you* just proved my point."

"You're glad I did. Admit it."

"I'm the dating expert who's terrible at dating, remember? I admit to nothing."

Day's lips twitched. "Who said anything about dating?"

Kellar punched his arm and took off down the trail. "Jerk." Was he playing games with her or what? One minute he seemed completely, seriously into her. That kiss! And the next he reverted to teasing her. No wonder she felt so out of balance.

"Hey, slow down. It's steep here. Watch out for the rocks."

Kellar thought about turning around and heading back. But she'd have to pass Day if she did. And she wasn't quite ready to face him. So, she kept going, barely keeping her feet under her as the dry reddish/brown dirt littered with stones kept her slipping and sliding.

"Kellar! Slow down!" Day called.

But her own momentum and the incline kept her brakes from working properly. She'd nearly reached a place where the trail forked off when she tripped over the point of a rock sticking up out of the dirt.

Her feet flew out from under her, and she landed hard in the brush and wildflowers, rolling twice before coming to a stop on her back.

She wasn't hurt or at least not badly, but she'd have a couple of bruises. She looked up at the sky, at the flowers with their tiny yellow and white heads and felt a moment of peace like she'd never known. Like everything was right with the universe, just like it was meant to be. Her anger evaporated.

Day plunked down next to her, and she turned toward him. He put his hand on top of her head. She smiled at him. The concern on his face vanished, replaced by suspicion. "What are you smiling about?"

She didn't know how to explain it, so she ignored the question and sat up, brushing off the dirt and leaves she'd collected.

"You're not hurt?"

"Only my dignity."

She made as if to stand, but he placed a hand on her arm, keeping her in place. "Why, Kellar? Why'd you take off like that?"

That she could have answered. *Because I'm terrified. If I move forward with you, I'll lose you. But if I don't? I'm afraid of what will happen. And we've got to stop sending each other mixed signals.*

When in doubt, attack. "Why'd you kiss me?"

Day stood and held out a hand to pull her to her feet, watching as she brushed herself off some more. She turned around, unable to reach her back. "A little help?"

Most of the dirt he brushed off her shirt blew back on him. He gave her shorts a couple of good swipes too, before he slid his arms around her and pulled her back against him, locking her in place. "Why do you think I kissed you?" he growled in her ear.

She turned her head in his direction. "You tell me."

"Because, like I said, I've been wanting to for a long time."

"And then you acted like it was a joke."

Day let go of her and she faced him.

He said, "I did, didn't I? Because that's what we do. That's how we keep it on the friendship level. Teasing. Jokes. One-upmanship. I can't believe I'm saying this, but I don't think I know how to move from that to something more with you. My God, woman. You've ruined me."

Kellar grinned. "I think you ruined yourself."

Day tugged her hand. "Let's head back."

She fell into step, letting him take the lead. He never let go of her hand.

Once back at his house, he said, "How about lunch?"

"Sure, but I'm going to shower first."

In what Day had designated as "her" room, Kellar stripped off her dusty clothes and stepped into the luxurious shower. They'd hardly talked during the drive back. Kellar honestly didn't know what to make of the morning, the kiss, Day's words. *This is why male/female friendships* never *work. One party or the other always wants* more.

And sometimes both parties, another part of her whispered.

She stared unhappily at her reflection. It wasn't fair. She liked Day so much. Enjoyed the time they spent together. He'd become one of the most important people in her life. And now she risked losing all of that.

She tried to imagine her life without Day in it. It was so much easier to imagine how that would feel than it was to imagine a romantic relationship with him. It wouldn't work. In her heart, that was her biggest fear. But, oh, how she wanted to try. She'd love nothing more than to stop fighting her attraction to Day. To give in, see where things went.

At the same time? What if the heartbreak she'd been trying to avoid since this all began lurked just around the corner?

You're conflicted, she told her reflection. *And scared.*

Damn right. Was it too much to hope that Day was too? That maybe even now he was trying to talk himself out of ever kissing her again?

She found clean clothes, didn't bother with make-up, and clipped her towel-dried hair back.

Day had lunch set up on the umbrella table on the deck. She stepped out to see a stunning charcuterie board with all manner of fruit, cheese, crackers, spreads, and deli meat. A pitcher of iced sparkling water with lemon slices swirling throughout sat next to it.

"This looks *amazing*."

She took a seat and gazed out at the ocean, where sunlight glanced off the water and waves rolled in with a gentle crash. The breeze lifted the heat from the warmth of the sun, and beneath the shade from the umbrella, she thought about never experiencing such a day again. "What a perfect day."

"Aww, you think I'm perfect?" His eyes twinkled.

She laughed. "Almost."

He poured water into two glasses. "Help yourself."

She did, going heavy on the fruit and lighter on everything else. "This is wonderful. Who put it together? Chazz?"

"Elsa." Day helped himself to a bit of everything. "Chazz left for Indiana this morning." Elsa was Day's housekeeper. She'd probably picked the board up from one of the restaurants or boutique delis and had it delivered so it was ready whenever Day was.

Kellar shook her head.

"What?" Day asked bemused.

"I'm not sure I'll ever adjust to the way you live. The servants. This." She waved a hand to encompass the house, the beach.

"It's not like I'm the lord of the manor. I don't consider Elsa or anyone else in my employ 'servants.'"

"I know. You don't have a title, but you have wealth and influence. It's like magic. Poof, whatever you want appears."

"I work hard for my money."

"I know you do."

"And money doesn't get me everything I want."

"Really? Like what?"

"You."

Kellar knew what he was going to say before he said it and could have kicked herself for giving him the opening. But there it was, and they had to have this conversation sooner or later. So, it might as well be right now.

"Let's try precise and direct language instead of teasing and jokes, ok?"

"Good idea." Day thought for a moment. "What if I weren't me. And you weren't you. Imagine we just met somehow. Would you go out with me?"

Kellar didn't have to think twice. "Without a doubt."

"Then there's nothing stopping us now, is there?"

Kellar looked out at the water again. They had somehow made their relationship extra complicated from the very beginning. It had seemed like such a safe proposition at first. Mutually beneficial. But if she were honest with herself, she'd known even then that such a situation couldn't last. One or the other or both would want to move forward or move on.

She brought her gaze to his. "You've become really important to me," she said. "I don't want to imagine my life without you in it."

"You don't have to."

"But I do." She reached across and covered his hand with hers. "Let's say you got serious about someone else. Maybe our friendship would survive, but it wouldn't be the same. It would only be natural we wouldn't spend as much time with each other. Eventually, I'd be phased out."

"I've stayed friends with Willow even when one or the other of us was in a serious relationship." Day wasn't exactly arguing with her. She refrained from pointing out that she and Willow would probably never be friends.

That could be a problem given Day's attachment to the woman.

"Let's say we move this friendship forward." He turned his hand over and squeezed hers. She gave a tremulous smile. "It would have to be all or nothing. If it works, it works. If it doesn't, that's it. We're done. We're out of each other's lives for good. The end."

"What you're saying is, either way, there's a chance we lose each other."

"Essentially."

"I don't want to lose you."

She gave his hand a squeeze. "I don't want to lose you, either."

They sat in silence, studying each other, guessing and second guessing where the other stood between these two options, until Day said, "We both want the same thing. I say we go for it."

Kellar laughed. "Just like that?"

"Just like that." He released her hand and started picking at his food. "You're saying there's a possibility we'll lose each other either way. Then why not give us a shot at being more than friends?"

"More than friends. I like the sound of that."

He grinned at her. "Me too."

"You'll have to concede I was right."

"Fine. You were right. About what exactly?" Day thought for a moment. "That thing about how men and women can't be friends?"

She popped a fat green grape into her mouth, letting

the sweetness explode as she bit into it. After a moment she said, "I hate to be a cliché, but I want to take it slow."

"How slow?"

"I don't know." She began to build a little sandwich with crackers and cheese and a thin slice of roast beef. "You just kissed me this morning. I can't go from zero to sixty in an afternoon."

"You wish to be *wooed*?"

Kellar giggled at Day's use of the old-fashioned word. But in truth, that is what she wanted. "Sure. Why not?"

"No reason. You want to be wooed? I'm your man."

"We'll see about that."

"No. I'm telling you. I'm your man."

Kellar smiled and bit into her cracker sandwich. Eating gave her an excuse to say nothing because she didn't know how to respond to Day's statement. The sand was shifting beneath her feet the same way it did every time the waves rolled into the shore. She wasn't at all sure what she'd just committed herself to, but at the same time she tingled with anticipation at the thought of another of Day's kisses.

Chapter Twenty-One

♥

The Friendship Thing: Why It Could *Work*

Kellar paused, fingers on her keyboard, debating about whether she wanted to write this, post it on her blog. She could write it, she told herself. That didn't mean she had to post it.

She started setting down the thoughts that had been swirling through her head since yesterday, typing fast. Some of it she'd already said to Day. Some of it, she feared, might reveal too much about her relationship with him. She could figure it out when she finished writing.

"...if both parties go into it with their eyes open to the possibilities, realizing that if the romantic relationship fizzles, most likely so will the friendship, then you have to ask yourself if it's truly worth it. If it works, you both get the best of both worlds. If it doesn't, you say goodbye to each other forever..."

A tear fell from her eye and the words on the screen blurred. She didn't want to contemplate a life without

Day. In truth, she couldn't imagine it. How had he become such a big, influential part of her life in such a short time, anyway?

And it wasn't just her. He'd impacted the lives of her sister, her niece. Her mother. Her readers.

What if she couldn't deal with her own fears, insecurities, and trust issues? She'd have to find a way. Because if she couldn't, the next time she saw Day she might as well kiss him goodbye permanently.

She'd survive, sure, like she had all these years with only her blurry memories to fuel the occasional fantasy of what might have been. But now she'd had a taste of how it could be if they were together, which would make it much harder to let go.

She swiveled away from the desk and picked up her cup of tea just as her phone rang. It was Day.

"An *actual* phone call? Not a text?" she asked.

"We're dating now, right? I'm attempting to behave like a proper gentlemen caller intent on wooing you. I'm calling to ask you out to dinner."

"You've always been a proper gentleman." *Except that one time,* that little voice in her head reminded her.

"Is tonight too soon? Or are you planning to wash your hair?"

Kellar laughed. "Mmm. I wasn't, but I don't want to come across as overly eager."

"Me either. But I am."

"So am I." She couldn't wipe the smile off her face. What was wrong with admitting that the idea of dating

Day, of anticipating another of his kisses, made her so giddily happy?

"I could pick you up at eight."

"Dress code?"

"Hmm. Upscale. Let's give them even more to talk about."

Kellar laughed. As if they hadn't given "them" enough to talk about already. "Sounds perfect."

"I look forward to it."

"So do I." They disconnected. Kellar turned back to her screen.

Maybe it *could* work.

"...the transition from friendship to romance can be laced with minefields. You already know so much about each other. You've already discovered things you love about the other person and things that might annoy you down the road.

Those same annoying traits you easily tolerate as a friend may end up driving you to distraction and beyond as a romantic partner. Your friend can be avoided. You step back and return to your own space for a bit. But in a romantic relationship, stepping back signals there's a problem. Especially if you've moved in together. Where are you going to go? Sooner or later, you'll have to learn to deal.

What if something you thought was annoying but cute

in a friend turns out to be something you can't live with in a lover?

Take it slow. Very slow. The time to begin negotiations is before *there's a problem so big you can't resolve it.*

You know I love hearing from you. If you've successfully (or unsuccessfully, for that matter) made the journey from friends to lovers or beyond, I want to hear from you. What worked? What didn't? Tell me your story in the comments section below.

As always, remember that your words are public and may appear in a context other than this forum.

Until next time,

KK

Kellar read over the post and made a few adjustments. She didn't think she'd given too much away, although her long-time followers would grasp the subtext. So would the entertainment media. She grinned at how much fun this could be despite her doubts. This whole thing with Day made her feel like she was playing with fire. She thought about the volatility of it. How easily it could slip from her control. She'd be more careful this time, she promised herself. No one was going to get burned.

She sent the post to Carol, checked the time, and called Adrienne. Her sister did medical transcription from home so she could be there for Gracie and have a more flexible schedule.

"How are things going?" Kellar asked. "How's Chazz doing?"

"I think he's napping at the moment, but he seems to

be bouncing back pretty quickly."

"That's good." She wondered if Adrienne could tell she didn't really want to talk about Chazz.

"Gracie's enthralled with him because he'll play games like Candyland and Chutes and Ladders with her non-stop. Yesterday he started teaching her how to play checkers. Oh, and don't tell anyone, but I think he lets her win at Old Maid.

Kellar chuckled. "Sounds like you guys are getting along well."

Adrienne hesitated before she spoke again in a near whisper. "He kissed me."

"*Chazz*?" Kellar nearly shouted. The reserved, fade-into-the-background personal assistant had kissed her sister?

"*Shhh!*"

In the background, Kellar heard the squeak of the mudroom door, which meant Adrienne had sequestered herself in there to guarantee privacy.

"Well? How was it?" Kellar decided she *did* want to talk about Chazz after all.

"The kiss? It was nice."

"Nice, huh?"

"Sweet."

Kellar waited for a better adjective. When no more were forthcoming, she said, "Is that what you're into now? Nice and sweet?"

"I'm not explaining it right."

"You didn't tear each other's clothes off."

"I'm not saying there wasn't any heat," Adrienne said. "To be honest, I think we're both a little gun shy."

"I guess I can understand that. Chazz is a bit of an enigma, isn't he?"

"He's reserved," Adrienne corrected. "But I'm getting to know him."

"Apparently."

"I don't want to rush into anything but, KK, there's something there. I really like him."

"Sounds like he likes you, too."

"He does. He told me so."

Kellar's eyebrows went up even though Adrienne couldn't see. "That's great, AK. You deserve somebody nice in your life."

"He told me about his childhood."

"Oh?"

"Drug addicts for parents. Did you know Day's mom and dad practically adopted him? They're like family."

"Uh-huh."

"He's been up front about going through rehab. I think the things he's been through have made him cautious. So, we'll take it slow and see where it goes. What's up with you?"

"Day wants to take things to the next level."

"What's the next level? A fake engagement?"

"Dating."

"For real?" Her sister's delight came through loud and clear. "And let me guess. You're overthinking it."

Kellar's laugh was anything but light-hearted. "How

can I not?"

"Run it down for me. Is this what you want?"

Kellar took a deep breath, stood, and picked up her mug. She looked out the kitchen window although there wasn't much to see except a strip of landscaping and the unit next door. "Age, I like him *so* much."

"Uh huh."

"And if this doesn't work…"

"Why wouldn't it? Wait. A better question. Why couldn't it?"

"You're kidding, right? With our track records? The number of women he's blown through? The number of times I've been dumped?"

"Anybody ever tell you your attitude sucks?"

Kellar smiled. "You. All the time."

"Have you ever been with me in the produce department?"

Adrienne's question gave Kellar pause. "I don't think so. What's that got to do with anything?"

"You come along some time and watch me pick out apples. Or better yet, grapes."

Kellar rinsed out her mug, waiting for the punchline.

"I pick up about ten apples for every one I choose. Grapes? It's worse. First, I squeeze them. Some are too soft. That happens a lot of times. There might be a bunch with good ones on the top, but the bottom ones are mushy. Reject. If I'm lucky, I find some that are just right."

"Goldilocks has nothing on you."

"Even someone with experience doesn't always make the best choices."

"Okay. I get it."

"I don't think you do," Adrienne said in her I'm-the-older-sister-and-therefore-wiser voice. "You keep saying you get dumped, but is it possible you unconsciously sabotage yourself?"

"What?"

"Maybe you're picking the apples that are all shiny on the outside, but when you bite into them, they taste like nothing. You thought you invested wisely, and you can't admit you made a mistake. Those apples weren't any good to begin with. They weren't the right ones for you."

"You're saying I wait for the apples I chose to get up and walk out on their own?"

"I don't know what you do. Maybe you think you can turn them into pie or applesauce if you wait long enough."

"I'm not sure this produce metaphor is particularly helpful." More irritating than anything, if Kellar was being honest. But she now had a craving for fresh fruit. "May I remind you I'm the one with the psychology degree?" She hated admitting Adrienne might have a point.

"I think Day's the real deal," Adrienne said. "I don't know him as well as you do, but from everything I've seen and everything you've told me, he's a genuine guy who cares for you. So, I'll ask again. What are you so afraid of?"

Kellar opened the fridge and pulled out the drawer

where carrots were growing pale yellow hair, and the mushrooms were shriveled to half their original size. "Have you seen the state of my produce bin?"

Don't blow it. Don't blow it. Don't blow it.

Kellar had no idea how she made it through the rest of the day. She did her best to concentrate on the work before her and stick to her schedule, but it wasn't easy, because that thought kept running through her head from the moment she and Adrienne ended their conversation.

At the gym, the music pouring through her ear buds did nothing to distract her. Her psychology degrees were worthless when it came to dealing with her own issues with trust and fear of abandonment, but she'd never wanted to explore those feelings too closely. She'd paid lip service to the therapy required to get her master's, glossing over the details of how her father leaving affected her.

Instead, she turned her thoughts to what to wear tonight. A few lesser-known designers had sent dresses to Day's stylist who'd approved a few and passed them on to Kellar. She had one in particular in mind which she hadn't worn yet and would be perfect for a first date.

Her appearance left Day momentarily speechless, when he stood in the doorway later holding a bunch of yellow tulips. His eyes widened as he tried to take in every inch of her. He stepped over the threshold and took her hand, turning her in a circle. The midnight blue dress suited her perfectly, hugging and plunging in all the right ways and sporting just enough bling that she didn't need jewelry. He especially liked the slit up one side that offered a discreet flash of thigh.

"You look fantastic."

Kellar must have believed him because she smiled. "Thank you. You look... hot." He hadn't overthought his own clothing, choosing a gray sport coat and a white button down over black slacks. But the way her gaze ate him up told him he'd done well. He was going to enjoy dating Kellar.

"Are those for me?" she asked, playing the innocent coquette to a tee.

Day looked at the flowers as if he'd forgotten they were in his hand. "Why yes. Yes, they are."

"They're lovely." Kellar took them from him and went into the kitchen. Day lagged behind so he could enjoy the sway of her hips and the plunge on her dress that showed off her upper back before draping in soft folds to her waist.

She reached for a vase on a high shelf in the cupboard. Day stepped up behind her and grasped it easily, pressing his front to her back. He brought the vase down and bent his head to brush his lips along the side of her neck, taking in her scent and the softness of her skin.

"I'm *loving* this dress," he growled. Wooing her was not going to be easy. Not when this was their first real date and all he could think about was getting her out of that dress.

"You're making my heart race," Kellar said so softly he could hardly hear her, almost as if she hadn't meant to say the words aloud.

Day took a step back as she ran water in the vase. "I guess we can check chemistry off the list."

She glanced up at him as she unwrapped the bouquet. "What list?"

"You're a dating expert and you don't know about the list?" Day asked in mock horror.

She began to arrange the tulips to her liking. "I don't know about *your* list."

"I don't exactly have a list, but chemistry has to be somewhere near the top."

"So far, we have mutual attraction and chemistry. On top of all the things we already know about each other, it's a pretty good start, don't you think?" She glanced his way again.

"It definitely is."

"Shariffe?" Kellar gazed at the restaurant entrance as the limousine slowed, then stopped at the curb.

"Since this is where it all started, I thought we could pay homage," Day said with a twinkle in his eye.

"Steak." Kellar sighed at the delicious memory.

"And frites. Sound good?"

"Sounds wonderful."

"You ready?" he asked just before the valet opened the door.

Kellar wasn't at all sure she was. Ready to get out of the car. Ready to date Dayman MacDay. Ready for what would happen next. But she tamped down her doubts and pasted her now well-practiced smile on her face. "I'm ready."

Day stepped out and helped her. Once they were on the sidewalk, he continued to hold her hand. They ignored the paparazzi who'd come to life at their appearance, pretended not to hear the shouted questions or requests to turn this way or that. There was no wait, and in seconds they were seated at "their" table.

Before Kellar could blink the sommelier appeared. "A lovely Pinot Grigio from the northeast of France for the lady."

He opened the wine and poured a small amount into her glass. Kellar caught Day's gaze and she couldn't help but grin. "I made a special request," he confided. She sipped and nodded and once he'd poured the wine, the sommelier disappeared.

"I feel so special," Kellar giggled.

Day gave her a wide smile. "That was the plan."

It wasn't a joke. Kellar truly did feel special. Day paid attention. He obviously remembered the snooty attitude of the server the first time around. *A man who made an effort.* It wasn't a huge gesture. Was it? Was it simply the fact that no other man had done such a thing for her? Had she ever been with someone who considered her special? Who believed her worth the effort?

Sadness for all the wasted time she'd spent dating the men who were wrong for her washed over her. Had her self-esteem been so low she didn't think she deserved a man like Day?

Day's smile disappeared. "What's wrong? Is the wine bad?"

Kellar shook her head. She chuckled, but at the same time her eyes were shimmering with unshed tears. So many regrets and emotions ran through her, she didn't know where to start.

A server appeared and set a glass of beer in front of Day, filled their water glasses, and left.

Kellar took a sip of her wine to fortify herself. "Don't let me drink too much."

"I'll look out for you." He drank some of his beer.

"It's just... the thing with the wine made me feel special. *You* make me feel special. And I don't think anyone else

I've dated ever did."

"Really? Is it possible some of the guys you dated did special things for you and you didn't pick up on it?"

Kellar's brow knitted.

"You should know better than anyone that dating can be such a minefield sometimes. It's so easy to misinterpret intentions and the signals get crossed. The wine thing? All I did was remember the time we were here before and made sure it didn't happen again. You picked up on it."

She rested her chin in her hand. "Huh. You could be right. Maybe I should sign my degrees over to you. I got sad for a minute there, wondering why I never expected to be treated that way. And *why* I didn't."

"I don't think it's just you," Day said.

"No. It's not. And that's even sadder. Why wouldn't you treat someone you're dating that way? If you're really interested in them, that is."

"I think you just answered your own question."

"I did, didn't I?" Kellar's brain kicked into gear. "Part of feeling special must be about expectations. Or feeling good enough about yourself to believe you deserve that kind of treatment. I think you've given me another blog idea."

Day lifted his beer in a toast. "That's why I'm here."

"I'll have to figure out what I can do to make you feel special."

"You're already doing it," Day said.

"I am?"

"You've been doing it since I met you."

"I have?"

"You listen."

"Oh, well, but that doesn't count. I mean—"

"No," Day said emphatically. "Don't discount it. It's important. Why do you think your podcast is so popular? You listen."

She lifted her glass in a gesture of agreement. "Psychologist. Listening is in the job description."

"It's a valuable skill. You don't give yourself enough credit."

Day was right. She'd developed a way of downplaying her abilities and deflecting attention. In some part of herself, she believed she didn't deserve accolades or praise while at the same time she craved both. *Second-best syndrome?*

"And as for wasting time with people who don't think you're special, that stops right now. With me."

His meaning was unmistakable. *He makes me feel good about myself.* It was the same feeling she got from him during that long-ago interview. And no doubt why she'd been so disappointed when he hadn't shown up for their date. Her self-esteem had still been pretty shaky back then and after that it had dropped to a new low. She'd been building it back ever since, brick by brick. Seeing herself through Day's eyes sped up the process.

"Maybe we have to go through certain things with certain people in order understand ourselves better and to weed out the undesirables." Kellar took another sip of her wine.

He lifted his glass again. "I think you've got the name for that blog post."

Weeding Out the Undesirables

♥

If you've been dating for a while and still haven't found someone you click with, don't lose heart, change your perspective. You're weeding out the undesirables.

We learn from every dating experience, every relationship, and mostly what we learn is what we don't want. We simply have to go through this process to figure out what it is we do want.

What we want is to feel special.

The first question to ask yourself is does this person see me as special?

Does s/he make me feel special?

Do they comment on those qualities that make me unique and valuable in their eyes?

In short, do you feel better about yourself because of the way this person treats you?

Are they helping you feel more confident/beautiful/desirable/capable? Fill in the blank!

Who wants to be with someone who makes them feel ordinary or who takes them for granted? Yet all too often, we settle for exactly that. We may not believe we are special and deserve to be treated as such.

If that's been your thought process, stop it! You can speed up the weeding process by simply asking yourself this question: Does he or she make me feel special? Do I feel special when I'm around him or her?

If you don't, it's time for a self-inventory. First, make a list of things you're good at. It will be longer than you think. Next, what do you need or want to work on for you? If your confidence or self-esteem has taken a nosedive lately, write down all the things you do well. Promotion at work? Compliments? A household project completed? Have you learned a new skill? Keep a success file or a journal for yourself and refer to it often to remind yourself of all that you have to offer.

Everyone's idea of "special" is different, but it's not about grand gestures or literally sweeping someone off their feet. The small things matter more than you realize. A bouquet of flowers, a unique brand of dark chocolate, a trinket from a favorite TV show or movie. You get the idea, right?

It doesn't have to be expensive, and it doesn't have to be gifts. For some, it's just listening. Being given their attention. Remembering details. A massage or a foot rub. The important thing is, once that someone knows what makes you feel special, do they try to provide it?

And beyond that, do they really, truly recognize those special things about you? Your gifts. Your talents. The things that make you uniquely you? Do you feel even better about yourself when you're with this person?

If not, that is a clue that tells you you're not that important to them. And if you're made to feel like you're not a priority during the dating stage, it's likely you never will. Ask yourself: Am I willing to settle for this?

I hope the answer is no. We should all hold out for someone who makes us a priority. Who makes us feel important and special. Because we are special, and we all deserve to be treated that way.

Chapter Twenty-two

♥

Kellar read over the draft and made a couple of minor corrections. Her eyes were drooping, but when Day first dropped her off, adrenaline was pumping through her system despite the two-plus glasses of wine she'd consumed with dinner.

She closed her laptop and finally prepared for bed. She didn't think she could have enjoyed dinner more. Day had arranged for the chef to recreate their first meal together, and interruptions by the server were minimal.

They were, however, interrupted by Jamie Falcon and his wife, who happened to be having dinner there at the same time. Jamie had to give both Day and Kellar some good-natured ribbing about what he called their "friends-only fibs" over the last few months, but it hadn't bothered either of them.

When dinner was over, Day held her hand as he escorted her back to the car and didn't let go until they were at her door. He stepped inside with her long enough for a very thorough kiss that left her wanting more.

She could tell Day did too, but she loved the way he

buried his fingers in her hair and looked in her eyes. "This wooing business? Taking it slow?"

"Uh huh?"

"It's fun. It's driving me crazy, but it's fun."

He kissed her lips again and stepped out, closing the door behind him. Kellar stayed where she was, leaning against the wall, trying to calm her racing heart, her every sense tingling and alive.

Day strolled back to the car, taking a deep breath of the cool night air.

He slid into the seat and put the window down. He considered hanging his head out on the drive home like a dog who'd played one too many games of fetch, who needed to lap up the breeze along the highway.

Dating Kellar, especially kissing her, was fun. But it wasn't easy. He wanted more. To kiss her for as long as he wanted before undressing her. Taking her to bed. Waking up next to her in the morning. Chatting over coffee. Showering together. He hoped his recurring fantasies would soon turn into his future.

But for now, he had to tread carefully. Not just because she wanted to take it slow. But because he was hiding a few too many things. Mostly about his relationship with her father, but a few other secrets he simply couldn't share with her.

She'd admitted to trusting him, but he didn't know how strong that trust was. To him, it seemed a fragile thing without roots or history. It didn't take a psychology degree to figure out Kellar. Rory had done a number on her, certainly, and she hadn't helped herself by apparently choosing men who repeated that same pattern.

He didn't think he'd imagined her sitting up a little straighter and smiling a bit broader when he mentioned her listening skills. He'd make a list of things he admired about her, he decided, and recite at least one of them to her every day. Her work ethic. The way she took care of herself by working out and eating well. Her drive and ambition and fearlessness. She was smart and sexy and *real*. Her overly chatty and funny remarks after a bit too much wine never ceased to entertain him.

Forget the "she completes me" rhetoric. "She entertains me" seemed much better.

He leaned back and stared at the ceiling of the limo, then slid the sunroof open. His thoughts drifted back to when he and Chazz had reconnected a few years ago. Like Kellar, Chazz's belief in himself had been undermined. Although still cautious, especially when facing new situations and people, Chazz had come a long way. He'd become confident in his instincts and abilities. It hadn't happened overnight. Day had done his best to support and encourage his friend, and finally Chazz began to flourish in his new environment.

Only a few stars were visible in the nighttime LA sky, not like on his property in Wyoming. He wanted to tell

Kellar about the stars there, take her to see them, see if she would consider relocating with him.

Ten years in LA had left him restless for wide open spaces. It was funny. He'd grown up in the sleeper cab of his parents' truck. A confined space surrounded by wide open spaces. He recalled the flat land of Kansas and Nebraska, where it seemed there was nothing but fields of wheat and corn. The mountains in Colorado and Wyoming, the deserts in Utah and Nevada.

He'd loved it all. Loved his unusual childhood, the way his imagination worked overtime as he considered living in any of the places they traveled through.

He had a vision for a house of rough-hewn timber, a barn and a stable for horses. Maybe a private airstrip. Heck, maybe he'd get his pilot's license. The possibilities were endless.

But he wanted someone to share it with him. No, not just someone. Kellar. But would she give up LA now that she was famous and in demand? He didn't know. There'd been no reason to broach the subject before. But he needed to know. Because now he could see her as part of his permanent future. They'd both still have to do some traveling and spend a lot of time online, of course. But at the end of the day, there'd be mountain sunsets, peace and quiet.

Assuming, of course, her father didn't become a road-block between them. Day felt he'd made a sticky situation even stickier by not telling her the whole truth about his relationship with her father. He'd signed that confidentiality agreement in good faith. Day had learned one hard lesson during his time in Hollywood—the less said the better. Everyone was after information they could leak to the press or rival studios. Everyone wanted to be in the know, because knowledge was power.

Kellar wasn't the only one with trust issues. If he shared confidential information with her, he wanted to believe it would go no further. And yet, his past relationships had proven that his instincts about people weren't infallible. He'd been fooled before.

The NDA with Rory protected him because he could always point to it as the reason he hadn't confided in Kellar. He comforted himself that he'd also promised Kellar he wouldn't mention her father again. Once the film was in the can, he'd explain and hope the truth wouldn't ruin everything between them.

Kellar didn't understand Day's relationship with Willow, either. He knew it made her uncomfortable and somewhat suspicious no matter how often he assured her they were long-time friends and nothing more.

Day hadn't heard from Rory, but his gut told him Rory was headed for a fall. Day had a tough love plan for Rory similar to the one that had worked with Chazz. He hoped Kellar's father would get on board with it. Because until her relationship with Rory healed, Day wasn't sure his own relationship with her could move forward in the way he wanted it to.

He stared out the window at the dark waters of the ocean as the limo wound its way along the PCH. His future with Kellar seemed just as murky at the moment. But each new day was an opportunity to build something lasting and real with her. If he didn't screw it up.

Day and Chazz had watched the rushes from the day's filming earlier and picked up pizza on the way home. Or what passed for pizza for Chazz. No flour. No cheese. Lots of veggies on a cauliflower crust and probably a sauce made from soy yogurt and crushed organic tomatoes. Something more conventional and which his trainer approved of for Day.

"I've got an idea," Chazz said.

Day's mouth watered at the aroma emanating from the boxes in the backseat of Chazz's car, tempting him to gnaw through the cardboard while assuring himself he could wait fifteen more minutes.

"Let's hear it." He hoped for a flash of brilliance to distract him from his empty stomach.

"Donate the proceeds from this film."

Day stared at Chazz. "What?"

Chazz spared him a glance. "Donate the proceeds."

"Are we running a charity or a profitable production company? Where'd you come up with this?"

Chazz carried on. "You've made enough money, haven't you? What if you donate a portion of the proceeds from this film to a good cause? Wouldn't it get you off the hook with Kellar when the time comes?"

Day relaxed a smidge. "I'm listening."

"She's going to hate that the film is more than inspired by her father. It's based on him. You never told her you bought his life story or that you used so many of the details she told you about her childhood."

Day winced as he did every time those points crossed his mind.

"But if you don't profit from using either of those scenarios, she can't be mad about it, can she? She might even understand about how much money you paid him."

Day ruminated on the possibility of releasing the film and keeping his relationship with Kellar unscathed. Not once had he been able to picture that happening. Kellar might never forgive him for going behind her back. Worse, he'd have destroyed her trust in him, and he might never get it back. Any way he looked at it, whatever he hoped to have with Kellar might die because of what he'd done and the way he'd done it.

"Where's the money going to go?"

"I've got two ideas," Chazz said as he turned onto their road. "What does Kellar care about?"

"Her family," Day said immediately. He snapped his fingers. "Her niece."

Chazz shot him an approving glance. "That's one. Do something that will impact kids like Gracie. Sick kids."

"Donate to that children's hospital, you mean?"

"Treatment for kids whose families can't afford it. Maybe a portion of it to benefit bone marrow transplants, specifically."

"And let me guess," Day said as they pulled into the driveway. "A gambling treatment center, too."

"Yes." He grabbed the pizzas and they went inside. "I was also thinking we could help the families who've been devastated by a gambling addict on a case-by-case basis."

Day pulled two mineral waters from the fridge. "Is there an organization that does that?"

"No," Chazz told him as they opened their respective boxes and surveyed the pies. "Not that I've been able to find, anyway. Most are support groups or counseling centers."

"So, say something happens like what happened with Kellar's family. A parent sucks up all the money and leaves the family high and dry. You want to build an organization from the ground up that could help them?"

"Why not?" Chazz took a big bite of his pizza. He chewed and swallowed before continuing. "Adrienne told me what a scary time that was for them. They didn't know if they'd be able to keep their house. Robin went back to work full-time. Adrienne put everything she made into paying the bills. Kellar was still in high school, but she got a job and even contributed her babysitting money. Don't you think families like that would appreciate practical help instead of just verbal support and online counseling resources?"

"Starting something like this will be a lot of work."

"It will be, but we can find a director with experience and let them worry about that. Put Kellar on the board if she's interested. With your connections? Who won't want to be involved with it? Heck, you can throw a ball or something every year to help raise money."

"A celebrity bowling tournament," Day put in. "That'd be fun. Maybe we can get it televised."

Chazz looked at him quizzically. "Whatever works, I guess. Once it gets going, it becomes self-sustaining. Gambling's a huge problem. It destroys families like any other addiction. You'd be making a real impact."

Given his background, it wasn't surprising Chazz would mount a soapbox for a cause like this. Who could blame him?

"I'll think about it. Talk to the accountants. But if we go ahead with this, I'm going to have one condition."

Chazz wiped his hands on a paper towel and reached for his water. "What's that?"

"I want you to sit on the board, too."

For Kellar the next several weeks were crowded with travel, phone calls, interviews, and meetings, punctuated by the few times she and Day managed to make a date. His schedule seemed to be even more crowded than hers, and she began to understand why celebrity relationships became strained with so much time apart.

Even though they were at the beginning of theirs, she wondered if that wasn't making things even harder, for sometimes she found herself questioning the depth of their connection with so many missed phone calls and interrupted text messages. They Facetimed occasionally but even their assurances to each other faded by the next day.

And so, Kellar's daydreams began again. What if they could both slow down and just be. What if they got married and relocated somewhere... else. She didn't know where, but somewhere besides LA. She wasn't all that attached to the city and could probably work from anywhere. But Day's life, career, and business was all Hollywood.

She tried and failed to picture Day on a farm in Indiana where she could be closer to her family. Pennsylvania didn't seem like an option, either. She knew some celebrities had forsaken the LA lifestyle and moved to the Southwest or places like Utah or Idaho to raise their families. It hadn't hurt their careers. So maybe...

Kellar knew she was getting ahead of herself. She and Day were far from making that kind of commitment. But in his absence, the daydreams were a comfort.

From the moment her appearance on Jamie Falcon went viral, her publisher had seized the day, scheduling book signings, seminars, personal appearances and squeezing her into every book festival possible. Meanwhile, Day had been overseas, first for two weeks of shooting for a film in which he'd taken a small but pivotal role and then on to Cannes before returning to LA for the shooting of exteriors as well as the final scenes for his film. He'd wanted her to join him in Cannes, but she couldn't escape her obligations.

At least they'd looked at their schedules together and discovered they would have a relatively quiet two weeks coming up soon. Finally, they'd have blocks of uninterrupted time to spend together however they wanted. Kellar couldn't wait. She'd missed seeing Day and talking to him. It didn't really matter what they were doing. Eating. Watching a movie. Hiking. Enjoying the sunset. She liked being with him.

Their time apart had proven one thing to her. She was ready to move forward with him. More than ready.

She wasn't connecting with Adrienne as often as she'd like either, and she missed sharing with her. Her sister texted her with updates about Gracie, but Adrienne had taken on extra work as Gracie's health improved so her free time became more limited. Kellar knew an increasingly large chunk of that time was spent communicating with Chazz.

The last leg of this trip was here in New York. She couldn't wait for it to be over.

There were a few diehard autograph seekers waiting outside when Kellar exited the radio studio. She still found it thrilling that anyone would want her autograph. Her celebrity status came via her connection to Day, but if they were fans or followers or readers of her book as well, she could afford the time.

The studio's town car sat idling at the curb. The driver waited patiently until she had attended to the small crowd to open her door. But once she was ready to go, someone calling her name stopped her from getting inside.

She turned to see her father. He must have been waiting for her. Must have known she was here. How? *Why?*

She watched him approach knowing there was no such thing as a happy reunion for them. Whatever his reasons for being here would be self-serving. Something of her feelings must have shown in her expression, for he slowed his last few steps and stared into her eyes. "How are you, honey?"

Typical. He'd already forgotten what happened the last time he'd called her honey. Annoyance warred with disappointment and longing. Did she really need to have it out with her father again and hope it was for the last time?? Apparently, nothing she'd said or done so far had gotten through to him.

Yes, she decided. She was ready now. Ready to tell him to go to hell and stay there. That she never wanted to see him again. Even if that was a lie. The more technical truth was she never wanted to see this version of him. The glad-handing, gambling, blowhard, who laid on the charm and spun entertaining, overly embellished tales about his experiences.

Kellar wanted to believe that somewhere, underneath this pseudo charmer was someone real. She clung to the memories of the fun dad he'd been during her early years. But she'd given up hope that he'd ever emerge. And until he did, she had nothing to say to him.

Except, of course, "Don't call me honey."

"Sorry," he said immediately. "You did ask me not to do that." He pretended sadness at the memory of their last meeting. "Kellar, then. Okay if I call you Kellar?"

"It is my name," she said testily, wishing he'd get to the point so she could say her piece and be done with him once and for all. A stab of regret pierced her heart. Was she ready to never see him again? *Never*? Would she always wonder what would have happened if she gave him one more chance?

"Do you have time for a drink? Cup of coffee? My treat. How about ice cream?"

I'm not five anymore.

She wanted to remind him of that, but ice cream might soften the blow of telling him off once and for all. Comfort food during a difficult time instead of after. She'd headed straight to the liquor cabinet after their last encounter. Might as well load up on sugar for this one.

"I passed a place a couple of blocks from here." Kellar noticed his wheedling tone, the only one he ever used on their rare meetings the past few years, was missing. Instead, he sounded practical, even reasonable.

Kellar glanced at the driver, still waiting for her to get in.

"We could walk there. It's a beautiful day. I'll pay for a cab back to your hotel," Rory added.

In truth, it was a lovely summer New York afternoon. Kellar had spent far too much time cooped up in hotel rooms and studios lately, and even with her father as escort, she didn't want to pass up an opportunity to enjoy the weather. She dismissed the driver, and they began to stroll.

Kellar enjoyed the chance to absorb the atmosphere of the city, to study the architecture, the pedestrians, even the traffic. The city hummed and vibrated and electrified. So different from laid back LA.

"Beautiful day, don't you think?"

Kellar offered a non-committal grunt. She dreaded the conversation to come. Why hadn't she excused herself the moment she'd seen her father? She could have gotten into the car and never looked back.

A glutton for punishment.

Fool.

In the middle of the next block, Rory pointed out the old-fashioned sweet shop and held the door open for her. At least that part hadn't been a con.

The walls were papered in turquoise and white stripes and there were several small round tables with spindly chairs. A pastry case anchored one the end of the counter and a display of decadent chocolates lined the other. In between were glass-covered cases displaying tubs of ice cream.

The place smelled like fresh-baked waffle cones and cocoa, a sugar-addict's fantasy vision of heaven.

Kellar took her time perusing the selection, delaying the conversation with her father as long as possible. From there, they crossed to a small park that appeared to exist mostly to accommodate the local canine population.

Nevertheless, they found an unoccupied bench beneath a tree that afforded them a bit of privacy. The surrounding hedge helped to muffle the traffic noise.

Kellar looped the strap of her purse around her elbow and concentrated on her child-size cup of the rich strawberry cheesecake chocolate truffle, scooping up tiny bites with the bamboo spoon. If Rory weren't next to her, she could almost be enjoying herself.

About halfway through, he set his cup aside and said, "I've come to apologize."

Kellar held in a snort of disbelief, but just barely. Her childhood had been filled with meaningless apologies. Back then her father could do no wrong, and she'd been the forgiving sort. But eventually she'd learned not to trust him or his false contrition. She had no reason to think he had changed.

She shouldn't have come with him. She'd wasted her time. Again.

Rory clasped his hands between his knees and turned his head to look at her. "There's no reason you should believe me, of course. God knows, I've said I'm sorry so many times before."

What changed? Kellar couldn't voice the question, too afraid this was just the start of another angle he wanted to play.

"I'm in Gamblers Anonymous," he said. "No fool like an old fool, I suppose, but I'm finally ready to admit I have a problem. I've hurt a lot of people. I don't know if I can ever make amends. I don't know how. But it's one of the steps, and I—"

Oh, brother. What else would he do to try to gain her sympathy so he could use it to his advantage? As much as she wanted to believe him, experience wouldn't allow it. "What changed?"

"Changed?"

"After all this time, what happened? You didn't just wake up one morning and decide to go to the nearest GA meeting, did you? I'm not buying it, *Dad*. What's really going on?"

"I realized how destructive I've been and—"

"You've spent years being willfully blind to the damage you caused, so what opened your eyes? Or should I ask *who* opened your eyes?"

Rory sat up. " I don't see what difference it makes. The fact is, I'm here now saying I'm sorry. I know the words don't mean much, and I don't expect you to forgive me when I've been a shit to you, your sister, and your mother your entire life. But I have to start somewhere, Kellar. I'm starting with you."

"Why me?"

Rory paused before he answered. "I hurt you the most. Adrienne was older, an adult starting to live her own life. Your mother and I had grown apart. By the time I left, she was ready to kick me to the curb anyway. I'm not saying I didn't hurt them. I did. But you were still in school. You were still a kid..." Rory trailed off.

"I guess I'm finally the first at something," Kellar said.

"That second best stuff? I never meant to hurt you."

"It doesn't matter what you intended. What matters is how it made me feel. Like I was never good enough. My whole life I've felt that way." Kellar didn't want to cry but she was close to losing it.

"I'm sorry," Rory repeated, but this time his voice was strained. He withdrew a pack of tissues from his pocket and yanked one out.

Kellar turned in time to see him wipe his nose, then under his eyes.

He addressed the sidewalk again. "I was a crap father. You deserved better."

Maybe he means it. Kellar wanted to believe him. But too many years of not being able to stood in the way. "Could I have one of those?"

He held out the pack of tissues. She dabbed at her nose and eyes but managed to hold herself together. That tiny sprig of hope that this was for real raised its head once again.

They sat in silence, crumpled tissues in their hands, melting ice cream forgotten. The air grew cooler as the sun dropped in the sky.

"I don't know where to go from here," Rory admitted. "But I'd like to take you to dinner if you're free."

"I'm not," Kellar said because it was true. The endless round of drinks and meals with her agent, editor, sales, and PR people never seemed to end. "You show up here and you spring this on me, and I don't know what to think." Seeing he was about to interrupt she held up a hand to stop him.

"No. Forgiveness isn't automatic. Not for me, anyway. Neither is trust. Not after you spent years either ignoring me or trying to use me. Saying you've changed means nothing. You'll have to show me."

"I will. I promise."

"Dad? Please don't make promises you can't or won't keep. You should know better."

"You're right. But I am going to try to prove to you that I've changed."

"Good."

The hope in her father's eyes told her she'd made the right decision. She needed to spend time with her father to find out if she could ever trust him again. Because the psychologist inside her knew that was the first step towards being able to fully trust herself.

"Kellar Kennedy. What a surprise meeting you here."

Kellar had barely entered the main terminal at LAX when she heard Jeanine Hartman's passive aggressive voice. She now knew how Day must feel every time Jeanine approached him. Trapped.

"Just back from NYC?"

Jeanine kept pace with Kellar, maintaining the conversational tone like they were old chums, and this was just a chance meeting. Kellar knew it wasn't. Somehow Jeanine had got hold of her itinerary or learned what day she was coming back and had staked out the airport. Kellar couldn't believe the nerve of the woman.

"How's your dad?"

Kellar might have missed a step. The question came out of left field, but she vowed to herself this woman wasn't going to get under her skin. Not this time.

"What do you want, Jeanine?" she asked. She didn't have to force the weariness into her voice. She wanted to get home and into the shower. Eat and sleep.

"Your dad just got out of rehab, right? Gambling addiction?"

Kellar kept walking, dodging the crowd along the wide corridor. She saw restrooms up ahead, but feared if she went in Jeanine would follow her into the stall. How did she know Rory had been in rehab when he hadn't mentioned it to his own daughter? If it was even true.

"Nice of Day to pay for it, wasn't it?"

Kellar stopped short. A businessman with a bulging briefcase who'd been following too closely almost ran into her. He *harumphed* and veered to the side.

"What did you say?"

"Centerstone. The facility outside of Tucson. Nice of Day to foot the bill. I hear it's not cheap."

Day paid for Rory's rehab? It was the craziest and most unexpected story Jeanine had come up with yet. She had to be way off base.

Kellar saw the triumphant gleam in Jeanine's eyes. "You didn't know."

Kellar didn't want to give her the satisfaction of

one-upping her. She started walking again.

"You don't believe me? Why don't you ask Day?"

I will. Day knew Rory. He'd admitted that much. He'd used Rory to get background for his movie. But pay for his rehab? She couldn't wrap her head around the possibility.

What were the odds that Rory had some sudden revelation to quit gambling and attend a rehab program on his own? He'd been decidedly vague about how he'd arrived in recovery. But Kellar hadn't pushed for an explanation, either. Not when, for the first time in her life, Rory had exhibited genuine interest in her as a person and not his second-best daughter.

"While you're at it, why don't you ask him what he and Willow Thorne have been up to lately?"

Even though she did everything recommended to counteract jet lag, once back in her own bed and her own familiar surroundings, Kellar couldn't sleep. Even her tried and true method of thinking of random words didn't work. Her brain wouldn't stop buzzing.

Except for a few erratic texts, Kellar had barely communicated with Day the past week. Even though most of the filming was done, Day spent long hours working with the editor.

In a way, she'd been relieved by the lack of pressure

between them, but she couldn't deny that she'd missed Day. Missed talking to him, holding his hand, his kisses. Missed their banter and the fun they could have in each other's company.

Now all she could think about was telling him about the meeting with her father. And about everything Jeanine had said. The woman's confidence troubled Kellar. Day knew Jeanine's penchant for spinning tales, and he would be able to clear everything up.

The one thing Kellar didn't want to bring up was Willow. Kellar knew Willow had attended Cannes. She could admit to herself that she still didn't feel secure enough in her relationship with Day to explain where her insecurity about Willow came from. Someday she'd have to tell him what she'd been hanging onto since the very beginning and why she had such a hard time trusting him.

Willow's possessiveness of Day and obvious dislike of Kellar fueled her insecurity. Except it wasn't a jealous vibe Kellar got from Willow. It was more like a mother lion protecting its cub, which made no sense. Why would Willow think Day would need protection from—*her*?

Maybe she'd just have to bite the bullet and put it all out there before she and Day became any more serious about each other.

She hadn't talked to Adrienne or her mother about Rory yet. She wasn't sure yet how to feel about her dad's supposed recovery. She didn't trust it and she didn't want to get anyone else's hopes up. A shockingly high percentage of people relapsed after treatment.

She flipped to her other side on the bed once again and tried to get comfortable. *Great. You don't trust Day. You don't trust your father. But most of all? You don't trust yourself.*

When had she lost her faith in people? She didn't like that about herself, feeling like she expected the worst from them even if they might be trying their best. She made a vow right then and there to stop it. With Day. With her father. Living with the disappointment if they let her down couldn't be worse than this constant guessing game she kept playing with herself.

On that note, finally, she fell asleep.

Kellar woke to see a text from Day welcoming her home and saying he'd missed her. He planned to work from home today, had a lot of calls to make and catching up to do, but he hoped to see her later and to let him know what her schedule looked like.

She grinned and stretched, remembering her vow to herself last night. Time to stop holding herself back. Why not believe in the possibility of a future with him? A permanent future. The one she'd daydreamed about for years?

She thought of one of Poppy's favorite sayings: poop or get off the pot. Crude, but accurate. Kellar knew she had to get out of the slow-moving state of suspension she'd put herself in. The time had come to go all in.

Coffee woke her and a shower revived her. She decided to grab her laptop and head to Malibu. She'd pick up some food in case Day wanted to take a late lunch break. If not, she could hang out on the deck which would be soothing after her hectic time away. Or maybe she'd lounge in the sun and catch up on her reading.

Sometimes Kellar thought about escaping city life for good. She couldn't argue LA had been good for her, but she'd accomplished what she'd set out to do career-wise. There was next to nothing that couldn't be done via the internet these days.

Maybe she could move somewhere with wide open spaces. She giggled to herself, thinking about living on a farm. Maybe not in Indiana, but a place not too far from a major city, so she could take advantage of amenities when she needed to, like an airport.

Would Day ever leave LA? Lots of working actors did, especially the ones who wanted a more conventional life for their children outside of the celebrity spotlight.

Kellar hadn't seriously envisioned herself with a family before, but maybe that was changing. Could she have a future with Day? One that included marriage and children? She still wasn't a hundred percent sure, but the very fact she was asking herself the question put a smile on her face.

Chapter Twenty-Three

♥

Kellar let herself in with the key Day had given her, holding onto the cardboard tray of smoothies and organic veggie wraps she'd picked up. As she gently closed the door, she paused and thought about pinching herself. She had a key to Dayman MacDay's house! She was in a relationship with the Sexiest Man Alive.

Even if they were still defining the terms of their relationship, at some point they'd become lovers. But beyond that?

You're doing it again, she warned herself. *Over-analyzing. Looking for a label. Why can't you just let it be what it is? Let it unfold... organically?*

Because I'm terrified of getting my heart broken, she answered back.

The moment she stepped away from the door, she heard voices. Men's voices coming from Day's home office, a large room facing the front of the house. Day had told her once during a tour of his place, it had originally been a library. Now it was part office, part mini-screening room. He'd installed a large functional desk, a seating area, and a small wet bar. At the far end was an automated screen that dropped to cover the bookshelves. A huge sectional sofa faced the screen, and a drop-down projector was set into the ceiling.

Curious, Kellar took a couple of steps toward the partially opened door.

First, she heard a voice she didn't recognize, although the words were clear enough. He was talking about a publishing house's expectations and a discussion he'd had with an editor.

"Okay. So, Rory, now that we've got you set up with a ghostwriter, that's going to be your priority. We'll be finalizing the release dates for both the film and the book next week, so it needs to be ready to go to the printer no later than the first of November." It sounded like Day was talking to her father.

"We feel confident we can get the rough draft done in six weeks, right, Nate?" That was her father's voice. "That should give us plenty of time."

Whoever 'Nate' was began outlining a schedule he'd come up with to complete the book by the deadline.

What book? What is going on?

Jeanine Hartman's words came back to her with haunting clarity.

What's going on with Day and your father?

They're pretty chummy, aren't they?

"And Mandy, you're going to work with Nate to minimize mentions of my involvement as much as possible."

"We've already discussed it and decided on a couple of

strategies that will keep you in the background." Mandy was Day's publicist, but what she said made no sense. "But initially at least, you're going to be the face and the spokesperson for the foundation. The genesis of the film, overlaid with Rory's memoir and your part in his recovery is going to give us the momentum we need to get the kind of exposure we're looking for.

"Anything to report on the Jeanine Hartman problem?"

"We're handling it," Mandy said. "That's what you pay us for."

Now Chazz was speaking, but there was too much noise in Kellar's brain to pay attention to what he said. She'd decided she'd stood here long enough. Been kept in the dark about whatever was happening. She took a step toward the door, planning to get some answers when movement from the hallway leading from the master suite snared her attention.

Willow Thorne appeared, wrapped in an oversized bathrobe, rubbing at her sleepy eyes. She caught sight of Kellar with her cardboard carrier of smoothies and a bag of food.

Willow yawned. "What's going on?" she asked.

"That's what I'd like to know," Kellar knew her voice was too loud, everyone in the office could no doubt hear her.

The partially closed door swung all the way open, and Day appeared, followed by Chazz. She got a glimpse of an oversized screen where her father's face and that of another man who must be the ghostwriter, along with Mandy's appeared.

It was too much. Suddenly, Kellar felt overwhelmed and stupidly, naively foolish. She'd wanted to discount Jeanine Hartman's questions and insinuations, but apparently the intrepid reporter knew more than she did not only about her father, but also about her boyfriend.

Kellar had been on the verge of trusting Day. No. Correction. She *had* trusted Day. She'd been ready to take their relationship to the next level, to truly open herself up to him, to see where they could go together. But Day apparently had gone in a completely different direction.

Without her.

Her gaze turned to Willow, then over Day's shoulder to where the Zoom call screen loomed behind Chazz.

Every nightmare she'd ever had about heartbreak came true. The crushing weight of Day's betrayal squeezed around her. She couldn't believe it.

Could. Not. Freaking. Believe. It.

She'd come full circle. He'd bailed on her once and she'd known deep inside he'd do it again. But being right did not make it hurt less.

Day took a step forward. "Kellar." He came toward her but stopped when he saw Willow.

"*No.*" The single strangled word worked its way out with difficulty. She did not want him to get any closer. To tell her the truth about him and Willow. About him and her father. To anything.

She sent the tray of drinks sailing in Day's direction.

Day jumped back as the smoothies splashed everywhere. She whirled away. The door. Where was the door?

"Kellar," Day called. "Wait."

Kellar got through the front door, slammed it behind her, and stumbled to her car. Day bolted out of the house while she fumbled with the ignition key. Oh God. She did not want a confrontation. She did not want Day to see the foolish, useless tears pressing for release. She didn't want his pity or his lame attempts to ease the pain she felt.

Day reached the car just as she tore out of the driveway, barely checking for traffic on the road.

Rage surged through her, and she pounded on the steering wheel the entire drive home. *Why?* Day could have any woman he wanted. She wasn't his type and yet he had pursued *her*. He'd been relentless, damn him, but *why?*

Her inner child sobbed. They'd been fine as friends. She'd managed to keep a lid on her feelings. She'd been realistic. Down-to-earth. Day was a player, and the very last thing she had wanted to be was one of his playthings. And yet, here she was... played.

And what in the world was her father of all people doing in the middle of this? What was that talk about a book deal? A ghostwriter? The *movie*? Just when she'd finally started to feel good about her father after all these years, apparently, he'd been in cahoots with Day. Behind her back. The two of them! She couldn't trust either of them.

She had no one to blame but herself. That truth burned worst of all. She'd started to believe in the sincerity of everything Day shared with her. She'd begun to think there was something real and *genuine* between them. Something they both sensed and wanted.

She glanced at her reflection in the rear-view mirror. "You are such an idiot. Some dating expert you are. You don't know anything. You're a fraud. A big fat fraud."

Her cell phone rang. Day. She let it go to voice mail. The phone pinged with a text message. She picked up the phone and turned it off. She rolled her window down because she was finding it hard to breathe. She took in the late morning air, making herself take deep breaths, willing herself to calm down.

She knew what Day would probably do now. He'd try to explain. Apologize. Or would he? Would he come knocking on her door? Ugh. She could just imagine the ensuing scene. What if he didn't knock on her door? Oh, God. That would be even worse, wouldn't it? Proof positive that she wasn't even important enough for him to have a scene with.

She didn't think she could live through either of those scenarios. Before she arrived at her townhouse, she had to make a plan.

Day pounded on Kellar's front door, feeling it shudder

slightly under his fist. He couldn't believe she'd run off without even letting him explain.

He'd been juggling a few too many secrets while walking a tightrope of half-truths and omissions. Knowing he'd never outright lied to Kellar was no comfort now. In hindsight what he should have done was sit her down and tell her everything. But how could he when events were still evolving with their friendship, the film, her father, Willow. He guessed Kellar wasn't the only one with trust issues. But if he were honest with himself, he'd feared she'd terminate their relationship and he didn't want that. He never wanted that.

Okay, he could see that it looked bad, her showing up unexpectedly and finding him on a Zoom call with her father, talking about a book deal. Plus, Willow's appearance made it clear she'd spent the night. As the saying went, the optics were bad.

As long as he lived, he didn't think he'd ever forget the look of devastation on Kellar's face. He hated knowing he had caused it. But still, she didn't have to bail on him.

He'd have loved it if the scene had played out differently, with the two of them sharing lunch, and maybe, finally, much more.

"Dammit."

The door to the unit adjacent to Kellar's opened

and her rumpled-looking neighbor appeared. "She's not there," the redhead said helpfully, cinching a knot in the belt of her bathrobe.

Day reigned in his temper. "Do you know where she is?"

"Not anymore. Tore in here earlier like a bat out of hell. Asked if I'd water her plants. Course I said yes. I always do. Tore out again. Funny thing is, she just got back yesterday."

Day sighed. "Thanks."

"Could you?" she asked hesitantly. "Would you mind?"

She edged toward him with a notepad.

"What?"

"Can I get your autograph?" from the pocket of her robe she produced a ball-point pen."

Day sighed. "Yeah, sure."

"I'm Cindy."

"K.K. What are you doing? You didn't even let him explain." Adrienne sounded annoyed, if not angry.

"Excuse me, A.K. Did you miss the part about where I found him in a meeting with our father? And another woman wandering out of his bedroom wearing his bathrobe?" She shouted the last part.

"I know. I know. It looks bad."

"Damn right it does."

"And I know he and Willow Whatshername go back a long way."

"Damn right they do."

"But I thought he told you they'd never been romantically involved."

"That's what he *said*," Kellar snapped.

"Well…"

"Well, what?"

"I know it's not the same, but you two weren't romantically involved for a long time, either."

"So?"

"But everyone thought you were."

"Your point?"

"Maybe it wasn't what it looked like—"

"If you are going to say he might have a reasonable explanation for all of this, I'm going to hang up on you," Kellar warned.

"All I'm saying is Day's a serial dater. A player. Whatever you want to call it. But I've never heard of him cheating on anyone before. Have you?"

Kellar mulled that over and silently conceded her sister might have a point. If Day had cheated on any of his girlfriends, the press would have exposed it. Or the girlfriend might have.

"K.K., come on. I've seen the two of you together, remember? You've got this, I don't know, this *way* between you. Like you *get* each other. Like you bask in each other's glow."

"Gag me."

"You're going to have to talk to him at some point, right?"

"Probably. If he even bothers to try to explain."

"You know he will. Don't be ridiculous."

"I don't know what's worse. Seeing Willow there or seeing that it was Dad he was talking to. Last I knew Day chewed Dad out for hitting me up for a loan, so what's that all about?"

"Speaking of Dad, he showed up here yesterday."

"*What*?"

"Yeah, I was going to call you later and tell you."

"He just showed up at the house out of the blue?"

"He did. Said he knew he didn't deserve it, but he wanted to talk to me. And to Mom. He told us he's in Gamblers Anonymous. He said he was sorry for how he treated us. He wants to make amends. That's one of the steps, you know."

"Did you buy it?"

There was a pause before Adrienne answered. "I don't know, but he seemed sincere. He talked to Mom in private for a little while before she left for work. He wanted to know how Gracie was doing. He even played a game of Candyland with her. It was kind of sweet."

Kellar tried to process what she was hearing. Tried to set her skepticism aside. "I wonder how he plans to make amends after all this time."

Adrienne chuckled. "I suggested if he was so interested in making up for the past, he could go get tested for bone marrow donation. I made sure he knew everyone else in the family, and even some of our friends did."

"Did he go?"

"He said he would. But I don't know if he followed through or not."

"It'd be pretty ironic if he turned out to be a match for Gracie, wouldn't it?"

"Considering he's ignored her up until now."

"He came to see me in New York."

"And you didn't tell me?"

"Same as you. I was going to as soon as we had time to really talk. I didn't know what to make of it or whether I believed him." Kellar felt more confused than ever.

"You could have stayed, KK. You could have let Day and Dad explain," Adrienne pointed out as gently as possible.

"No, Age, I couldn't. Right at that moment, I honestly couldn't. After the stuff Jeanine Hartman said and then hearing and seeing what I saw? It was just—too much for me to take in."

"But now you don't have answers."

"What I do have is a headache. God, how did I screw this up so bad?"

"I don't think you have. Not permanently, anyway."

"I'll see you tomorrow night," Kellar said. She didn't want to talk anymore. To anyone.

"I can't believe you're driving here," Adrienne said.

"I'm hanging up now." Kellar disconnected and dropped the phone in the passenger seat.

She really did have a headache because, thanks to Day, she hadn't had any food. She needed massive amounts of caffeine and a big greasy breakfast. And she was going to get it at the next truck stop she came across.

"Day's here."

Kellar rolled over and stared at her sister. "*Here* here?"

Adrienne nodded and sat at the edge of the bed. "Gracie's ecstatic. He said he'd try to come for her birthday, remember? You have to talk to him."

Kellar rolled away. Suddenly her brilliant plan to get away from Day didn't seem so brilliant anymore. She'd been there when he made that promise.

"I know," she said to the pillow. But she didn't want to. She was exhausted. She'd arrived late last night feeling bloated from all the food she'd eaten on the road, upset at the interruption of her schedule, and emotional from too many feelings and too much uncertainty. She'd spent most of the driving time crying and questioning her own behavior. Hadn't she just vowed to stop expecting the worst?

Footsteps sounded in the hallway and there was a tap on the door Adrienne had left ajar. It eased open and her heart went into overdrive. Adrienne patted her on the thigh and Kellar felt her weight leave the bed. Then her footsteps retreated. The door closed softly behind her.

Oh God. She didn't know what to say. She didn't want Day to see what a mess she was. Didn't want him to know that she regretted choosing her familiar reaction at the first sign of trouble.

Seconds ticked by. She didn't move. She thought he'd stopped at the foot of the bed. He must be watching her. Maybe he didn't know what to say either? Surely, he did, though. He was an expert at breaking hearts, right? Maybe he'd been rehearsing a new line just for her.

"Hey. Are you going to talk to me or what?"

"What." She said it like a petulant teenager.

"I can't believe you bailed on me," he said.

She shot up, forgetting her puffy eyes, messy hair, and reddened nose. "I bailed on *you*? I think you got that backwards, buddy."

"One bump in the road and you run away," Day said. "Isn't that exactly what you accuse men of doing to your many female followers?"

"*Excuse* me? Another woman spending the night in your bed is more than just a bump in the road to me."

"I've told you Willow is a friend, and yes, she spent the night, but I've never slept with her. And as for your father, I met him a year before I met you. I told you he helped me with research. Now we're working on a project together. You didn't give me a chance to explain anything."

Kellar looked into his eyes. He looked rumpled and weary with a day's worth of scruff along his jaw. She wanted to believe him. She wanted to trust him. Could he fake that kind of sincerity? He was an actor, but still…

He sat on the edge of the bed next to her. "Kellar, I would never do anything to intentionally hurt you."

"That's what you said to all the women you hurt."

The dagger hit home. "I can't win, can I? Because I've had relationships that didn't work out, because people got hurt, I *must* be a liar and a cheat, is that it? Did you ever think maybe *I* got hurt, too? Did you ever think maybe I wanted a relationship to stick, and I was sad when it didn't?"

"Of course, but—"

"But what?" Day didn't hide his exasperation.

Kellar cringed at his tone.

"What were you going to say? That it's not the same? That men never get hurt the way women do? That it's easy for us to walk away and never look back?"

"Something like that," Kellar admitted dully.

"Damn you," he swore softly. "Why do you think I'm here?"

"For Gracie?"

"You haven't got a clue, do you? You don't know love when it comes along and blows up in your face. You're not an expert in dating. You're an expert in disappointment. Because that's what you expect. You look for it. You seek it out. And you're happy when you find it. Because then you get to be right. Why don't you put that in a blog and post it?" He got up and walked out.

"Day, wait," she called. But his footsteps pounded away.

Hours later, Kellar dragged herself out of bed and into the shower. She did her best to make herself presentable, but she still felt disoriented, sluggish, and heartbroken. Especially heartbroken. She made her way downstairs and found Adrienne in the kitchen with Gracie.

"K.K.!" Gracie exclaimed. "Look what Day got me!" Kellar forced herself to *ooh* and *aah* over the extravagant princess playset.

As soon as she could, she escaped to a bar stool. "Is he gone?" she whispered to Adrienne.

"Yes. He said he had to get back to LA, and he didn't mention anything about coming back." Adrienne opened the refrigerator and removed a bottle of pinot grigio from the door. She poured two glasses and slid one in front of Kellar.

Kellar stared into the glass wishing the pale liquid could give her some answers.

He left you this. She held up a DVD case.

"What's that?" Kellar asked dully.

"I don't know. He suggested we watch it after Gracie goes to bed."

By eleven that night, an empty bottle of wine held place of honor on the coffee table, surrounded by crumpled tissues. The credits were still rolling when Adrienne hit the pause button on her laptop.

"Wow," she said. "Look at that. Proceeds from this film will be donated to the Grace Finley Fund at Bartlett Children's Hospital, Centerstone Recovery Center, and to The Families of Gamblers Foundation." Adrienne stared at her. "He's established a charity in Gracie's honor. Can you believe that? I don't know what The Families of Gamblers Foundation is, but it sounds impressive."

Kellar had no words. Too stunned to speak, she continued to stare at the frozen screen.

"He *really* nailed it," Adrienne said, her voice filled with awe.

Kellar agreed one hundred percent. It was like Day had taken what she'd written in her journal, taken everything she felt about her father and somehow transformed it so that anyone who saw this film would know and feel exactly what she'd known and felt. How had he done that? Day wasn't lining his own pockets by exploiting her experience. He was giving back.

"And the guy that played the character based on Dad," Adrienne went on, her voice now one of admiration. "Sean Harrison. He was amazing. The way he spoke, the mannerisms, every detail. At times I thought I was watching Dad."

Adrienne chanced a look Kellar's way. "Are you okay?"

"This explains the meeting," Kellar said her tone dull. "Why Dad was there. At Day's house. Why there's going to be a book."

"I don't get why he wouldn't tell you, though."

"He did tell me he met Dad in Vegas and that Dad helped him with background for the film. After Dad came to see me and wanted money, after I told Day about our whole history, I gave him the journal I kept back then. I also told him I didn't want to talk about Dad ever again. Day tried a few times, but I shut him down."

"You think he was looking for an opening? To explain about whatever deal he made with Dad and about the movie?"

Kellar leaned her head back on the sofa cushion and looked up at the ceiling. "Probably."

Day's words from this morning continued to play in her head. *You're an expert in disappointment. Because that's what you expect. I can't believe you bailed on me. One bump in the road and you run away.*

"I thought I could trust him, Age. He's the first guy I was ready to trust, and I talked myself out of it."

"This still doesn't explain why Willow Thorne was there. Or why it looked like she'd spent the night in his bed."

"I know. But..."

"But maybe there's a reasonable explanation? Maybe

you should have given him a chance to explain because it wasn't what it looked like?"

Kellar nodded. She'd felt awful since she'd hightailed it out of LA, and even worse since Day's visit this morning. Something nasty continued to churn and slither around inside her, even though she felt hollowed out and empty. Most likely, it was the realization that she'd been wrong. That her trust in Day hadn't been misplaced at all. That once again her fear had pushed that trust aside, and she'd beaten a hasty retreat rather than face him saying something she wouldn't want to hear.

Day's words came back to her. *Why don't you put that in a blog and post it?*

She would have to do an entire series of blogs and podcasts on self-sabotage, something she'd been practicing for a long time, but refused to admit to herself.

Doctor, heal thyself. What an example she was. Sharing her supposed knowledge and expertise with her audience, all the while ignoring her own destructive patterns.

Way to go, Kellar. Day didn't break your heart. You did.

The following day, Adrienne barged into Kellar's room and shook her awake. "Get up. There's something you need to see."

Kellar tried to push her away, but Adrienne was insistent. "It's noon! Get out of bed and get your ass downstairs. *Now!*"

"Fine!" Less than forty-eight hours back home and Kellar had turned back into an uncooperative teenager.

She put a robe on and stomped down the stairs to the kitchen. Adrienne shoved a mug full of reheated coffee at her and turned her laptop around so Kellar could see it.

Willow in all her usual stunning glory, looped a strand of hair behind her ear, her gaze uncertain, stating in a soft voice, "I am a gay woman."

Kellar sat riveted after the first sentence, as Willow briefly outlined her struggle with her sexual identity and her fear for the future of her career if the truth were known as well as the effect it would have on her family. She'd initially placed the post on her social media pages, but apparently it had since gone viral, "But I have realized that living a lie isn't really living. Talent has nothing to do with sexual preference. Not being authentic is self-destructive and I don't want to live that way anymore. I'm extremely thankful for the good friends who've always been there for me.

"I'm ready to face the future, whatever that may be. Thank you all for your support and understanding."

"Oh, shit." Kellar looked at Adrienne.

Her sister was biting her lip, obviously trying to hold back her laughter. "Looks like they really are just friends."

"Thanks for *your* support and understanding," Kellar echoed in response to Adrienne's obvious amusement.

"I gotta say, when you mess up a relationship, you do

it in style."

Everything in Kellar deflated. She'd been in a funk after Day left yesterday and not even time with her sister and a shared bottle of wine could pull her out of it. Day showing up, even his anger, had somehow given her hope.

He wouldn't have bothered even trying to talk to her if he didn't care at least a little. He wouldn't have been angry if she didn't have the ability to hurt him. In the back of her mind, she'd nursed a hope that somehow, they could explain themselves to each other and...what? Have a future together? That's what Kellar wanted, but she couldn't make herself believe in the possibility. Or, perhaps more accurately, Day was right. She expected to be disappointed and created a situation where it became a self-fulfilling prophecy. She was so certain that every man she allowed herself to care about would walk away just like her dad, she ended up pushing them away before they had the chance.

The very definition of self-sabotage.

She'd been awake for hours last night, replaying scenes from Day's movie, *Poker Face*, over and over in her head. She'd re-examined every encounter she'd had with Day from the moment they'd been in Jamie Falcon's green room.

She'd liked him. Then she'd loved him. And finally, she'd trusted him, or thought she had. He'd earned her trust, yet she'd been so quick to throw it away.

What the hell is wrong with me?

Day had been honest with her from the start. She'd

wanted to trust him despite his history, despite *their* history, but she'd been too afraid to put her heart on the line. Too afraid of being hurt.

Except she was hurting now.

"...living a lie isn't really living... Not being authentic is self-destructive and I don't want to live that way anymore."

Willow's words resonated with Kellar. Wasn't that what she'd been doing for years? Living a lie, building a career around dating, but never believing in happily ever after for her followers or her fans...and especially not for herself. She pretended to applaud dating successes, while at the same time celebrating failures. She could more easily identify with failure.

"I don't want to live that way anymore either," she said aloud.

"What?"

Of course, Adrienne couldn't know what she was talking about. Kellar wasn't going to take the time to explain it. "I have to go," she said. She jumped off the stool and headed upstairs.

"You're leaving? Where are you going?"

"I have to find him. I have to try and make it right. Assuming he'll even talk to me."

"I'll help you pack."

Kellar had the drive across several Midwest states to contemplate her conversation with Chazz, who'd finally answered her call. He'd told her Day wasn't available.

"Where is he?"

Chazz gave her the runaround. Kellar had to remind herself that Chazz had never really warmed up to her. She didn't know why, but that was a subject to be explored later. Right now, she wasn't above using anything and everything she could think of to make Chazz give up Day's whereabouts.

"Chazz, you saved a little girl's life. Now I'm asking you to save mine." She thought for a moment. "Also, Adrienne will be pissed if you don't help."

Chazz didn't respond, but he hadn't disconnected.

She closed her eyes a moment, taking a deep breath. "I love him."

Chazz groaned. "Oh, man..."

"It's true. I love him and I screwed up. I want a second chance."

"Don't tell me that. Tell him."

"I would. But I don't know where he is."

She sensed Chazz's internal debate. Clearly, he was torn between protecting Day's privacy and the more personal issue at hand.

"I don't know where he is, either," Chazz said finally.

"Not exactly. He's camping."

"Camping?"

Chazz sighed. "Somewhere on his property in Wyoming."

"How do I find him?"

"That's the problem, isn't it? He turned off his phone and it's not like I have GPS tracker on him anymore."

Kellar blinked. "*Anymore*?"

"I take his security seriously. He thought it was... excessive."

"Chazz, please. I really need your help."

"I don't want to be in the middle of this."

"Please, Chazz. I've got to make this right."

Chazz sighed. "His SUV has a tracker—in case of theft," he added quickly. "He's probably camping not too far from it. I'll send you the location."

"Thanks Chazz, you're a sweetheart."

"You better not screw this up. Because it's my ass on the line."

He disconnected. A few minutes later, she knew where to find Day.

By the time she arrived, exhaustion swamped Kellar. Driving, along with her wayward emotions, had done a number on her. She'd also worn out her swearing vocabulary as her satnav sent her on one wrong turn after another. She'd wound up in the middle of nowhere on the unmarked tracts of Day's property. She'd begun to wonder if Chazz had sent her off on a wild goose chase just to keep her away from Day.

She imagined herself running out of gas, food, and water. When they finally found her, the headlines would read: "Crazy Dating Coach Found Eaten by Coyotes."

She'd done a lot of thinking during her long drive. About herself. About Day. About Willow. She decided to invite Willow to be on her podcast. Not to talk about dating, but to discuss her journey and how her effort to live authentically was progressing.

For her part, Kellar had never had a worse case of imposter syndrome than she had right now. She'd have to come clean with her audience about the trouble she had getting out of her own way. She chuckled when Taylor Swift took over the radio and started singing about how she was the problem.

Kellar liked to believe she'd known all along that she was the problem, she just hadn't wanted to admit it. It was so much easier to live in denial, blame others, and not take responsibility for her own part in relationships.

She wouldn't do it anymore. She'd find Day. Apologize. See if a second chance was even possible. It occurred to her that's what her dad wanted. Maybe she could cut him some slack and see where things went.

The wild land spanned the gap from meadow to forest, flat land to rocky foothills, ravines and streams. Or maybe the same stream snaked through the area and Kellar kept crossing it. She'd lost cell service over an hour ago. At the same time, the sun began to set. Darkness moved in swiftly because of the mountains, and she felt her first moment of panic when she thought she saw a flash of red in her headlights.

She drove her car carefully over the rocky clearing and almost cried out in relief when she saw the taillights of a giant black SUV parked with its nose aimed toward the stream some distance away. She got out and made her way over the rough ground. Day didn't appear.

Where was he? What if this wasn't him? What if she'd stumbled on some hunter who'd shoot first and ask questions later? She didn't have a flashlight except for the one on her phone, which she'd left in the car. The rocky ground pressed up against the thin soles of her shoes as she pressed on toward the SUV.

The doors were locked. She couldn't see inside because of the tinted windows and the waning light.

"Day?" she called hesitantly.

Surprising him didn't seem like a particularly good idea, given the way they'd parted. Or, more accurately, the way he'd departed.

You wouldn't know love if it blew up in your face!

She hadn't been able to get that line out of her head since he'd uttered it. That's exactly what had happened—love *had* blown up in her face, and she had no one to blame but herself. She been afraid to believe in happily ever after.

But with Day, I'd be willing to give it a shot. If he'd forgive her. If he'd give her another chance. And if he didn't? She refused to go there. She'd find a way to convince him. If she could *find* him.

She stumbled on, her gaze sweeping left and right even though she couldn't see much in the dim light. She could hear the trickle of the stream as she drew closer. Why hadn't she left the car's headlights on? She wasn't even sure she could find her way back now. Oh, God, she was an idiot.

"Day?" she called into the growing darkness. The rocks and trees and water seemed to swallow the sound of her voice.

She heard a rustle. Movement. Up ahead. Was it him? Or was it a bear? Or a coyote? Or Bigfoot?

"Kellar?" At least bears and coyotes were off the list. Probably Bigfoot too.

"Day?" She heard something skitter behind her. "Where are you?" she asked, fear making her voice wobble.

"Right here."

With her imagination working overtime, she half ran down an incline, slipping and sliding over rocks and fallen branches and patches of grass and dead leaves until she barreled right into a shadow that turned out to be solid.

He staggered back when she slammed into him, falling straight down the rocky bank, and landing in the stream. Chilly water splashed over her, soaking her from foot to knee and from hands to elbows. But Day's whole body was wet.

"For Pete's sake, Kellar. You'll do just about anything to be on top of me, won't you? What the hell are you doing?"

"Letting love blow up in my face?" Kellar said softly. "Or trying not to let it blow up. I'm not exactly clear about how that metaphor was meant to work."

"Can we discuss literary devices when I'm *not* soaking wet?"

"Oh. Sorry." She got to her feet and offered him her hand. The light from a waxing moon and a few stars reflected off the water and helped her to see him now that her eyes were adjusting to the dark.

Day took her outstretched hand and tugged, so she fell face first into the stream next to him. She spluttered at the shock and the mouthful of water she'd almost swallowed.

She scrambled to her knees and smacked his chest. "What'd you do that for?"

He laughed and got to his feet. "Now we're even."

"Even? I drive out to the middle of nowhere to look for you and you're worried about getting even?"

"Trust me. It's all part of my plan."

She began to shiver from the cold. "Does your plan include hypothermia?"

"No. But it does include getting you out of those wet clothes."

He, of course, had a flashlight app on his water-resistant cell phone. With it he located the proper flashlight he'd left nearby, took her hand, and led her back to the

SUV. Her teeth were chattering by the time they reached it. He popped the rear hatch and started to undress.

"Come on," he urged when she just stood there and watched. "I've got blankets in here. I'll crank the heat so we can warm up and dry off."

At the promise of warmth, Kellar started stripping.

"Back seat," Day said as he opened the driver's side door and started the engine. He adjusted the temperature settings and joined her in the back. She'd wrapped herself in a flannel blanket and shook out the other one for him. He draped it over himself while Kellar's teeth kept chattering.

She sat with her feet tucked under her thighs, trying to generate some body heat, but the cold water and the mountain climate had left her chilled through.

"I'll never be warm again." She shivered.

"Oh, I think you will," he teased, his breath warm against her neck.

The glow from the dashboard lights allowed them to see each other.

"Come here," Day commanded. He hauled her into his lap and wrapped his arms around her. "We can share our body heat until it warms up in here."

Warm air blasted from the vents, making a slight dent in her level of discomfort. She couldn't even enjoy being in his arms, she was so miserable. Still, she drank in the scent that was uniquely him, now mingled with pine and wood smoke.

"I'm sorry, Day. I shouldn't have left. I should have let

you explain," she stuttered, trying to control the chattering of her teeth.

"Damn right you should have. I thought I deserved at least that much from you. You should have trusted me."

She looked away, blinking to keep the tears clouding her eyes from falling. "I know. I thought I did. I wanted to."

"Kellar." With gentle fingers under her chin, he turned her back to face him. "Why didn't you?"

The tears spilled over. She wasn't sure she could explain or if she could if it would make any sense to him. But she had to try or be sorry for the rest of her life that she hadn't. "You were right. I didn't believe in what I was selling. I'm a fraud. I expect be let down, so I set myself up for it. I thought it was going to be different this time. I told myself I would be different. But it turned out I was lying to myself all along. I was afraid to hope. Afraid of having my heart broken again."

"Who broke your heart to begin with?" Day asked tenderly.

She sniffed and smiled at him sadly. "Besides my dad? In a way, I guess it was you."

He stared at her, mystified. "Me?"

"Ten years ago. When I interviewed you for my college newspaper."

"I remember."

"You do not."

She saw the flash of his teeth when he smiled. "I admit, I didn't at first. But you seemed so familiar, and I couldn't figure out why."

"Go on."

"After Chazz discovered your connection to Rory, I wasn't at liberty to explain everything to you, but I did try to talk to you about it a few times, if you'll remember."

"But I didn't want to talk about my father. I shut you down every time."

"I'm glad you figured that much out."

"It took me a while, but I figured out quite a few things."

"Anyway, Chazz kept digging. Eventually, he got hold of the article you wrote in college. And there you were with the byline. Kellar Kennedy. That's why you seemed familiar when I saw you again. But you never said anything about meeting me before. How come?"

"Because even though I never forgot you, you didn't remember me. You didn't recognize me, anyway."

Day reached up and smoothed her hair. "I never forgot you. Just some of the details blurred. Like your name. I knew it wasn't a common name."

"But you never said anything, either."

"By the time I found out, I didn't know how to bring it up. For all I knew you'd forgotten you met me before, too." His hand in her hair stilled. He looked into her eyes. "I asked you to meet me for a drink that night."

"But you never showed."

"Something came up I couldn't get out of."

"I know."

"But I went to the pub. The bartender said he knew

you. He promised to give you the message that I couldn't make it."

Kellar stared at him. "You did? He did? Who was the bartender?"

"Beats me. Some guy. I admit I couldn't remember your name, but I described you. Mentioned that you wrote for the college paper, and he said he knew who you were. I left my phone number."

Kellar's mouth dropped open. "You did?"

"Of course, I did. I wouldn't just ditch a girl."

"No, you wouldn't, would you?"

She rubbed her thumb over his bottom lip thoughtfully.

"You never got my message, did you? Or my phone number."

She shook her head. "I waited and when you didn't show, I walked home. Along the way I passed a restaurant and I saw you." She lifted her eyes to meet his.

"The director put together a party for Willow's birthday at the last minute, and he made it clear he expected me to be there."

"You looked like you were having fun."

"I'd rather have been in that pub getting to know you. But you're probably lucky I wasn't."

"Why?"

"I wasn't terribly mature for one thing. Pretty self-centered and full of myself. If we'd gotten together back then I'd probably have reinforced every negative belief you had about men. My friendship with Willow took off that night and she's really helped me view relationships differently. I guess you could say we kind of grew up together. Without her I might be one of those shallow un-gettable men you're so interested in.

Kellar released a humorless laugh. "I'm not *interested* in them. I'm interested in you. And just for the record, that bartender? Talk about players. I'd shut him down a couple of times."

"So, of course, he's not going to give you a message from me."

"Nope."

"But still. We'd just met. Tell me how I broke your heart?"

She feathered her fingers through the ends of his hair. The car was getting warmer and so was she. "You weren't the first guy who'd stood me up. There'd been others before you. Before that, of course, it was my dad. But what happened with you back then... that was like con-firmation that everything I feared about men was true."

Day returned the favor, sliding his fingers into her hair, cupping her cheek. She leaned her head into his hand. "I really liked you," she said, her voice cracking. "I know it was just one interview, but I thought we had this... connection or something. I thought you felt it too."

"I did," he said so softly she had to strain to hear him.

"Then I saw you in the restaurant and I thought, of *course* you'd choose someone like Willow over me. She was beautiful—"

"She doesn't hold a candle to you."

Kellar wanted so badly to believe what she saw in his eyes. "I stopped believing in the fairy tale ending. Stopped trying to connect with anyone because I was sure it had all been one-sided anyway. I was sick of being hurt and disappointed. I swore I'd never put myself in that position again."

Day pulled her closer. She laid her head on his shoulder and sighed. "You know what I remember about you in that interview?" he said. "You were being yourself. You were funny and you asked interesting questions. I'd just landed my first big movie role, but I was already getting sucked into the posturing and the pretending required to make it in the industry. You were like a breath of fresh air, and it didn't hurt that you liked me."

"I did," Kellar admitted. She sat up. "I still do. I love you, Day. It scares the hell out of me, but I love you and I'm sorry I bailed on you. Please, please, please, give me another chance. Please." There were those damn tears again. She sniffed and tried to brush them away. "You're the only guy," she paused to swallow a sob. Her voice turned high and squeaky in her desperation to make him understand. "The only one who ever came after me. The only one who didn't just walk away after I screwed things up."

She felt a thousand times a fool, sitting here naked in the back of this car in the middle of nowhere. The wool of the blanket scratched against her skin. The heat from the vents began to make her uncomfortably warm. She found no reassurance from Day's silence. She had clean clothes in her car. She could still make a relatively dignified exit. Find her way out of here. Try somehow to pick up the pieces and pretend she could have a life without him.

No! She wasn't going to bail again. Not going to give into that knee-jerk reaction she'd fallen back on too many times. This time she was going to stand and fight for what she wanted.

He held her head in his hands and swiped at the tears with his thumbs. He stared into her eyes. The tears continued to seep over the edges. "You know all those other women I dated?"

She sniffed. "You're bringing them up? Now?"

He grinned. "Yes. I am." He stared into her eyes some more. "*None* of them ever cried over me."

"You don't know that."

"That's true, I suppose. But none of them ever cried in front of me, or chased after me like you did."

"Really?"

"Really. Mostly they shouted about how I didn't deserve them. How sorry they were they'd ever gotten involved with me. Then they packed up, slammed doors, and left. You know what else?"

"What?"

"Not one of them ever asked me for a second chance."

"Fools."

His teeth flashed white when he grinned. "Right?"

"Well, I'm asking," Kellar pointed out. "And I might be asking for a third chance or a fifth or a fifty-sixth. Because

I might screw up. But I'm going to learn to stop sabotaging myself. That's what's made me so bad at dating.

"You're bad at dating? I had no idea!"

"Jerk." She rubbed her thumb along his bottom lip again wishing he'd kiss her and put her out of her misery.

"I think I've got a solution for you."

"Being a jerk?"

"No, your pitiful dating skills."

"Well, as you often remind me, you're more of an expert than I am."

"I say we stop dating."

"Huh?"

"I say we go straight to the permanent happily ever after. I think I can make a believer out of you."

Kellar's heart swelled. "Maybe you can. Are you ever going to kiss me? I'm dying here."

Day swooped in, capturing her mouth in a kiss that seared her soul. The blankets fell to their waists in a tangle, so that finally they were skin to skin.

Day tilted sideways, pushing the blankets away until he was half-lying across the seat. Kellar gave him a shove. "You know I'll do anything to land on top of you, right?"

He looked into her eyes with a wicked grin. "I gotta say. It's a helluva view."

Chapter Twenty-Four

♥

They drowsed and dozed in a sleeping bag in the back of Day's SUV as the first wisps of dawn light swept through the mountains and curled around the trees.

Kellar had been awake for a while. She still had so many questions, but one was prodding at her now. "It was you, wasn't it?"

Day spooned her from behind and she played her fingers over the sprinkle of hair on his forearm. "Me what?" he murmured sleepily.

"You helped my dad give up gambling."

Day's silence spoke volumes. It was the only scenario that made sense. "I'd like to know what happened. How you managed to reach him when no one else could."

Day shifted and so did she, so they were lying face to face. "Did he ever tell you the details of how we met?"

"No," she said. "And neither did you."

"You never gave me a chance," he reminded her.

"I know."

"Like I told you, we met in Vegas. He literally ran into me, trying to escape his loan shark's enforcer. Dragged

me into a bar and used me as a human shield." Day
chuckled at the memory. "I thought it was some kind of
joke at first. Then he admitted he was into the loan shark
for a hundred grand, which he didn't have. Something
about his story and the way he told it intrigued me. I got
him up to my suite and Chazz recorded him telling us
how he got where he was. I bought the rights to his life
story the next day."

"For enough money to pay off the loan shark."

"And then some. Fast forward a year later. I'd already
started working on the film by the time I met you."

"But you didn't know I was his daughter."

"Not at first. By the time Chazz found out, I didn't see
how it would matter. All you and I had was an agreement
to attend awards shows together for the season and that
was going to be that as far as I was concerned. Kellar,
even if I'd wanted to tell you, ethically, I couldn't. Rory
and I had a contractual agreement to keep our association
confidential. It's standard in the business, although, of
course, not everyone abides by them.

"And by then, I saw things differently. By paying him
for his story, I was also enabling him. Later I was afraid
you'd see it that way, too. Or that you'd think I'd taken
advantage of him, used his addiction for my own benefit, and you wouldn't forgive me." Kellar kept her eyes
locked on Day, which made him shift a bit uncomfortably. "Then Rory showed up and asked you for money."

"And you convinced me to talk about it."

"Turns out, that was the key to everything."

"What do you mean?"

"I told you there was something missing from the film. Some indefinable something that kept it from coming together into the vision I had for it. That indefinable something was your perspective. Showing Rory's own self-destruction was easy, but the character was clueless about the destruction he'd wrought on others. I needed to show that through another character's eyes."

Tears welled up in Kellar's eyes. "Like his daughter."

"Like his daughter." Day swiped at the tears dribbling across her nose. "Him telling you you were second best, then walking out on you. I had to use it and hope you'd understand."

Kellar couldn't speak. She nodded.

"The day after he showed up at your place, I read him the riot act. I don't think I'd realized until then how low he could go. I think maybe that was when I started to realize how much I cared about you. He was going into a big game, and I knew he wasn't going to come out on top. So, I told him if that happened to come to me, and I'd bail him out. But then I'd own him."

"He never thinks he will lose," Kellar said.

"Exactly, but sure enough he showed up, tail between his legs, so I told him I'd pay off his debt, but he had to get help. Admit he had a problem and at least try to deal with it."

"Let me guess. He didn't agree to that."

"Not at first. But he didn't want two broken kneecaps, either. I made him watch the rough cut of the film. That's what pushed him into accepting the help. Chazz had found a rehab place in Arizona for gambling addicts. Rory went without a fight."

"Probably figured he'd do what you wanted and go right back to Vegas and to his old life."

"Probably," Day agreed. He smoothed a lock of her hair back. "He may still."

Kellar appreciated the gentle warning. "He came to see me in New York. At least he's trying to make amends."

Day continued to focus on running his fingers through her hair. "It's a start."

Kellar held onto his wrist. His gaze came back to her. "But you knew I needed to reconcile with my father if we were ever going to have a chance. You and me, I mean."

"Don't give me so much credit. I'm not a psychologist."

"You wanted me to trust you."

"Well, your problem with trusting men started with Rory, right?"

"Heal the father, heal the daughter." Kellar saw so much love in Day's eyes right now.

"I wanted you to give us a chance. Give me a chance. "

"Give myself a chance."

"Exactly."

"And then you donated the profits from the film."

"Chazz's idea. But I thought it might soften the blow of me not being up front with you about all of this."

"Why didn't you tell me?"

"Like I said, at first, I thought it wouldn't matter. And

then later, I was afraid it would matter too much. Plus, after that one time when you told me everything you refused to talk about your father at all."

"I didn't want to talk about him because it wouldn't change anything. It never had in the past."

Day looked at her from beneath his lashes. "So, I'm forgiven?"

"I think I should be asking you if I'm forgiven."

"You are. But you have to promise to stick around and that you'll never bail on me again."

"Oh, yeah. You're forgiven." She wrapped her arms around his neck. "I promise. I love you, Day. So much."

Day smiled as the sun came up and his whole life came together. "And I love you."

As much as those words meant, Kellar pulled back. "There's one thing you still haven't explained."

Day waited.

"Why Willow walked out of your bedroom wearing your bathrobe and looking like she'd spent the night."

Day's eyes twinkled. "I like it when you're jealous.

"I'm not jealous," she insisted. "At least not anymore. Well, not of Willow anyway."

"Willow struggled with her sexuality for years. As long as I've known her and before. She grew up in an ul-tra-conservative family and their approval meant every-thing to her."

"I can't believe I didn't figure it out before," Kellar said.

"She went to great lengths to keep her secret, but it's been eating her up inside. Even an actor can only fake it for so long before it starts to do some real damage. She met someone also in the business who'd been urging her for a couple of years to come out. She knew they couldn't have any kind of genuine relationship until Willow made that decision. She finally did, but a couple of days before she was set to make that announcement, she had a major meltdown."

"So, she came to you," Kellar said, understanding what Day's friendship and support must have meant to Willow all these years. The knowledge that she could trust him with her deepest secrets, knowing he'd never betray her.

"She needed to talk. And talk. And talk. It got late. She stayed over. And in the interest of full disclosure, that's not the first time she did. Sometimes you just need someone, you know?"

"I do." She wrapped her arms around him. "You're the best man, Day. The very best man."

"Yeah?" he said, nipping her earlobe. "I can't wait to be the groom."

EPILOGUE

♥

The glint of her wedding ring momentarily distracted Kellar from the wedding ceremony. Swirls of platinum encased a stunning setting of aquamarine and sapphires. Day couldn't have designed a more perfect piece.

She glanced up to see him smiling from the arbor-covered platform where he stood near Willow and her soon-to-be wife. As it turned out, Day became a groom first and a best man not too long after.

The grounds of the private estate were perfect for the day Willow and Mirabelle had planned. Kellar estimated there were a couple hundred family members and close friends in attendance for the evening ceremony and the reception to follow. A cool breeze swept in from the ocean and a piano quartet provided exquisite accompaniment as needed.

The women looked stunning in their wedding finery. Willow appeared even more wispy and angelic in lace, and Mirabelle chose a raw silk ensemble that enhanced her dark hair and olive complexion.

Kellar contemplated how relaxed and genuine Willow seemed ever since she'd publicly declared her relationship with Mirabelle and shared the struggle she'd experienced.

Kellar found she could relate because she'd also learned her lesson about keeping secrets and not being her authentic self. They both had Day to thank for that.

She wondered how long it would be before another wedding took place. Peripheral vision allowed her to see Chazz and Adrienne seated further down the row, their hands clasped. Kellar allowed herself to dream. Maybe they'd all relocate to Wyoming and share in Day's vision for a retreat for artists as well as a camp for kids like Gracie. "Maybe some of those attending the artists' retreat can get involved with the kid's camp. It might be therapeutic to teach rather than perform," she'd suggested. Day thought it was an idea worth considering.

Their plans were still in the talking stage. Sometimes it seemed like she and Day had so much to say to each other they'd never run out of conversation.

The ceremony concluded. The officiant offered a final blessing and encouraged them to seal their union with a kiss. Applause broke out. The brides beamed. The quartet played. Day made his way toward her.

"Not a bad gig, being the best man," he said as he escorted her down the aisle.

"I thought you'd enjoy it," Kellar replied, her eyes dancing with one more secret she was ready to part with. "How would you feel about being the best dad ever?"

Acknowledgements

My thanks to the following who are those who inspire and support my creative endeavors:

Kellar Carmouche for her hilarious story-telling ability which inspired me to write Those Who Can, Date.

Adrienne Carmouche, Kellar's older sister, who shares her own interesting stories. Together, they are known as "the girls."

I started this book in 2015 and finished it in 2023, so for those of you wondering how long it takes to write a book, sometimes it takes years. And it might not have been written at all if not for Sandy Carmouche, a dear friend and mother of "the girls."

Author Rosanna Leo shared her invaluable insights and experience, which were exactly what I needed to make the character of Rory what he was.

CurtissAnn Matlock and Alison Nissen both read early versions of this book and offered useful feedback.

Lakeland Writers group, and especially Sofia Simpson, read scenes out of order, offered feedback, and also helped me fashion the blurb.

God was and is always there to provide inspiration and has bestowed upon me every bit of writing talent and ability I have.

Social media followers, especially those on my personal Facebook page are always ready and willing to provide answers to research questions and offer their opinions on cover art.

My fans, who show up at in-person events, who buy my books, review my books, love my books, are the best and the reason I keep writing.

Bill, who's stuck it out for 40+ years, understands nothing about what I do and has never read a word I've written, but still gives his opinion on career decisions and cover art when asked.

Editor Noah Chinn and cover artist Steven Novak who are infinitely patient and make my books the best they can be inside and out.

Afterword

A Note to Readers

Dear Readers,

Those Who Can, Date was inspired by my friend, Kellar. She is the one who told of a blind date that went on much longer than expected, so long in fact, that she ran out of dating talking points. It was one of the funniest things I'd ever heard.

That was back in 2015. I started the book shortly after, but I didn't have a plot, as I so often don't when I start a project. It took awhile for the story to come together. Here we are eight years later. Well, nine, because even though I had this book edited and ready to go in 2023, I hit a wall that lasted almost six months, and I didn't do any fiction writing or publishing.

I am so happy to name my entirely fictional characters after Kellar and her sister, Adrienne.

I hope you enjoy this fun story and that it puts a smile on your face.

Thank you for reading Those Who Can, Date.

Feel free to reach out to me via my website barbarame yers.com. I'm always happy to hear from readers.

Wishing you all the best,
Barbara Meyers

Also by

<u>Look for these titles by Barbara Meyers</u>
Books Now Available:
Misconceive
Scattered Moments
Not Quite Heaven
Cleo's Web
White Roses in Winter
Training Tommy
A Family for St. Nick (Christmas Novella)

The Braddocks Series (Connected, Stand Alone)
A Month From Miami (Book One)
A Forever Kind of Guy (Book Two)
The First Time Again (Book Three)
What A Rich Woman Wants (Book Four)

Red Bud, Iowa Series (Connected, Stand Alone)
If You Knew (Book One)
If You Dare (Book Two)
If You Stay (Book Three)
Coming Soon: If You Touch (Book Four)

Phantom (Romantic Suspense, Manuscripts Under the Bed)

The Color of Nothing (Young Adult, Manuscripts Under the Bed)

Barbara Meyers writing as AJ Tillock:
The Grinding Reality Series:
The Forbidden Bean (Book One)
Cool Beans (Book Two)

www.ingramcontent.com/pod-product-compliance
Lightning Source LLC
Chambersburg PA
CBHW021234190726
48289CB00005B/1325